The Curse of Kaninjanga Island

By
Scott Jones

The Curse of Kaninjanga Island
First Edition 2020

Published By KABooks
www.kabooks.co.uk
S. Jones

ISBN 978-1-909191-85-3

Text copyright © Scott Jones
Cover design and Illustrations by Sara Valsar

Printed and bound in England by Clays Print Ltd

Sequel To:
Secret Of The Dark Woods

Dedication

For Lola, who started me out on this incredible adventure.
No matter how much you grow, you will always
be my baby girl.

I love you

What is a Cornish Knocker?

Knockers were goblin-like creatures who used to live in mines. Legend had it they used to knock on walls to warn miners that a cave-in was about to occur, thus saving them from certain death. To express their gratitude they would throw their pasty scraps to the Knockers.

However...
There was another train of thought that Knockers were nothing more than mischievous beings who actually knocked on the walls to cause the cave-ins. But I guess we will never know...

In the following story, you will meet Terry - a Cornish Knocker. However, Terry is not like other Knockers. He is unique, some might say, a little bit too unique...

Prologue

Why? Why had they trusted him? He continually misbehaved. From the moment he'd emerged from the bush in the playground, he had done nothing but try to land the boys in trouble. The first day he came up to visit their school, he played enough pranks to last the entire year.

He turned up to some classes in fancy dress and mocked the teachers behind their backs. He sat on teachers' laps, wrote rude words and drew funny pictures on the blackboards. The teachers would then ask who was responsible for the graffiti? And, as they tried to discover who the culprit was, he would stand next to them at the front of the class, with his hands on his hips and a frown upon his face, as he disapprovingly shook his head from side-to-side. He would stare at the boys and laugh as he wiggled his hips and give them a double thumbs up. The boys looked away as they struggled not to laugh.

He also had a tendency for changing subject books during lessons, partly to confuse the teachers, but also to see if the boys could contain themselves.

During one such lesson (on Greek gods), Mrs Halligan was standing at the front and addressing the class in her normal manner - arms folded across her chest and a stern expression on her face, while she surveyed the room to ensure they were giving her their undivided attention.

As she was telling one boy to stop prodding the girl in front of him and pay attention, Terry reached up and removed the book on Greek mythology, which lay on her desk, and replaced it with one hidden down his top. He stood and watched as Mrs Halligan reached behind her, grabbed the book, and brought it around to the front, ready to show the class. As she continued to talk to the students, she opened the book and stopped. She was not staring at Athena, the Greek goddess of wisdom and war as she was expecting, but a step-by-step guide on how to make the perfect Cornish pasty.

While the rest of the class sat there wondering what was going on, Billy and Austin continued to stare at him. The small creature at the front of the class looked at the book and then back to the boys. He had a smile on his face and began rubbing his belly as he pretended to drool. Billy and Austin looked away before they burst out laughing.

However, his best prank was reserved for the

first PE lesson of the year. The children were in the middle of a game of rounders, when a whirring noise came drifting over. There was a crashing sound, and part of the hedge collapsed. Seconds later the school tractor came bursting through the gap it had just created. All the children started screaming as they ran away from the out of control tractor that was heading in their direction and swerving all over the field. The boys looked closely and there he was, bouncing up and down on the spring-loaded seat. Tears were streaming down his face and he was laughing out loud as he struggled to control the vehicle's big steering wheel. The children reached the playground where they continued to watch the incident unfold with their faces pressed up against the fence surrounding it.

The tractor continued weaving all over until it hit a tree on the far side of the field with an almighty crash. Its wheels continued to spin and churn up the grass, as its driver sat there, laughing his head off and grabbing his belly.

The school caretaker, Mr Tacklebum, who was trimming the hedge around the field, came to the rescue. He dropped his shears and made his way over. He removed the block of wood that had been used to wedge the accelerator down, turned the engine off and looked around to see if he could identify the culprit, but there was no one to be seen.

Little did he know that the culprit was, in fact,

inches from his face, still holding his belly, that was now starting to hurt due to his continued laughter. How could he know, how could he possibly know who it was and how close he was to him?

As Mr Tacklebum bent down to examine the accelerator, the creature smiled, turned around, dropped his trousers and let rip, right into Mr Tacklebum's face. The caretaker continued with what he was doing, but involuntarily screwed his face up as the noxious gas filled his nostrils. He stood up and looked around for the cause of the offensive smell, but he could see nothing. Billy and Austin looked on from the other side of the fence, watching in disbelief as the creature sat there pointing at the caretaker with tears streaming down his face, and howls of laughter bellowing from his mouth.

The problem was, nobody could see or hear him, nobody except Billy and Austin. And what if they told the teachers and other students what was going on, how would that look? What would everyone think if the boys said the trouble was being caused by a cheeky Cornish Knocker they met in the woods, who had the ability to do whatever he wanted because he owned a magical stone that he found lodged in the wall of an old mine? They would have to explain that he was responsible for what had happened in the playground on the second day of the school year. No, they couldn't. They needed to keep quiet and continue to look shocked and flabbergasted at every weird situation that occured. They needed to act as clueless as everyone else. It was their only option, unless they wanted to get into serious trouble for lying to the teachers.

Terry was full of mischief and he liked nothing better than playing a few childish pranks to land the boys in trouble, but nothing came close to what they were doing now, this was beyond funny and the consequences, if it went wrong, would be catastrophic. This was a step too far. If they got caught, how on earth were they going to explain what they had done?

It was meant to be the best school trip ever, but little did they know that Terry had planned it all for this very moment. He concocted the entire trip and then planted the idea in Mr Horrocks's brain. The Headmaster thought he had come up with an amazing excursion for his pupils. They would be visiting so many exciting and historic places. He was so excited for the children and wished that he was going too. Only, it was nothing to do with him, none of it was actually his idea. Everything had been put in place by the school's very own troublesome Cornish Knocker. It was all his doing. From the time they left school to the time they arrived back home again. Well, by the time most of them arrived back.

Terry planned the trip because he needed the boys with him, even if they did not know it. They would be vital to the success of the adventure they were about to embark on. He couldn't do it all by himself. So he had tricked the Headmaster, and now he had tricked the boys. But there was no other option, he needed to take it, sail it on the open seas, and go back to find the treasure.

So, here they were. The school trip had been hijacked, exactly the way he had planned it. The three of them sat listening to the creaking of the ropes as they struggled to hold on to their moorings on the jetty. The ship was gently rocking from side-to-side, then the last rope's gave way as the tension held in them released. Seconds later, the ropes came flying back over their heads and crashed on the deck in front of them. They heard screaming and shouting coming from the workers and sailors on the jetty. A massive clattering sound came drifting overhead as the gangway and support struts fell from the ship and hit the dry dock. Billy and Austin sat there, watching, as Terry took one finger and slowly moved it towards his nose. He looked at them, winked and asked one question.

'Ready my ansums?'

Then he started laughing as the finger entered his nose.

Chapter I
And So It Begins

All the trouble began on the second day of term, the day after the boys met Terry in the woods. Austin had been getting a lot of funny looks from the other students, and even Mr Robertson, as he filed in and sat down quietly, waiting for the teacher to start calling out names. He sat there dressed in a brand-new uniform, complete with a school blazer and a new rucksack. He had even managed to tie both of his shoelaces. His previously long, greasy, brown hair was now cut, washed and styled. His deep blue eyes, that once were filled with sadness, were now sparkling away, as if they were alive.

Throughout registration he sat bolt upright, at the front of the class, with a contented smile on his face. At the rear of the class were his fake friends. They called for him to join them, pointing to an empty seat on the back row. He looked at them and declined, and instead remained at the front next to Billy. The boys at the back all looked confused. Why did their troublesome leader have no interest in sitting with them?

Sue leaned towards Billy and whispered in his ear.

'What is he playing at?' She asked, sounding confused.

'No idea, maybe his parents heard about what happened yesterday and he got a right telling off last night. Who knows?' Billy said, trying not to smile.

Mr Robertson, who was halfway through the register, paused before he called Austin's name.

'James?' He called, and waited for a sarcastic comment, as this was obviously some strange prank. Mr Robertson waited for the punchline, but all he got in return were two, unexpected words.

'Yes, sir,' Austin answered. Nothing else. Mr Robertson looked up at him and found himself thinking, *What on earth happened to him last night?*

Their teacher finished the register and placed it back in the cupboard before turning around to address the class. As he did so, he removed a tissue from his trouser pocket, took off his glasses and cleaned the lenses. After checking they were clean, he put them back on and returned the tissue to his pocket. He looked at Austin, waiting, once again, for the sarcasm to start, but it didn't.

Austin just sat there, smiling at his teacher, who stared at him for a few seconds longer, before starting the class.

'Good morning,' he said.

'Good morning, sir,' they all chimed back, including Austin. Mr Robertson cast a wary eye his way once again, still unsure what was going on.

'Now, this morning we are going to—'

'Aaaaaaaahh,' came a scream from the back of the class, everyone turned around, just as a frog jumped out of a boy's rucksack. Billy looked at Austin and they both tried their hardest not to laugh, while the other children all started screaming. Mr Robertson hurriedly grabbed a container from the sideboard and chased around after the frog that was now hopping around the classroom, causing the screaming to increase. Some children lifted their legs up, while others climbed on top of their desks. Austin had his hands over his mouth to stifle his laughter. Billy smiled and shook his head at him.

Mr Robertson finally caught the creature, walked over to the window, opened it and released the frog into the bushes. The children started talking amongst themselves and discussing what had just happened. The boy who owned the rucksack from where the creature materialised was sat at his desk in tears, casually wiping his running nose with the sleeve of his jumper.

'Okay, okay, settle down, it was just a frog, Wilkinson, dry your eyes. It's gone now,' Mr Robertson said as he waited for the children to settle back into their seats and the Wilkinson boy to stop sniffling. Billy gave a sideways glance to Austin, who was grinning from ear to ear. The boys both started chewing on their pens. It was all they could do to stop themselves from bursting out laughing.

'Okay, so as I was saying, today we will concentrate on—' Mr Robertson was interrupted again.

Bang!

The noise from outside was closely followed by a flash of light that lit up the early morning sky and caused the classroom windows to rattle. Mr Robertson rushed to the windows at the back of the classroom to see what had caused the sudden explosion. It was followed by another loud bang which caused the children to stand and join their teacher in trying to see what was going on. Seconds later an intense light burst through the windows as the sky filled with a multitude of colours shooting off all around and fizzing past their windows. Nearly every child was in shock, unsure what was happening outside in their playground. Some were screaming, some were crying, and some stood there watching. No-one had a clue what was going on, except two of them - Billy and Austin. The boys, who had remained seated, slowly rose from their chairs and looked at one another, as the other children and Mr Robertson stood staring and gasping as the fireworks show continued outside. Billy and Austin looked at each other, smiled, and simultaneously muttered one word.

'Terry.'

******

Mr Robertson rushed from the classroom and headed outside to see what on earth was happening, closely followed by the children. The corridor was filled with teachers and students, all hurriedly heading for the exit. Loud, overlapping voices, children talking excitedly, and comments of 'What's going on?' filled the air. The teachers were so interested in trying to get outside that they had forgotten to tell the children to keep the noise down. Billy and Austin were in no rush. They waited at the back of the crowd. After all, they had seen all of this and much more the previous day.

'Why do you think he is here?' Austin asked.

'No idea, but it's going to mean trouble. Can you imagine having him at school? God, it would be a nightmare,' Billy said as he shook his head.

'Might be fun though,' Austin replied, smiling.

As the boys approached the exit, the lights and fireworks vanished, the whizzing sounds ceased, and all that remained was the smoke that had engulfed the playground. Billy and Austin stood there, waiting for the children in front of them to exit the building. Suddenly, all that could be heard were mumbled gasps and enthusiastic shrieks from the children as the surrounding smoke cleared. Some girls started letting out high-pitched screams and the boys were all shouting and fist-bumping each other. What had Terry done?

Finally, the children in front of them filtered out of the exit and headed into the early morning sun. More gasping and howling could be heard as the smoke dissipated and the playground filled with children and teachers. Billy and Austin reached the door and as they looked around, they could not believe what they were seeing. Their old, tatty, worn-out playground was gone. It had been completely replaced. They watched as all the children started hugging each other and jumping up and down. Billy and Austin remained on the top step, hands thrust deep into their pockets, as they both cast an eye over Terry's latest creation.

In the far corner there were a gaggle of teachers, scratching their heads and pointing at areas of the playground as they gesticulated with their hands. Just like the children, they too looked confused. The school's poor excuse for a playground, with the solid white line separating boys from girls and the worn-out jungle gyms at either end, was gone. The faded sports lines and broken fence were no more. What stood in its place was a playground any child would love.

The previously worn-out concrete floor with its weeds protruding from it was now a soft-black-rubber surface, marked out in fresh colours. Along both sides were zones for playing interactive games. There were squares, circles and ladders, all marked out in the brightest colours. On the far side there was a 20-ft high climbing wall, harnesses hung in a locked cage next to it. A sign above it read, 'USE OF THIS WALL MUST BE SUPERVISED BY A TEACHER'. Children were running around everywhere, and an electrifying buzz filled the air. The teachers were too busy trying to work out what had happened that they forgot all about their lessons.

The boys' attention was drawn to the sound of more screaming, this time it was coming from the far left-hand side of the playground. All the children and teachers stopped what they were doing and headed over. Pandemonium broke out as more pupils and teachers arrived.

Billy and Austin headed down the steps and followed the crowds. As they approached, they could see the top of a black fence that was not there the day before. More of the fence became visible as they got closer. This area was once a field full of bushes, trees, and old school equipment ready for the dump. Not anymore. Sat there, in the previously overgrown wasteland, was a brand new 20-foot-high fence, which was half as wide as it was long. Inside the fence was a full-size artificial football pitch, complete with 11-a-side and five-a-side goals, as well as hockey goals. On the near side, there were two bus-stop-style seated dugouts, and on the far side there was a spectator stand, full of seats. Lined up along the fence was a wealth of fitness equipment. Bags of different balls, hockey sticks, poles, cones, bibs, netball posts and much more. Brand-new kits, for a multitude of sports, also hung on the fence. More children started shouting as they entered the gate and flooded the pitch. The entire school was now standing inside the new sporting arena, unable to make any sense of it. The teachers were all looking around, speechless about the transformation. They had abandoned lessons for the day, or so it seemed.

Billy and Austin stood with their hands thrust deep into their pockets. As they looked around, they noticed something even more surprising. Stood there, in the middle of the pitch, was a strange creature. He was wearing a green miners' garb and a red bandana was pulled tightly over his small round head. Around his huge belly he wore a tatty brown belt, with a pickaxe tucked into the right side, and a sack hanging on his left hip. The creature stood there, looking around with a finger shoved up his nose. He spotted the boys, removed his finger, wiped it on the trousers of a boy stood next to him, raised his hand and waved.

Terry had outdone himself this time, but what if he was seen? The boys rushed over, both pleased to see him, but wondered why he was here.

Chapter 2
Here's Terry

'Ello my ansums, long time no see,' Terry said, as he chuckled.

'What are you doing here, and will you hurry up and hide?' Billy said, causing Terry to frown.

'Well, that's blinkin' charmin' that is. I come 'ere, does your playground up, and that's the fanks I get. Wants me to go an' hide in a blinkin' bush. The cheek of it,' he placed his hands on his hips and shook his head, disappointed at the welcome from his newfound friends.

'What if someone notices you?' Austin asked, joining the conversation.

'No one is goin' see me,' Terry said, rolling his eyes in a 'don't be stupid' way. The boys both frowned at him. They did not say a word. Terry sensed they didn't understand what he was saying and let out a sigh.

'Watch this,' he said. The boys watched as he headed towards Mr Horrocks, the school Headmaster, and Mr Robertson. They were standing in the corner scratching their heads and looking around, unable to comprehend what had happened. Terry bent down, undid both laces on Mr Horrocks' shoes and tied them together. He looked back to the boys, smiled and gave a double thumbs up. Billy and Austin watched as Terry walked behind and gave their Headmaster a shove. He lost his balance as he tried to take a step forward, causing him to bump into Mr Robertson. Mr Horrocks toppled forwards, flailing around as he tried to grab on to his colleague to stop himself from falling over, but all he succeeded in doing was pulling Mr Robertson over with him. They both crashed to the ground, and lay there on their backs, totally confused about what had just happened. As quick as a flash, Terry jumped onto Mr Horrocks belly and started bouncing up and down. Then he leaned forward, removed the Headmaster's thick glasses and put them on himself. They were far too big and only just fit over his ears. Terry grabbed onto the teacher's bushy beard with one hand and raised his other hand in the air.

'Yeeehaaa, giddy up boy,' he shouted, like he was a rodeo cowboy. He continued to hold on to the man's facial hair, laughing as the glasses flapped around his face before falling to the ground.

A few seconds later, Terry climbed off, as Mr Jackson and Miss Thompson came running over to help their stricken colleagues. The boys continued to watch, as Mr Horrocks was helped to his feet, looking flummoxed at what had just happened to him. Miss Thompson picked up his glasses. The dazed teacher put them on, brushed himself down, and tried to take a step forward. Unfortunately, in his haste to move on from the embarrassment of his fall, he forgot all about his laces being tied together. As he attempted to leave, he stumbled again. Seconds later, the school Headmaster was once again on the floor, this time lying on top of Miss Thompson, who he had knocked over.

As the teachers scrambled to help the Headmaster up for a second time, and rescue Miss Thompson, Terry looked at the boys, smiled and muttered one word.

'Invisible.'

******

Mr Horrocks composed himself and demanded that all students return to their classrooms, immediately. The children reluctantly did as they were told. They may have a new and exciting playground, but the same old strict, grumpy Headmaster remained by the looks of it.

As they reached the playground, Terry looked up at the boys.

'Go on then my ansums. Get back to class,' the boys eyed him suspiciously.

'Don't worry, I'll explain all dreckly,' he smiled at them before strolling jauntily off to the far end of the playground. The boys turned around and headed back towards the doors.

As they reached the top step, they heard shouting coming from behind them. They turned around and what they saw made them realise that Terry's presence would be a bad thing for all of them. Over on the climbing wall, right at the top, was a small Cornish Knocker, hanging upside down in a harness. His miners garb had fallen over his head and his bum was on show. He started laughing out loud, turned around, and gave the boys a wave.

'See you dreckly my ansums,' Terry shouted, as he lifted the garb and tried to free himself from the safety apparatus. The boys looked at one another and shook their heads. What they didn't know was that this was only the start of it.

The children finally reached their classroom and sat back down. They were still talking excitedly about what had happened when Mr Robertson interrupted them.

'Right then,' he began. 'I am as confused as you are with what has happened outside, but we will get to the bottom of it. In the meantime, what do you say we all do a bit of, what I like to call, Maths?'

Groans filled the room.

'Okay, settle down,' he went on. 'Books out and open at page six please.'

The children removed the lesson books from their bags and placed them on their desks. Suddenly, the door burst open. Everyone looked up to see who had just entered their classroom, but there was nobody there. The only thing outside was an empty corridor. Even Billy and Austin couldn't see anything this time, although they had an idea about who was responsible, but they had no idea what was about to follow.

Mr Robertson continued looking at the door, unsure how it had opened. The children watched as he walked across, closed it, and gave the handle a tug to ensure it was shut. He made a little *humph* sound, and shook his head.

'I'm not sure what is going on today. Maybe we have been invaded by gremlins ?' he joked as he stood, scratching his head.

'Right, let's get started,' Mr Robertson said while glancing at the door one last time to ensure it would not interrupt him again.

It didn't.

As he continued with the class, Billy gave Austin a nudge with his elbow. Austin looked at Billy, who turned his head towards the teacher's desk. Austin could not believe what he was seeing. Sat there, in the teacher's chair, was Terry. He was wearing a tweed, cape-style jacket with a matching deer stalker hat perched on his head. His feet were up on the desk and his right hand was wrapped around the bowl end of a pipe, with the other end clenched between his teeth. Terry sat there puffing away with a look of intense concentration on his face, as plumes of invisible smoke circled around his head. Billy leaned into Austin and whispered.

'He thinks he's Sherlock blinking Holmes,'

Billy said. Suddenly Terry started coughing as the smoke filled his lungs. He coughed so hard that he toppled backwards and fell onto the floor.

As Mr Robertson continued to talk to the class about the day's subject, (Fractions) Terry peered over the desk and waved at the boys, as he climbed back up onto the chair.

'Ere' what you fink of me new 'at? Does I look proper dapper?' He said as he tapped the peak, whilst putting the end of the pipe back into his mouth and taking another puff. Billy put his finger to his lips, warning him to be quiet. Terry removed the pipe from his mouth and shouted at Billy.

'What you shushin' me for, 'e can't 'ear me. Can you, ya gaet oaf?' he shouted at Mr Robertson, who continued to deliver the lesson without flinching.

'See, told you. Ere, I got a joke for you,' he said, as he leaned back and put his feet back up on the teacher's desk.

'If Sherlock Holmes was Cornish, what would his assistant be called?' The boy's continued looking at Mr Robertson and tried to ignore Terry, but it was no use, he continued anyway.

'He would be called Dr Wasson,' the boys struggled hard not to laugh. Terry was in fits of laughter though.

'You get it? See, Sherlock's assistant is Dr Watson, and Wasson is Cornish for 'what is happenin',' he said, in a fake posh accent. 'So, that would be 'is name,' Terry explained needlessly while continuing to chuckle at his own attempt at humour.

Throughout the entire lesson, Terry wandered around the classroom looking for mischief. He inspected everything from the teacher's desk, to the children's bags. After a while, he walked over to the open window, sat down and dangled his feet out of it. He was holding a sandwich in his hands that he had just removed from Mr Robertson's lunchbox. With his back to the children he started poking the sandwich, then he held it up to his face, turned around, and peered at the boys through two of the three holes he had just made.

'Coooooey,' he shouted at them.

As they looked over at him, he stuck his tongue through the third hole. They both laughed and then quickly started coughing to hide their sniggers.

Next, after taking two bites, Terry put the sandwich down and climbed out of the window. He tapped on the glass to get the boys' attention and when they looked over, he pressed his open mouth against the glass and blew out hard, causing his cheeks to inflate. The boys could see the inside of his mouth and started chuckling as he wiggled his tongue around and went cross-eyed. Mr Robertson glanced in their direction.

'Something more interesting outside is there boys?' they both turned to look at their teacher who stood at the front of the class with his hands on his hips and an unimpressed expression on his face.

'Sorry, sir,' they both chimed.

'Well, get on with the task I have just set the rest of the class. Page eight,' he then shook his head and made a tutting sound, before going to help a child at the back of the class, who had her hand in the air. Billy and Austin looked across at Terry. He was stood on the teacher's desk with his hands on his hips, shaking his head from side-to-side, and tutting at them, mimicking their teacher. They both looked away and got on with the exercise on page eight before they landed themselves in more trouble.

******

Billy and Austin were glad to finish the lesson. However, the rest of the day proved no different.

During English, Miss Thompson set the children a writing exercise. While she sat watching intently, Terry burst into the room. The boys sat there, staring at him, mouths open. What was he doing now? Miss Thompson got up from her desk, walked towards the open doorway, looked out into the corridor and, after seeing nobody there, shut the door. The boys hid behind their books as they started laughing. Terry had climbed up onto the teacher's desk where he stood in another outfit. Their furry friend was dressed in a pink baby costume, complete with a matching bonnet on his head, a rattle in his hand and an oversized dummy in his mouth.

Miss Thompson surveyed the room to ensure the children were working, then walked back and sat in her chair. Terry turned around, looked at her and climbed onto her lap. Billy and Austin watched as he nestled into her chest, removed the dummy, looked up at her and muttered *Mumma*. The boys started sniggering, causing Miss Thompson to glare at them over the top of the glasses perched on the end of her long, thin nose.

'Something amusing you two?' she quizzed them.

'No, miss,' the boys said together.

'Then get on with the exercise,' she scolded them. The boys did as they were told and did not look up from their books for the rest of the lesson.

******

With English finished, the boys headed to the sports hall for the disastrous P.E. lesson, that would end with the school tractor, driven by the invisible knocker, bursting through the hedge and charging across the field. The lesson finished early for obvious reasons, leading to the children having an extra 20 minutes for lunch.

History was their first afternoon lesson, where they had been learning about Greek mythology, until Terry interrupted the teacher's thought process by changing her book for one about Cornish Pasties. And then finally, it was their last lesson of the day - Design Technology with Mr Tebble. During the lesson, the boys kept looking around for any furry creatures that might want to interrupt and try to land them in trouble, but thankfully the lesson passed without Terry making an appearance.

After an hour, the bell rang to signal the end of the lesson and also the end of school for the day. The boys put their books back in their bags and made their way to the exit. The corridor was filled with conversations about the day's events. Obviously, the prime subject for discussion was the magical transformation of the outdated playground and sports facilities. Everyone had a theory about what had happened. One boy suggested aliens had come down and stolen some children for experimental purposes and as a thank you, they updated the playground. According to the school know-it-all, (or Pinocchio as he was known, because of his constant lies) the modification was because of a hi-tech overlay and when they came back tomorrow, it would be back to normal.

As Billy and Austin listened to them, they looked at each other and smiled. It was a smile that said *we know something you don't know.*

Chapter 3
Where's Terry?

Billy and Austin followed the other children outside and looked around. There was no sign of Terry. He had not appeared in the last lesson of the day and they wondered why he was not outside waiting for them. The playground still looked the same as it did after the transformation that morning. Some children made their way over to the climbing wall, but as soon as they got close, Mr Jackson's voice started shouting from an upstairs window.

'Get away from that wall! Now.'

The children huffed and made their way towards the exit. The boys looked over to the football pitch, but the only person they saw was Mr Tacklebum. He was standing beside the tractor, scratching his head, still unable to work out how it had driven through the hedge and across the field.

The boys stood, looking around, but there was no sign of Terry anywhere. Today had been crazy - the transformation of the playground, the pranks Terry had played on the teachers, the headmaster flailing around on the ground with Miss Thompson, and the tractor bursting through the hedge during P.E.

'Where is he?' Austin said, as he continued searching.

'He must have gone back home. Fancy a quick game of FIFA?' Billy asked. Austin thought for a moment and realised there was no need to rush home and wait, hand and foot, on a slob anymore. Things had now changed, thanks to the events in the woods the day before.

He smiled.

'Sure, why not?' The boys left together and were heading out of the gate, when they heard a voice behind them.

'How come you two are best friends?' They turned around and discovered Sue standing behind one of the gate pillars.

'Oh, hey,' said Billy, awkwardly.

Sue glared at him.

'Ok, so what happened last night?' She asked, crossing her arms and glaring at Billy whilst she waited for an answer.

'Oh, um, nothing,' Billy said, as he stood there scratching his head, searching for an appropriate explanation.

'Oh, I'll tell her, you chicken,' Austin interjected.

'Your boyfriend here slipped down the hill behind his house and ended up stuck between two trees until I arrived to help him. I heard him screaming like a girl while I was on my way home. You're lucky I did, or else he would have been a right mess, especially if he had slipped all the way to the bottom. God know's what's down there,' Austin explained. Billy bit his lip to stop himself from laughing. If only Sue knew what had really happened.

'Oh, right and now you're best buddies are you? After the way he treated you yesterday, and me. I'm very disappointed in you, Billy. I thought you were better than that,' she didn't even wait for a reply. She glared at Austin, pushed her way through the pair of them, and headed home.

'Jeez, you were lucky there mate. She's a bit highly strung that one,' Billy smiled but said nothing. He wished he had handled it differently because he really liked her.

Austin saw he was upset.

'Look, she'll be fine once she's calmed down. She's a girl. You know what Terry said, '*they is all blinkin' nutters,*' he joked, imitating Terry, causing Billy to laugh.

'So, dry your eyes princess, and let's get going so I can kick your butt at FIFA.'

'You wish.' Billy replied.

As they walked to Billy's house, they couldn't

help but wonder what had happened to their little furry friend. He had simply vanished.

******

The boy's arrived at Billy's house and after a quick hello, they made their way up to his bedroom. As they entered, Billy picked up the washed and folded laundry on his bed and threw it onto his chair. Most of it toppled over and fell onto the floor, where it stayed. Billy then picked up the PlayStation controllers from his desk.

'Here you go,' he said, passing one to Austin. As Billy set the game up, Austin looked around.

Billy's room was not the biggest. On the wall opposite his bed, he had two shelves. One of these contained assorted Lego figures; *Marvel, DC, Star Wars, Lord of the Rings and Harry Potter*. Several computer games occupied the second shelf; *Fortnite, The Uncharted Series, Assassin's Creed, Spiderman, Lego Harry Potter, Tiger Woods, and FIFA*. He had a small football clock just above the shelves, and his curtains displayed Marvel Avengers characters; *Thor, Ironman, Hulk, Spiderman, Black Widow, Captain America, and Captain Marvel*, all in different battle poses. One corner contained a double wardrobe with clothes spilling out from the bottom of the open door. Next to this his desk was cluttered with several items; pens, paper, computer boxes, and books. There was also a crumpled up football kit underneath it.

'What do you think happened to him?' Billy asked, distracting Austin from his thoughts.

'Who?'

'Who do you think? Terry.'

'Oh... no idea, maybe he went back home for feeding.' Austin offered.

'I suppose,' said Billy.

Both boys sat in silence until the game loaded up. Billy wasted no time in selecting his team – Liverpool. Austin did likewise and picked Manchester United.

'Ready to be annihilated?' Billy smirked.

'So boring,' Austin joked back. The boys played a few games and soon forgot all about Terry and the antics he had pulled at school that day. After an hour, Billy's mum shouted up the stairs to ask if Austin wanted to stay for dinner.

'I would run for it before it's too late if I were you, mate,' Billy said.

'I can't anyway, I need to get home. Mum will kill me if I'm any later, and besides, I want to have dinner with them.'

Billy nodded. He could understand that.

The boys made their way downstairs. Austin said thank you to Billy's parents and headed out of the door.

'See you tomorrow,' Austin said as he pulled

his blazer off the coat hook, picked up his bag and slung it over his shoulder.

'Yeah, see you there,' Billy said as he opened the door. Austin walked down the path, waved, and then disappeared around the corner. Billy stood there, looking around. He half expected Terry to be waiting for them, but there was no sign of him.

Billy's mother called from inside the house to inform him dinner was on the table, so he closed the door and headed into the kitchen. As he sat down, he couldn't help but wonder what had happened to Terry. He was sure he was ok, but there was something at the back of his mind niggling him.

Chapter 4
Billy Explains

The next day, the boys arrived early for school, as had most of the teachers and pupils given yesterday's strange events. Everyone was eager to look around their new playground, which despite the claim from the boy known as Pinocchio, was the same as when they had left the previous day.

Billy noticed Sue standing on her own, so he made his way over. He wanted to clear the air with her.

'Hey,' he said as he approached her.

She looked up at him but didn't say a word. Instead, she folded her arms and waited for an explanation.

'Look, I'm sorry. I got stuck in the woods and he helped me out, that's all. Then we got talking, and it turns out he's not as bad as we first thought.' The fact they were stuck in the woods made him feel better as technically he was not lying. Sue continued looking at him, but still didn't say a word. He started batting his eyelids and turned his mouth down, pretending to be sad. Finally, she started laughing, then caught herself and stopped.

'I was just disappointed. He was so rude and obnoxious to us on the first day and there you were acting like best friends. I still don't trust him,' she said, glaring in Austin's direction.

'I get that, I do, but give him a chance, you might even like him,' Billy replied.

'You think?' she said with a frown.

'Yes, trust me. I promise to protect you if he's rude again,' he said, puffing his chest out and giving it a double pump with his fist. Sue laughed at him.

'You idiot,' she said.

'Now that's just rude,' he joked. 'So, you want to come over?'

'OK. But if he starts then I'll give you a thump, and I can hit hard,' she raised her hand to threaten him in a joking manner.

'Ah, not in the face,' he said, pretending to cower. They both laughed and walked over to see Austin.

He was leaning on the railings leading up to the doors. When he saw Billy and Sue approaching, he stood up straight.

'Ooooh, you two lovers made up have you?'

Sue glared at him.

'Mate, don't be an idiot,' Billy said.

Austin rolled his eyes and tutted at him.

'I'm only messing. Look, I'm sorry we got off on the wrong foot. I was just trying to be funny and show off as you were new,' Austin said as he held his hand out towards her.

She looked at him, still unsure. However, she took his hand and shook it.

'Ok, but the minute you're that rude again, that's it,' she warned him.

'No problem, sister,' Austin joked as he let go of her hand.

'Anyway, either of you two got an idea of what happened here yesterday?' Austin asked, looking from Sue to Billy.

'Not a clue,' Billy replied as he shrugged.

'It wasn't only the playground. What about the doors opening when we were in lessons? There's something weird going on,' Billy said, looking at Austin and struggling not to smile.

'It's not just that,' Sue said, joining the conversation.

'What do you mean?' Billy asked.

'Well, after I walked off yesterday...' she started.

'You mean when you stormed off in a huff because I stole your boyfriend?' Austin interrupted as he smirked at her.

Sue just glared at him, again.

'Anyway, as I was saying, on the way home

yesterday, I saw the strangest thing.'

'What?' asked Billy.

'Well, I went to check out the lane in the woods,' she continued.

The boys glanced at each other.

'Right, and?' Austin asked.

But before Sue could answer Billy interjected.

'Why did you go that way? That's not on your route home?'

'Because, I wanted to see if you two were telling me the truth yesterday. I hate being lied to,' she said as she looked from Billy to Austin.

'Go on,' Austin said.

'Well, I walked along the path that runs around the back of the woods and I came across an area of disturbed earth. There were footprints, and a broken tree branch down the slope, which backs up your story from yesterday, so I believe what you told me.'

They both sighed.

'Is that all?' Austin asked, letting out a groan.

'No, that's not all. If you will stop being so rude and let me finish,' she said, crossing her arms again.

The boys looked embarrassed after their telling off.

'As I was saying, on the way out of the woods I heard something rustling a few feet to my left, so I edged my way between two trees. At first,

I thought I was seeing things,' Billy and Austin were eager to hear more, but just at that moment, the school bell rang, interrupting Sue's story.

'What did you see?' Asked Billy.

'I'll tell you later. I don't want to be late for registration.'

And with that, she walked past the boys, headed up the stairs and disappeared through the door. Billy and Austin stood there for a second, looking at each other. Both of them had an idea about what Sue had seen, but hoped they were wrong.

The boys' thoughts were disturbed by Mr Jackson, who was on morning playground duty. He informed the last remaining children that they should start heading in to avoid being marked as late. 'Only three late marks to receive a free detention,' he announced as if it was a special offer at the local supermarket.

The boys turned and headed up the stairs, taking the same route Sue had. Billy was thinking about Terry. They had not seen him since yesterday afternoon, and he wondered where he was and what had happened. He only hoped Terry was ok.

Little did they know, Terry was on an adventure and it would prove far more dangerous than they could have possibly imagined.

Chapter 5
Sue's Discovery

During Geography, Billy and Austin sat on either side of Sue. They were keen to hear what she had seen the day before and wanted to be close enough in case she started talking, but she didn't. Her education was far too important to talk about the strange events in the woods the day before.

During the lesson, Billy and Austin kept looking around, waiting for Terry to enter or appear at a window dressed as a superhero, but he didn't, nor did he turn up during their next lesson, Art, with the aptly named, Miss Tittlebrush. In fact, as the day went on, they forgot all about their furry friend.

Once the bell rang for the final time that day, the three of them made their way out of the gate and headed along the path towards home. The boys didn't bring up the subject of the previous day or ask Sue about it, despite being desperate to find out what she saw, as they were worried about

Terry. Finally, Sue broke the awkward silence that was surrounding them.

'I can feel the tension in the pair of you. Let's go over there and I'll put you out of your misery,' she said, pointing to a bench next to a grassed area to their left.

The boys removed their bags and placed them on the floor as they sat down, leaving a gap in the middle for Sue.

'I don't know why you two are so keen to hear my story. It's nothing interesting. Just strange,' she said as she looked from Billy to Austin before sitting down.

'Well, just tell us anyway, it may be nothing, but we're both intrigued,' Austin said. He looked over at Billy who was staring intently at Sue. Austin wasn't sure if it was because he was interested in the tale she had to tell, or because he fancied her.

'Well, as I was saying this morning, I went to the woods to check out your story and as I was heading back out, I heard a scuttling and rustling noise coming from behind the trees that separate the path from the woods. I thought it was an animal.'

'Yeah, it must have been,' Austin said.

'It wasn't.'

'Did you see what it was?' asked Billy.

'Not exactly,' she said, leaving the boys to wander what she meant.

'So you saw nothing? You just heard a sound coming from the woods, but you know it wasn't an animal?' Austin said, as he shook his head. He wasn't sure where she was heading with this conversation.

Sue looked at him, annoyed.

'That's right. It wasn't a woodland animal, or a cat, or a dog, or a monkey, or even a flipping rhinoceros,' she said in a sarcastic tone.

'I'm sorry,' said Austin. 'But if you didn't see it, how do you know it wasn't an animal?'

Sue was tiring of the boys questioning her.

'Because, when was the last time you heard an animal, burp, break wind and then laugh as they said something weird like, *gate on my lager?*' The boys looked at each other. They knew what she had heard.

'Gate on my lager?' said Austin as he chuckled.

Sue, not for the first time, glared at him.

'Was it more like, *getton my lover?*' he said, imitating Terry's accent.

'Yes, that was it,' she said as she pointed at him.

'What happened then?' Austin asked.

'Well, I started walking towards the sound, but the trees were in front of me so I couldn't see clearly. Then there was a flash of light, just like the one we saw yesterday, only a lot smaller. That's where I found it...'

'Found what?' the boys said simultaneously.

'As I edged around the trees I saw a small stump which had a plume of smoke circling above it,' she replied.

'That it?' asked Austin.

'No, that is not it. There was also this, lying on the floor next to the stump.'

Sue reached into her pocket and pulled out a small white scrunched up bag. She unfolded it as the boys watched in silence. When Sue finished unravelling the creased-up bag, she passed it to Billy to examine. He looked over at Austin, who was staring down at it. The bag was the kind that bakeries use and had a picture of a pasty printed on the front. Billy and Austin looked at it but didn't say a word.

'So, who would have been in the woods eating a Pasty and then just vanish?' Sue asked the boys.

'I wonder,' said Austin. Then, he stood up, put his backpack on and waited for the others to join him.

What was Terry playing at and where was he?

Four Months Later...

Chapter 6
Terry's Predicament

The beast stood there, motionless, as blood dripped from the ripped flesh still wedged between its teeth. He gave another deafening roar that bounced around the walls of the deep ravine. Terry cowered behind the cover, with his eyes shut and his hands firmly cupped over his ears as he tried to block out the intense noise circling all around him. How had he ended up in this position? Cornered, with the stone lying directly under the belly of the beast. Then came another roar, louder than before. He crouched low to the ground, keeping under the blanket of smoke.

As Terry peered out, the three-headed Chimera spotted him and growled once again. A long wavy mane framed the ferocious looking lion's face, which contained a mouthful of razor-sharp teeth. Red fiery eyes were firmly fixed on Terry's current location, as if waiting for him to emerge so that he could pounce. The head of a goat, was situated next to the lion. Two thick-curled horns rose from the top of it and its ominously black eyes seemed soul-less. To the rear a 10-foot-long tail curled all the way up from the base of its back, to the vicious serpent's head located at the end. Its mouth contained four oversized fangs that twinkled whenever the sunlight caught them as it continued to hiss and sway from side-to-side, ready to strike at any moment.

The Chimera had followed him into the ravine, and now it waited, it had to finish him, it needed the stone, that was the key to everything. Only, nobody could use the stone. Not unless Terry transferred ownership. He was the custodian and the use of its powers lay solely in his hands. The lion roared and the serpent lurched forwards whenever it caught sight of him.

Terry peered around his cover again. The stone was still there, resting on the open flap of his sack. The Chimera was standing over it, guarding it. Why had he taken it off when he went for a quick poop? Stupid Knocker. He had to get it back somehow. He couldn't get home without it, and he couldn't let them have it, not now, not ever!

There was no way of getting to it though, not whilst the beast continued to guard it. To his right he spotted a small rock lying on the ground, just within his reach. Beyond the rock there was a deep gully that ran from the bottom of the ravine to his sack. He had an idea, but he would have to be quick. The only chance would be to get to the gully and pray he could scoot along, unseen. It was dangerous, but right now it was his only option.

He closed his eyes, and took a couple of deep breaths, then opened them and made his move. As he reached out and grabbed the rock, another roar echoed around the ravine. The creature had spotted him and lunged forwards. Luckily, Terry pulled his arm to safety, just before the serpent's head swung around and sunk its teeth in. A hiss of disapproval followed as it struck the dusty surface of the floor and recoiled.

Terry began to chuckle as he thought *at least it can't get any worse*, but it was about to get much, much worse. Suddenly, he heard hissing, but it was not coming from the serpent. This sound was continuous and much louder. Soon it was joined by popping and fizzing noises, and seconds later there was a loud explosion. Terry felt himself getting very warm, so he stood up and took a peek. The Chimera growled at him again, but that was the least of his worries. What he saw filled him with dread, and he started panicking. He had to act. Now!

'Oh bugger,' he muttered, and then looked at the small rock sat in the middle of his hand. He only had one chance, and he had to make it count.

The lava was pouring down the hill and would fill the ditch around the ravine in seconds. A quick check confirmed his fears. The Chimera was going nowhere. It was still guarding the stone and seemed happy to give up its life for it.

Terry gripped the rock tightly in his right hand, turned and launched it across the ravine. It hit the wall and disintegrated on impact. The lion roared, and the serpent hissed towards the sound. The lava continued to hiss and spit as it flowed into the ravine, melting anything it touched. Terry was running out of time. He cupped his hands over his mouth and screamed as loud as he could in the opposite direction to where he had thrown the stone. The sound reverberated off the walls and echoed around the ravine as the serpent continued swaying from side-to-side, searching for the source. Terry screamed a second time causing the lion to turn. Once again, the echo did its job and bounced around the walls. The beast was frantically looking around, no longer sure of where its prey was. Lava had now filled the left and right-hand sides of the ditch and was pooling at the bottom. It would soon start filling up the entire ravine. Terry needed to move. He had to get to the gully. It was now or never. He filled his lungs, cupped his hands again and threw his voice as far as he could. The beast's roaring seemed angrier and its movements had become more frantic as the echoing continued to bounce off the walls, confusing its senses. Meanwhile, the sizzling lava kept pouring from the volcano. It was only a few feet away now and the heat was intense. Terry prepared himself.

Now. He had to move. Now.

Terry launched himself towards the gully. The floor was dusty and full of loose stones and fragments of rock, which made moving forward difficult. The lava had already filled the bottom of the ravine and was moving up towards him. He was in trouble. The beast was still turning, still looking, the serpent continued to hiss as the lion roared.

Terry needed to move faster, but he continued slipping. He could not get any purchase to pull himself forwards. He was eight feet away from the stone, with the lava continuing to rise as it filled the ravine. The hissing and spitting sounds were getting louder, more rocks evaporated and melted away as the lava consumed them. It was no use. Terry was losing the battle and he would be next.

Just then he had an idea. He reached down with his right hand and removed the pickaxe from his belt. He raised it above his head and drove it into the ground. He began to pull himself along. It worked. Now that he had fresh impetus, he didn't stop. He pulled the axe out and repeated the action, and again. Three swift movements and he was almost there. The lava was right behind him. He was so hot, sweat was pouring from him and his feet were burning, but one more strike with the axe and Terry was almost within touching distance of the stone. As he glanced in front of him, there was the serpent, looking directly into his eyes. It hissed, giving him a perfect view of its over-sized fangs, which glowed red from the reflection of the lava all around them. Terry drove the axe into the ground one last time as the serpent lunged towards him with a final hiss. All Terry could see was the inside of the serpent's mouth as he reached for the stone and wrapped his fingers around it. He closed his eyes tight, waiting for the vicious-looking fangs to sink into his arm, but all he felt was the soaring temperature reduce. Terry could no longer hear the hissing sounds of the serpent, or the sizzling of the boiling lava as it rose towards him. There were no uncomfortable rocks under his body, only soft undergrowth.

Terry slowly opened his eyes and realised that he had made it back. He did not understand how, and couldn't believe that he had survived, but he was home, safe and sound in the clearing, just outside of his village. He lay on the grass for a few minutes thinking about what had just happened. Why had he gone on his own? Why had he risked it? He really was a stupid Knocker sometimes.

As he lay there, he started laughing, small chuckling sounds at first, but soon he was holding his belly as it continued wobbling and hurting because of his continued laughter. He couldn't stop. Terry began howling as the tears streamed down his face.

Once he had regained his sanity, he began to think about what he had been through, what he had seen, and what he now knew. He realised he would have to go back, leaving it there was unthinkable. There was no other option. When he returned, he would take the boys along with him. They would be vital to the mission. He knew they would refuse, so he wouldn't ask them directly. In fact, he had already put the wheels in motion and the boys knew nothing about it. This was something that he needed to do. Everyone's future depended on it.

Terry got to his feet, dried his eyes, dusted himself down and then took a deep breath. Taking on the creatures he had encountered over the past few months had been a piece of cake compared to what he was about to face. He cocked his leg, farted, and started picking his nose as he headed home, ready to lie to his wife about where he had been and what he had been doing for the past few months.

******

Back inside the ravine, the Chimera was perilously

perched on top of the boulder as the lava continued to rise. It was marooned with no way out. It panicked as the red fiery liquid continued to pour down from the volcano. The lion roared, and the serpent hissed.

The lava had filled the entire ravine. The Chimera awaited its fate, holding onto as many precious seconds of life as possible, before it was gone, forever. Suddenly, the lava stopped rising. It was not pouring down from the volcano anymore, but instead flowed backwards. The lava continued to move away and slowly, inexorably returned to the volcano.

The Chimera stayed where it was, as the volcano continued to fill up with the red-hot substance. A loud roar from the distance filled the ravine. Moments later, the sky turned black as an enormous creature floated overhead. A female figure stood on top of the dragon. In her left hand she held a chain, which was wrapped around its neck and in her right hand she held a staff, the base of which was resting on the dragon's back. She was wearing a long cape that stopped midway up her knee-length boots. The dragon continued to flap its gigantic wings as it hovered above the Chimera.

'He will be back and we will finish him. You will not fail me next time. We need the stone and when we have it, he will die.'

She pulled on the chain in her hand, causing the dragon to let out another roar and, as a ball of fire exhaled from its mouth, it departed. The Chimera climbed down from the boulder and headed out of the ravine.

As he reached the top and turned the corner, the volcano started bubbling once again, and erupted for the second time that day, sending boiling lava back towards the empty ravine below.

Chapter 7
Billy, Austin and Sue

The boys had not seen Terry for four months. In fact, they had just about forgotten all about him. He popped into their heads sometimes of course. How could he not, after what they had been through together? However, it seemed their furry little friend had moved on, as had they. The three of them, Billy, Austin, and Sue had become very close friends. They had forgotten all about the confrontation on the first day of the school year and had built a genuine friendship.

Austin had turned the corner in his schoolwork. He was hitting all of his targets, getting rave reviews from his teachers, and had even received an attitude improvement award. He was enjoying life and on one occasion came close to beating Billy at FIFA. Billy was definitely using some sort of cheat. Austin watched his friend's fingers when they played, looking for a certain button combination, but he didn't see anything.

His home life had also vastly improved. He and his dad did everything together, from messing about when washing the car, to hiding in cupboards and jumping out on each other. Austin once hid in the clothes rack at the local supermarket and waited for his dad to come around the corner. When his dad appeared, he jumped out and let out a loud scream. His dad leapt backwards, lost his balance, and went crashing through a display of baked beans, sending them all over the floor. Austin burst out laughing and quickly hid in another aisle so he could watch his father try to explain what had happened to the staff.

Sue was excelling. She was top of the class in almost every subject and first in with homework, which was always presented in pristine condition. She was enjoying her life in England since moving from South Africa in the summer. Her dad had relaxed slightly and allowed her to stay out with Billy and Austin, but only for one hour, maximum. Then she would have to be home, sat at her desk and doing her homework before dinner. Billy had taught her how to play conkers and some other traditional English games. However, the boys could still not tempt her to go apple scrumping. Stealing apples from trees in people's gardens was a step too far for Sue.

Billy was also settling into life in his new school. He had made the school football team and was their star player. Scoring goals, he had discovered, gave him the biggest buzz, especially if Sue was watching. His dad had finally found a job, which made Billy's home life a little less stressful, as his mother was now much happier. He was even helping his little sister with her homework. Billy spent a lot of time chilling with Austin. He was good fun, and getting better at FIFA, but Billy always made sure he won. There was one-time Billy had a big scare when Austin nearly beat him though. Luckily, Billy knew a few secret moves to ensure he still won. Not that he would ever tell Austin his sneaky tricks.

The new playground was going down a treat at school. Rival schools had commented on it and applied to have their own playgrounds transformed. The parents would often ask Mr Horrocks how he had funded it. He would tap the side of his nose, wink, and tell them it was a secret. Technically, he was right. There were so many more sporting events taking place than before thanks to the new facilities. There were new school teams for football, hockey, rounders, rugby and also netball. It had completely transformed the school. There were so many more students applying to study there than ever before, which raised the profile of the school even more. The teachers seemed a lot happier too. They had relaxed slightly and this led to the students enjoying their lessons far more than they had previously.

Things were on the up. The atmosphere around the school had improved immensely and there was also the school trip to look forward to. A trip organised by Mr Horrocks, after a day out to the Maritime Museum in Falmouth, had proven very beneficial. Afterwards he had arranged for the school camping trip this year to take place in Hampshire. The best part of this was that the children would get to spend a day onboard HMS Victory, one of the Royal Navy's most famous ships.

Billy, Austin, and Sue were so excited. The visit to the ship would be the highlight of the school trip, and they would also have four nights away from their parents. Sue had been researching the ship for weeks and she took great pleasure in informing the boys about all the facts she had discovered.

She told Billy and Austin about the famous battle of Trafalgar and the exploits of Lord Horatio Nelson while they listened intently. Although, when Sue announced this would be the most exciting adventure any of them had ever been on, the boys glanced at each other and gave a wry smile.

Little did they know Sue would be proven right. This would be the most amazing adventure any of them had ever been on. It would be exciting, eventful, but above all else, it would be fun. What they didn't realise was that it would also be dangerous. All thanks to a little furry creature who had recently gone missing. A creature who had not disappeared for good, but who had been on an adventure of his own. A creature who had been battling beasts and escaping erupting volcanos. A creature who had discovered a secret treasure that lay hidden inside a deep, dark cave on a tropical island.

Terry had recently returned, but he would be going back, and this time he would take the boys. The problem was, Terry couldn't transport all of them that far. The stone wasn't strong enough, not on its own. He also couldn't tell the boys where they were going and why, because they would refuse if they knew how dangerous it was going to be. He had to get them there a different way. It was at that moment, he came up with a brilliant idea.

Terry knew all about the school trip. In fact, even though he had been away for months, he knew everything that had been happening and what they had been up to. The stone showed him whatever he wanted to see, whenever he wanted to see it. The school trip was his chance to get the help he desperately needed. It was also a chance to go on another adventure with his best friends.

So he planned the trip, all of it. He had to make it the most amazing school outing the children had ever been on. He needed them to want to go, so he had to make it very special. During their trip to the Maritime Museum, they had shown a very keen interest in many aspects of it. They were talking with Museum staff members, interacting with teachers and seemed to have an amazing time. Watching them on that day gave him a brilliant idea. Later that night, he used the stone to watch their teacher, Mr Horrocks. He would never sanction the trip that Terry needed them to go on. The other teachers had a hard enough time getting him to approve funds for the Maritime visit, so there was no way he would sanction what Terry had planned. There was no other option though. Terry knew he would need to intervene. That night, just before bedtime, Mr Horrocks settled down with his hot cup of cocoa, as he did every night. Terry, who was sat thousands of miles away, rubbed his hands together and went to work. He used the stone to teleport a bolt of light into Mr Horrocks's cup. Luckily, the teacher was leaning back in his favourite chair, resting his eyes, so he never saw it. He finished his drink and then made his way to bed. Just as he was drifting off, he sat bolt upright.

'Yes!' he screamed out, forcing his wife to wake with a start and fall out of bed.

'That will be amazing,' he said to himself as his wife climbed back into bed, punched him on the arm, and called him an idiot. And that was that. Terry had planted the seed. There was no going back, not now the headmaster was already planning the trip.

******

Terry had just reached his village. Taking a deep breath, he lent to one side, farted, and took his finger out of his nose as he prepared to face his furious wife.

He stopped momentarily, looked at his finger, wiped it on his garb and then stuck it up the other nostril, before entering his village.

Chapter8
Terry's in the Doghouse

'Four months! What on earth 'ave you been doin' for four blinkin' months? Come on, I can't wait to 'ear this one,' Terry's wife asked. She had one hand on her hip and the other on top of the broom she was using to sweep the path. Terry removed the finger from his nose and wiped it as he prepared to explain to his wife where he had been.

'Well, you won't believe me if I tell you, so woz the point?' he said.

'Try me!' she demanded.

As he looked at her, he knew he couldn't tell her the truth, she would string him up. It was then that he decided that he needed to do what he was good at. Lie.

'Well, I was in the woods, you know, lookin' for stuff for the village and a woodland imp found me and asked if I could 'elp them with a lil' problem. They found this new mine but needed 'elp wiv diggin' and preparin' it as they heard there woz loads o' gems in there. Well, o' course, minin' is what I do, so I ended up goin' to 'elp him. Before I knew it four months had passed. Got some set-up now though they 'ave. All thanks to me,' he said puffing out his chest. 'So that's what I 'ave been doin', 'elpin' others. Woz problem wiv that?' He answered as he extended his arms out, insinuating it was no big deal.

It was unfortunate that he could not transport back to the exact moment he had left four months before, but there wasn't enough time. He was lucky to have made it back at all. He just had to get out of the ravine.

His wife stood there, glaring at him.

'Oh, well, that's alrigh' then. As long as you 'as 'ad fun, leavin' me 'ere to look after the lil' ones while you go off gallivantin' 'round the place. I 'ope you enjoyed yourself?' She asked sarcastically.

Before Terry could answer she continued.

'I mean tis not like there's loads to do 'ere is there? Cookin', cleanin', washin', tidyin', it all does itself. I turn my back and when I turn 'round 'gain, as if by magic, tis all done.' Her sarcasm was increasing. Terry smiled and joked as he scratched his bum.

'Well, I always thought you woz a bit of a witch,' as soon as the words left his mouth he regretted it.

'A witch, a witch! How dare you?! You come

'ome 'ere after bein' god knows where, doin' god knows what, and you call me A WITCH? How dare you!' She then tightened her grip on the broom as she rose it above her head and chased her husband down the path and around the clearing with it. He was in fits of laughter, while she screamed at him with the broom raised high above her head like a giant sword. The clearing was full of Knockers who were looking at them and laughing. The women were egging Hazel on, whilst the men were cheering for Terry. He smiled and waved at them before risking a quick look behind him to poke out his tongue and blow a raspberry at his wife. Just at that moment, he tripped on a corn cob and came crashing down on the ground, stricken and helpless, as his wife pushed the head of the broom under his chin like it was the point of a sword.

'Not so funny now, is it, my ansum? Please, remind me, in front of all our friends, what you just called me?' she stood, glaring down at her husband. He looked at her and smiled before he replied.

'Well, I just said you was the most beautiful woman I 'ad ever seen and I want to spend the rest of my life starin' into those big beautiful eyes o' yours.' There were *'oohs'* and *'aahs'* from the Knockers watching. Hazel just looked at her husband. She pushed the broom up under his chin.

'You are on very thin ice Terry Trevithick, so, get yer butt off the floor. Tis work to be done and don't you ever call me a witch again, okay?' She waited, with the broom still firmly held in place. He didn't answer. He couldn't because he was biting his lip so hard trying not to laugh.

'OKAY?' she reiterated.

'Okay, Okay, I 'pologise. That was too far. I should have been more 'foughtful. I didn't mean it. You is the love of my life, not a witch,' he lay there on his elbows looking into her eyes. Hazel looked at him, as a wry smile crept across her face. She removed the broom and helped her husband to his feet. She then gave him a kiss on the cheek.

'That's more like it,' she said, before turning around and walking back towards their home. Terry couldn't help himself, he stood there, brushing himself down and smiled as the words tumbled out of his mouth.

'I'd love you even more if you could shave that moustache off, 'tis most unladylike and always tickles when you kiss me,' he began to chuckle just as his wife raised the broom above her head, and started chasing him around the clearing again. Terry continued laughing as she shouted obscenities at him.

'Chase me, chase me, if you catch me please don't kiss me,' he said through his laughing.

Their children just stood in the doorway of their shack, munching on cookies, watching as their mum and dad played *catch me if you can* around the clearing.

Chapter 9
Sue's Controlling Father

'But dad. Everyone from my class is going. I'll be the only one who isn't, PLLLLEEEASEEE!'

'Sue. I said no and that's the end of the matter. I'm allowing you to stay out for an hour after school with your friends, but you are not going on a trip for five days. It's out of the question,' her dad was remaining firm on his stance about the trip. He would not buckle. Sue looked at her mother for support.

'Mum, please?' Sue begged.

'I'm sorry sweetie. Your father has spoken. It's disappointing, but you must respect his decision,' her mum then drank the rest of the coffee in her cup, stood up and walked over to the sink.

'This is so unfair. What am I supposed to do?' she said as she folded her arms and lent against the fridge.

'Young lady, that is enough,' her dad said, as he looked sternly at her and held his hand out in a *stop* gesture.

'Aaah, this is not fair! We're not living in South Africa anymore. I don't see what the problem is. You're so controlling.'

Sue threw the permission slip on the floor, stormed out of the room and stomped up the stairs. The tears started before she had even reached the first step.

'You're going to have to cut those apron strings at some point,' Sue's mother said to her husband as she turned to face him. He removed his glasses and rubbed his eyes.

'She is not going and that is final. You need to back me up on this, Amanda,' he replied as he put his glasses back on.

'I am! But I don't think it would hurt for her to join her friends. You're excluding her from having fun. If you're not careful you'll drive her away. She's growing up so fast and you need to allow her to do that.'

'Maybe, but I can't. I have to protect her and you know why. It can't happen again. I won't allow it. It's my responsibility to protect her,' he explained. 'It's for her benefit.'

'Hers or yours?' his wife asked.

'That's not fair, I'm doing this for her. I can't take a chance on the same thing happening, not to our own daughter.'

'Yes, I know that, but there was nothing you

could have done. It wasn't your fault, you need to realise that. We came here to get over it and move on as a family, but if you continue to suffocate her, she will resent you for it,' his wife said. She walked over and put her arms around her husband, as he stood there staring blankly at the floor.

'You're right, and I'm trying, but it will take time. I'm not ready yet, she is not going on that trip. My decision is final,' he said as he hugged her back and kissed the top of her head. Then he let go before turning to leave. 'Let me know how she is when she comes downstairs,' he said as he reached the door. 'I'll be back in a couple of hours.'

With that, he picked up his bag, opened the door and walked down the path to his car. His wife walked into the living room and watched him leave.

He reached his car and gave it a quick once over then pressed the button on his keys and seconds later the boot automatically opened. Mr Johnson placed his bag inside, removed his vehicle inspection mirror and walked around his car, checking to see if he could find anything suspicious hiding underneath it.

Once he had finished, he put the mirror back in the boot, closed it and walked around to the driver's door. He climbed in and seconds later the reversing lights illuminated. He backed out of their drive, swung the car around and headed down the hill and out of sight.

When was he going to let it go? It had been almost two years since the incident and he was not getting any better. He was throwing himself into his work as a distraction, so he didn't have to deal with it. Mrs Johnson blew out her cheeks and went to check on her emotional daughter. Once again she would have to try and tidy up the mess that her husband had created.

Sat outside on a rock in the front garden, a furry creature started shaking his head. He had used the stone and watched the entire episode unfold. He did not understand why her dad was so protective. It seemed over the top, but he must have his reasons. Terry knew he would have to intervene. Sue was Billy and Austin's best friend and she was so excited about the trip. He knew what he had to do. They would all go on the trip, and they would have an amazing time. But when they got back, she would have to face her father and explain why she had disobeyed him. He would be furious. There would be repercussions, outrage, and arguments. She would be grounded and the hour after school with her friends would stop, probably forever.

However, Sue would have the time of her life and her father would know nothing about denying her the most amazing school trip ever.

Terry then jumped off the rock, thought about

what he was about to do, smiled and made his way home.

******

When Sue and her parents sat down to dinner that night none of them said a word. Sue didn't look up from her plate for a second as she was so upset with her father. She didn't want to engage in conversation with either of her parents. Her mother attempted to talk to her a few times, but all she got in return were one-word answers.

Sue finished her dinner, asked to leave the table, and immediately headed back upstairs, giving an excuse that she still had homework to do and needed to get ready for school the next day. She was not looking forward to tomorrow, seeing everyone get excited about handing in their permission slips. It was going to be painful for her to watch, knowing she couldn't go. How was she going to explain it to Billy and Austin? The three of them had spoken of little else since they found out where they were going. While the class was away on the trip; she would have to attend school and complete tasks set by the teachers. She'd probably have to help the younger children too. It was so unfair.

Sue went into her bedroom, sat on her bed, and put her head in her hands as she thought about everything she would be missing. After a few moments, she stood up, walked over to her chest of drawers and opened the bottom draw. She removed a box from inside, walked back over to her bed, and sat down. On top of the box written in pink pen were the words, 'School trip, Hampshire - EEEEEEK'.

Sue took the lid off and removed a pile of paperwork. She had been researching it for weeks. There were several paper clippings, articles from the internet, leaflets the school had handed out, and an information pack covering their itinerary.

The school was staying at a local campsite, complete with log cabins, a massive BBQ area and, best of all, a water park. She was so excited about paddle boarding and the assault course on the water. It would have been so good. She picked up a leaflet for their second day. They were due to visit the 170-metre tall Spinnaker Tower. Underneath this were several articles about the D-Day Museum, their destination for day three. Sue read two articles and placed them on top of the Spinnaker Tower leaflet. Next, she picked up cuttings and a small booklet on the best part of the trip, the visit onboard HMS Victory at Portsmouth Naval Base. She had plans and drawings of the ship, information on Lord Horatio Nelson, including the plaque marking the spot where he fell during the battle of Trafalgar in 1805, and information on the ship's weight, length, and the date she was first launched. Sue let the papers fall from her hands back into the box and sat there in silence for a while.

She had gathered so much information about the trip, but it was all useless now. She was going nowhere. Her dad had seen to that. She ripped the sign from the lid of her box and placed it on top of the paperwork, picked it all up, looked at it once more, and let out a long sigh before walking over and dropping everything into the bin. She then returned the box to the bottom draw and closed it.

Sue shuffled back to her bed, got under the covers and pulled them over her head, as the tears rolled down her cheeks. This was so unfair, why did he have to be so controlling?

Chapter 10
The Magical Light

That night, just after Sue and her parents had fallen asleep, a ray of light emerged from the woods and splintered the darkness outside. It flew through the trees and across the green. It reached the house with the solid blue door, where it paused for a few seconds. The letterbox flap lifted, just enough to allow the ray of light in, and then shut again. It floated through the hallway and headed into the kitchen, moving from one side of the room to the other. It was searching for something specific. After looking on top of the table, it found nothing and darted over to the worktop instead. Still nothing. Where was it? The light shot across to the fridge but it couldn't find what it was looking for among all the notes attached to the door with magnets. After a couple of seconds, it stopped in front of the drawer underneath the microwave and started to glow brighter. Suddenly, the drawer flew open. The room filled with banging and clattering as the cutlery contained inside bounced around. Just then, there was the sound of a door opening upstairs, followed by footsteps on the landing.

'Hello, is there somebody down there?' A male voice, likely belonging to Sue's dad called out, followed by the sound of movement as he descended the stairs. The light started darting around the room, frantically looking for somewhere to hide. A few seconds later Sue's dad entered the kitchen and switched on the light. As he stood there looking around, he tried to identify where the noise had come from, but there was no-one around and nothing to be seen. The room was empty and quiet. He must have been hearing things. The cutlery drawer was open, so he walked over, closed it and turned back around. The reading lamp, which his wife always left on, was shining in the far corner, but apart from that, there was nothing out of the ordinary. Mr Johnson yawned, rubbed his eyes and left the room, flicking the light switch off as he passed it. The stairs creaked as he climbed them, one at a time, until he reached the landing, then came the sound of a door closing as he re-entered the bedroom.

The ray of light jumped out of the reading lamp and resumed its search around the room. It wrapped itself around the handle of another drawer next to the oven, and this time pulled it. As the drawer slid open, there was what it was looking for, lying on top of a pile of paperwork.

An envelope and pen slowly floated up out of the drawer, drifted through the air, and came to rest on the large, oak kitchen table in the middle of the room.

The envelope then stood on its end as the ray of light moved around. The brightness of the light increased as it moved over the seal causing the flap to magically open. Two sheets of paper slowly emerged from the envelope, unfolded themselves and lay flat on the table. The words written on the letter would have brought joy to so many children. All except one that is. Sue. She was fast asleep upstairs and had no idea what was going on in her kitchen. Yet tomorrow, she would discover something magical had happened while she was in bed, dreaming about the school trip that she couldn't go on.

Or so she thought.

Chapter 11
The Letter

Dear Parent / Guardian,

Please find below details for this year's school camping trip. We request you complete the attached permission slip, confirming whether your child will, or will not, be attending. We hope that you see fit to allow your child to attend this fantastic school excursion.

This year, we have a very exciting trip planned. We will stay for four nights at the New Forest water park. There are several amazing activities for your children to take part in, from wakeboarding, to kayaking and also canoeing. On-site there is also the water park assault course, reserved for our school, once we have arrived and completed the check-in process. Wetsuits and other safety equipment is available, and we will also have four qualified water-sports instructors on the course to ensure the children's safety. It will involve 30 minutes of free play, to allow the children time to get to know the course, and then there will be a competition for each team, to allow them to score house points. The session will conclude with a further 15 minutes of free play.

On the second day, we will visit the amazing 170-metre tall, Spinnaker Tower, which has stunning views over Portsmouth harbour and the surrounding areas. On a bright day the views are spectacular, and you can see all the way to the Isle-of-Wight.

Day three will see us attend the D-Day Museum, where the children will learn about preparations for the historic Normandy landings during the Second World War.

The last day will involve a visit to the Royal Naval Base at Portsmouth, where we have arranged a tour around the Royal Navy's most famous Ship - HMS Victory. On completion of the tour, there will be a full three-course meal for all children. This will be on-board the Ship itself!

This will be a magical experience and give the children an insight into the history of the Royal Navy and one of its most famous leaders, Lord Horatio Nelson.

Once the meal has concluded, we will head back for one more night of camping. The evening will involve a BBQ, followed by a talent show, Marshmallow toasting and storytelling. The following morning, we will head back home, complete with a bus full of tired and grumpy teenagers - no change there.

I hope you will allow your child to attend and experience what Hampshire has to offer. The day visits will be fun, but also educational, which should make them all proud of our magnificent country. The school is providing most of the fees, therefore, the cost for the trip is only £100.00 per child.

Please complete the attached slip and return it with payment for the full amount by 14th of February.

Yours,

Mr D Horrocks
Headmaster

Permission slip - Hampshire Camping

~~My child will be attending the school trip; I attach payment of £100.00.~~
Or
My Child cannot attend the school trip.

Child's name: Sue Johnson

Signed: *David Johnson*
Name - David Johnson
Relationship - Father

The light hovered above the slip, as if reading it, when suddenly the pen lifted from the table and began to float in mid-air. The button at the top of the pen then disappeared, depressing the ink cartridge contained inside the chamber. Once the nib emerged, there was a tiny click, and the brightness increased as the ray of light started moving across the page.

The bright light continued to drift over the paper, and as it did, something amazing happened. The line, denying Sue a place on the school trip, faded away. It reduced in colour, and before long, had disappeared completely. The pen then lowered and made the necessary adjustment to confirm that Sue would attend the trip. Once it had finished, it moved to the bottom of the slip and started writing again.

As the pen was doing its work, the light drifted back over to the drawer. After a period of rustling, a rectangular pad came floating out of it. The light led the cheque book over to the table where it set itself down, under the raised pen that had finished its previous task. The front cover of the cheque book flipped open, and the pen lowered itself and started writing once more.

When the pen had finished, there was a small tearing sound, as the cheque detached from the pad. There on the table was a cheque, made payable to the school, for £100.00, signed by Mr D Johnson.

The cheque drifted over and lay on top of the

slip, which folded over and re-inserted itself into the envelope. The flap closed and the light rolled over the seal, securing the permission slip inside once more, along with the freshly written cheque.

As the light hovered above them, the pen, cheque book, and envelope lifted off the table and floated back over to the drawer. The light lowered, pushed the drawer closed and made its way towards the kitchen door.

With task one complete, it was time for part two of the plan.

※※※※※

Mr and Mrs Johnson were now sound asleep. How Sue's mum slept at all with the snoring coming from her husband was amazing. He sounded like a motorbike racing down the road. The handle of the bedroom lowered and the door opened. It made a slight swoosh sound as the bottom dragged along the plush grey carpet.

The light entered the room, and reached the bottom of the bed. It worked its way up the floral bedding and headed towards the snoring beast. Sue's dad started tossing and turning as the light moved upwards, causing it to pause and wait for the moving and fidgeting to stop. As he moved onto his side, the most horrendous sound escaped his rear. It made his snoring sound like a whisper.

When the hurricane had passed, the light continued on its journey, heading up the duvet and resting on Mr Johnson's chest. Suddenly, it shrunk in size and shot straight up his enormous nose. This was followed by a popping sound as the light bounced around inside his head, like a ball in a pinball machine. Mr Johnson sat bolt upright and sneezed, causing the ray of light to shoot out of his nose and hit a lamp, which smashed against the wall, waking Mrs Johnson.

'For god's sake, David. Will you stop fidgeting and get to sleep?' she shouted sleepily at her husband, before turning on her side, and pulling the duvet over her.

'Umm, what?' he replied, disorientated. He lay back down and drifted off to sleep again.

The light slid along the carpet and back out of the room. As the door closed behind it, the motorbike noises started again. The light headed back downstairs, slipped through the letterbox and escaped.

Moments later the light reached the darkness of the woods and disappeared once more.

Chapter 12
I'm Not Going

The following morning, Sue woke, stretched, yawned and lay there dreading the day ahead. She loved school and was always straight out of bed, but not today. She was even contemplating playing the sick card. Sue never missed school, but today would be horrible. Seeing everyone handing in their signed permission slips and talking excitedly about the trip would be too much to bear.

She climbed out of bed and headed to the bathroom. The mirror normally showed a bright, vibrant young lady, but not this morning. Today's reflection showed a girl who looked like all was not well in her world, as if there was something troubling her, which of course there was. Sue ignored the reflection and turned the shower on. As she showered and got ready for school, thoughts of South Africa filled her head. Something bad had happened out there, but she did not know what. Her dad had changed so much since two years ago, as had her mum. They had been such a fun, loving, content family, living the perfect life in Durban.

They would fill their weekends with activities, family visits and fun. On Saturday mornings, her dad would jump out of bed, smile and tell the family they were 'off out'. Sue and her mum never knew where. It was always a surprise. It would be a visit to somewhere Sue or her mum had said they wanted to go, or something they wanted to do. They would have been talking about it weeks before. Her father would act as if he wasn't paying attention, but he was really listening to every single word, saving the information up, ready to unleash it when he was ready, much to the delight of Sue and her mother.

However, everything changed on the day of the incident. Her father had returned from work, looking so grey, so shocked, and so vacant. He was always dressed so immaculately, but now he looked disheveled, and he was not even wearing his tie - a must for any upstanding citizen, according to him. Sue was sent to play with her friend next door as her parents had a chat. Sue returned home for dinner a few hours later and it was obvious her mother had been crying, as had her dad. Sue asked what was wrong, but they both ignored the question as they walked around the kitchen like zombies.

Things were never the same again after that day. Her father became very withdrawn and quiet, and her mother was never the same again either. The surprises and the fun evaporated from their home and Sue never knew why. After two years of an unhappy and stressful life, they left Durban and moved back to England. The incident, that had ruined their lives in South Africa, was never spoken of. Sue always wondered what had happened, but she was too afraid to ask. Previously her dad wouldn't have batted an eyelid about the school trip. Not now though. There was no way he would let her out of his sight for five days.

******

Sue finished her breakfast and made for the door. Luckily her dad was still in bed, so she didn't have to ignore him during her morning routine. Her mum was busy scanning the latest gossip from Facebook and updating her daughter. Gillian had now bought herself a car. Last week she had treated herself to a new wardrobe and booked a holiday cruise around the Caribbean, and now she had taken delivery of a brand-new car. The perks of having a little win on the lottery, according to her mum. Sue did not know Gillian and did not want to know about her joyful, happy life. Not today.

She put her coat on and shouted goodbye to

her mother, who didn't seem to hear her. Jenny had done something appalling at the office party last night apparently. Sue stepped outside and was about to close the door behind her when she remembered what today meant and how important it was. She turned around, walked back into the kitchen, opened the drawer, and removed the envelope that was sat at the top of it. She pushed the drawer closed with her hip and once again said goodbye. She didn't even bother checking her hair in the hallway mirror before opening the door and heading off to school.

In the distance, Sue saw Billy and Austin waiting for her. She quickened her pace and cut across the common. Normally she would not walk on the morning grass as the dew would make her socks wet, but she was in a hurry to get today over with and didn't care about her stupid socks.

'Aye-Aye, here she is,' said an enthusiastic Austin.

Billy sensed there was something wrong. They had got to know each other well over the past few months and could always tell when one of them had something on their mind. He watched her walk across the grass. Her long flowing hair, her immaculate uniform and that radiant smile that made his heart race. Only, this morning there was no smile and her big brown eyes were not full of life as they normally were. All Billy could see this morning, was sadness.

'What's up?' he quizzed her.

'Nothing, I'm fine,' Sue snapped back.

'You don't seem it,' Billy said, concerned.

'I told you, I'm fine,' she said, sounding even angrier than before.

'The lady doth protest too much,' Austin said.

'What?' Sue said, snapping her head in his direction this time.

'You say you're fine but we both know you're not, so you might as well tell us,' Austin said, as he ran his right hand through his hair.

'I told you, I'm fine, now drop it. We need to get to school,' she then pushed her way past the pair of them and marched off towards school. Billy looked at Austin, who rolled his eyes.

'Women,' he said.

Billy turned and went after her. Austin sighed and followed them.

'Hey, here's an idea. How about we do more research at lunchtime, you know, about the trip?' Billy asked, trying to get Sue engaged in conversation.

'Why?'

'I dunno, just an idea. I thought it would be exciting.'

'Well, it won't. It will be a waste of time. We should all be concentrating on our schoolwork, not going away for a week and playing stupid games,' she shouted over her shoulder as her pace increased.

Austin had heard enough. He jogged around and stood in front of her. He wanted to know why she was so grumpy, especially today.

'Right. Stop.' He said as he put his arms out to the side, blocking her path. She tried side-stepping him, but he moved over. He looked like a crab walking along the pavement, shuffling from side-to-side as she tried to get around him.

'Ahh, ahh, ahh. No, you don't,' he said. 'You need to tell us what's going on.'

Billy watched as she just stood there glaring at Austin.

'Will you just move,' Sue screamed and tried to push past.

'Nope,' Austin said, standing firm. 'We're your friends, so tell us what is going on, moody guts.'

He smiled at her, which only infuriated her more, but she knew she was going to have to explain herself. Sue looked at the floor and let out a sigh.

'I'm not going on the school trip anymore.'

'What?' Billy said, sounding astonished.

Austin dropped his arms.

'Why?' Billy asked.

'My dad said no. He refused to sign the permission slip. He is so controlling, I hate him sometimes,' she said as she put her head in her hands and started crying. Billy and Austin didn't know what to do. Billy looked at Austin who was waggling his finger to his temple and pulling a face to insinuate that Sue was crazy. Billy frowned at him and shook his head sternly, which made Austin drop his hand quickly.

'Why?' asked Billy. Sue sniffed and removed her hands.

'Because he doesn't want me to be out of his sight for five days. He thinks that something bad will happen. But everyone is going. I'll have to stay and do menial tasks while you're all off having fun,' Sue barged past Austin and headed off to school, as the tears started again. Billy made to walk after her, but Austin stopped him.

'Dude, just give her some space. She needs to be on her own.'

Billy knew that Austin was right, but he hated seeing Sue upset. He only hoped that she would be ok. Unbeknownst to all of them, she would soon be smiling from ear to ear, just like the rest of her class.

Chapter 13
Sue's Surprise

'Morning, all,' said Mr Robertson.

'Morning, sir,' the students all chimed together. An excited buzz filled the air as the children sat there gripping their envelopes, ready to hand them in when requested. The school had never arranged a trip like this before. In fact, the school had never been as much fun as this before.

'Okay, as you are all aware, today is the day. Du-du-duuuuuu,' Mr Robertson said, sounding a fanfare. 'So, if you would please place your envelopes on the desk, I can give you your responsibilities for the trip.' He seemed more excited than the students.

The children stood up from their desks and jostled about as they moved to the front of the class. Sue remained seated. After all, she was in no rush to hand her slip in.

'Do you want me to put yours in with mine?' Austin asked her. Sue shook her head.

'No, it's okay thanks,' she strained as she smiled up at him. Sue stood and put her envelope on the pile then mooched back to her desk and sat in silence.

Mr Robertson opened all the envelopes and separated them into different piles. He opened the last one, and after reading it he looked in Sue's direction, and gave her a warm smile. She felt herself sink into her seat. Mr Robertson must have felt bad for her now that he knew she would not be going on the trip. Next, he started calling out the names of the children. When they answered, he gave each of them their jobs for the trip.

'Wilkinson?' he called.

'Yes, sir?' answered the boy who had brought the frog into school on the second day of the year.

'You will be in charge of ensuring we clean the bathrooms each morning before we set off.'

'Williams?'

'Sir?'

'Laundry room duty.'

Their excitable teacher called the children one-by-one until there were only a few forms left.

'Gibson?'

'Yes, sir?' Billy answered

'Daily mustering of all sports equipment and NO kicking the balls into the lake,' Mr Robertson added with a smile.

'No problem, sir,' Billy smiled.

'James?'

'Yes big-man,' Austin quipped.

In the past, he would have received a severe reprimand for the way he had answered the teacher, but because of his newfound enthusiasm for school and improved attitude, Mr Robertson let it pass and smiled in his direction.

'You, young-man, will be in charge of ensuring that everyone is accounted for when we leave each activity. Understand?'

'Yes, sir,' Austin beamed. There was only one form left. Mr Robertson had given every child their task, meaning that every other student was going on the trip.

'And last but not least... Johnson?'

Sue closed her eyes, waiting for the laughter to begin when he said she had to work with year 8 or 9 for the week.

'Yes, sir?' Sue answered, eyes closed, head down, waiting for the inevitable mockery to begin.

'You, Johnson, have the star prize young lady,' he smiled.

Sue couldn't believe that he was ridiculing her in front of the entire class. She slid further down in her seat.

'Yes, sir,' she answered, the sadness clear in her voice.

'You, Miss Johnson...' the teacher said, before having a slight coughing fit to clear a tickle in his throat. '...will be...'

Sue closed her eyes even tighter.

'...in charge of ensuring everybody is in place before the meal onboard HMS Victory is served. Everyone is to be in their seats ready to eat five minutes before they serve the starter. The Royal Navy is meticulous for good time-keeping, as are you, therefore, it seems to be the perfect task for you,' Mr Robertson said.

There were murmurs through the class, but not from Sue she did not say a word. She sat there, as if hypnotised.

'Miss Johnson?' Mr Robertson asked, snapping her out of her daydreaming.

'Umm, yes sir?' she asked, still in a daze. Sue was trying to comprehend what had just happened. Mr Robertson must have made a mistake.

'I said you have the most important job of the trip. Are you okay? You don't seem yourself today.' Mr Robertson looked puzzled as he addressed the normally unflappable Sue.

'Ummm, yes I'm... I'm fine, sir,' she answered, sounding surprised, but very excited. Mr Robertson didn't believe her but nodded and carried on going through the rest of the details for the trip.

The entire hour was taken up with information, key points, equipment and clothing requirements. Mobile phone and electronic policies, travel times, and a complete, comprehensive breakdown of the trip. As the bell rang to signal the end of the lesson, the children all stood up and made their way outside for break time. Billy and Austin hadn't spoken to Sue for the entire lesson, but they would finally get their chance to talk to her in the playground now.

On their way out of the class, Sue approached Mr Robertson.

'Sir?' she asked as he was tidying his desk.

'Yes, Sue?' he answered, not looking at her.

'May I check my permission slip, please?'

He looked up at her, puzzled.

'Any reason in particular?' he quizzed her.

'I just need to check something, if that's okay?'

'Yes, here you go,' he picked her form out and passed it to her, then went back to arranging the paperwork on his desk.

Sue didn't read the front. She turned the page over and looked at the second page. The important one. There, giving permission for her to attend, was her father's signature. Not a forgery written by her mother, not a rushed signature, and not a mistake. It was the same signature she had seen so many times in the past. It was his. And attached to the front of the page was a cheque for £100.00, made payable to the school and signed once again by her father. It was as clear as day. Her father had signed and given her permission to go. And just for good measure, at the bottom of the page, he had written a personal message to her teacher.

Dear Mr Robertson,

The improvement I have seen in this school over the past few months is vast. Sue often comes home and tells me and her mother all about her day and how enjoyable she finds it and, in particular, your teaching.

Re-adjusting to life since returning to England has been difficult. However, the school, by organising amazing trips like this, and ensuring Sue is happy and content, has made our transition so much easier. I just wanted to pass on my appreciation for everything you are doing. Thank you.

Keep up the outstanding work.

David Johnson

Sue stood there with her eyes wide. She couldn't believe it. As she studied the cheque, a smile broke out over her face. He must have reconsidered last night. After she had taken herself off to her bedroom for the night, her mother must have convinced him to let her go. Her mum must have talked him around. She was so excited, but how would she explain to Billy and Austin? After acting like a petulant child in the morning and storming off like that. They might not want to talk to her. Billy and Austin were her best friends, and she

94

needed to make sure they were okay. They had not spoken to her all lesson.

Sue passed the slip back to Mr Robertson, who gave her another warm smile. Before she exited the room, she turned back to her teacher.

'Mr Robertson?'

'Yes?' he replied as he looked up at her.

'Thank you so much for my task. I promise I won't let you down,' she said with a smile.

'I know you won't. That's why I gave you the best task of the trip,' he winked and returned her smile. She turned and headed for the exit with a newfound spring in her step.

Sue reached the playground and looked for the boys. She had to apologise, explain that she must have been mistaken and say sorry for her behaviour earlier that morning.

Little did she know, but Billy and Austin already had an idea about what had happened. They knew who had signed the slip and that it was nothing to do with her father.

As Sue made her way down the steps, the boys stood in the playground and waited for her, thinking about what this meant. They looked at each other and smiled as Billy said what they were both thinking.

'He's back.'

Two Months Later...

Chapter 14
Terry's Little Fib

Terry had been home a few weeks now and had been keeping a low profile. His wife had only just forgiven him for disappearing for four months. He promised he would be more thoughtful in future and let her know his plans and whereabouts in advance. It had taken a full two weeks of groveling and pleading, but he had finally got himself out of the doghouse. Since returning home, he had kept checking on Billy and Austin with the stone, but he had not popped up to see them. He wanted it to be a big surprise when the time was right.

As Terry lay in bed, he thought about seeing them again, and what he had planned. He was so excited. Although he must keep it quiet from the wife. If she knew what he was up to, she would not be happy. Not at all.

He swung his legs out of bed and as his feet hit the floor, he stepped into something squishy. Terry looked down and right there on the floor was a ball of sticky cookie dough. It was all over the floor and now it was squirting between his hairy toes. He wiped off as much as possible and made his way to the bathroom, being careful not to step on any of the toys scattered around the room. Terry went in, looked around, and sighed at the carnage that greeted him. They'd done it again. His children had made a total mess, no doubt singing, and doing the full actions for '*row-row-row your boat*' in the giant turtle shell they used as a bathtub. Water and bubbles covered the floor, and they had blocked the tiny drain with all sorts. Hair, more cookie dough, and some weird homemade green slime.

Terry picked up the wet towels, mopped the floor with them and chucked them into the laundry shoot. He removed all the cookie dough, slime and hairs from the drain and threw it in the bin, but not without getting some dough stuck under his fingernails. He looked for something to wipe his hands with, but there was nothing. He had already discarded the dirty, wet towels, so he had no choice but to place his fingers into his mouth and suck them clean. After he pulled his fingers free, he felt something tickling the back of his throat. He put his index finger and thumb inside his mouth and removed a long curly hair. Terry looked at it for a second and wiped it on his pants.

After he finished clearing the drain, he pulled on a chain to the left of the door and a swooshing sound followed as a flap underneath the turtle shell opened and the water disappeared down the hole. A sloshing sound could be heard as the water flowed down the pipe on its way to the gully that led deep into the woods.

Terry grabbed a clean towel, showered, dressed, and thought of the day ahead. He was sure it would all work out. The children had been having a wicked time so far and now the final day of their school trip was finally here. It was the day they had all looked forward to more than any other. What they didn't know was that the trip was about to get even more interesting. Terry couldn't wait to see Billy and Austin again. He had not seen the boys for months and had so much to tell them.

He went downstairs and sat with his children at the table, as his wife put his breakfast in front of him.

'Much planned for today?' she asked him.

Previously, she would not ask where he was going or what he was up to, as she didn't really care. However, since his four-month disappearing act, she now wanted to know what he was up to every day, and as he explained his plans to her, she would watch him like a hawk, looking for any clue that he was up to no good.

'Well, I fink I is goin' go on a lil 'venture,' he

said.

His wife turned and scowled at him.

'I am goin' pop up top, and I is goin' steal a ship and take it to sea. A famous ship no doubt. I 'ave 'eard of summfin 'idden on an island and I need to find it and brin' it 'ome. Our entire future depends on it and I is the only one who knows where 'tis, as I 'ave the map. Tis magical and only I can use it.' After explaining his plans, Terry took a bite of his grapefruit, wincing at the bitter taste. His wife glared at him and then chuckled.

'You are a blinkin' idgit, Terry Trevithick,' she said, as she shook her head, turned around, and carried on cleaning the kitchen.

'I might 'ave to stop askin' you wot you is doin' if you is goin' be silly 'bout it,' she said as she stood there shaking her head and chuckling.

Terry sat there, smiling. He looked down and noticed that there was a piece of paper poking out of the top of his sack. He quickly pushed it back down and buckled his sack tighter, before his wife noticed the map protruding from it.

Chapter 15
The School Trip

Sue sat fidgeting for the entire journey. They had been on the bus for 30 minutes, but to her it felt more like 30 hours. Today was the day she had been more excited about than any other part of the trip. The week had gone so fast but it had been such good fun. From the moment they first boarded the coach outside of school, they had not stopped laughing and enjoying themselves.

They arrived on the first day, checked in, and headed straight for the water park. After putting their wetsuits and lifejackets on, they received a safety briefing, and then headed out on the water. Mr Robertson was not a teacher this week, he was the biggest child in the water park. He would run along the walkway shouting *cannonball!* and launch himself into the water, bombing as many kids as he could.

Despite his love of water, he was useless on the paddle board though as his balance was shocking. According to him, this was because the board he was using was unbalanced and there wasn't enough air in it. The truth of the matter was he was simply rubbish and couldn't stand-up. The one time he did manage it, he threw his arms in the air to celebrate with the paddle held above his head in both hands, like one of the sand people in Star Wars. However, Austin, who was right behind him, extended his paddle out and gave the teacher's board a gentle shove. That was all it took to send Mr Robertson's board shooting forwards and the hapless teacher into the water. When he emerged, the paddle board drifted back and hit him square on the forehead, much to the delight of the children, who started shouting and laughing. Thankfully, he also saw the funny side and gave Austin's board a shove in mock retaliation. Austin however maintained his balance and stayed upright.

'I did that on purpose,' said Mr Robertson. 'I'm a stunt paddle boarder.' This caused the children to laugh even harder. He was so much fun outside of school.

Billy and Austin were joined at the hip. Playing on the air bag was their favourite activity. One of them would lie at one end of the bag and the other would then jump from the top of the inflatable pyramid that hung high above it. They would then land on the other end, shooting the person about

20-feet into the air, before they crash-landed in the water with a huge splash.

Sue loved the wakeboarding. It wiped her out a few times, but the buzz from taking off made it all worthwhile. She missed not having this much fun with her parents anymore.

The visit to Spinnaker Tower had also been an excellent day. The views were spectacular, and it was a cloudless day, which increased their enjoyment. Austin was not a fan of heights, so he stayed as far away from the window as possible. Billy, on the other hand, was almost hanging out of it.

The D-Day museum visit was very interesting and sobering. Sue could not believe some things that happened during the Second World War. It was awe inspiring seeing what the nation had dealt with. The heroism displayed by so many made her realise how proud we should be of our country. She walked away with such admiration for the people who had lived through those times, and the sacrifices they made. It was an amazing experience.

And now here it was, the day she had been looking forward to the most. The day she was most annoyed and upset she would miss - the trip onboard HMS Victory. Her father's reaction to the trip and sudden change of heart still confused her.

The day she found out she would be going, she

rushed home to give him the biggest hug. She raced through the door, dropped her bag on the floor and ran into the kitchen. She saw her father standing there with his back to the sink, reading the paper. As she walked in, he looked up and smiled at her. He did not have time to ask how her day was before she ran forward and flung her arms around him.

'Thank you, thank you, thank you so much,' Sue said as she hugged him as tight as she could.

'For what?' He asked, not having a clue what his daughter was going on about.

'For letting me go on the trip,' she said.

'What trip?' He asked, sounding even more confused. Sue stepped back and looked at him, frowning.

'The trip to Hampshire, for five days,' she explained with a tone that suggested it was obvious.

'Oh, right. Who is that with then?'

'Dad, stop. We're having a school trip to Hampshire, as you know. We're going to a water park, the Spinnaker Tower, the D-Day Museum and HMS Victory. You know all this already... Are you alright?' She asked, frowning slightly.

'Oh, fantastic. That will be so much fun. Do you need any money to pay for it? It can't be cheap?'

'Dad, you already paid. It's £100.00 each. I handed it in this morning,' she stared into his eyes, looking for some recognition, but there was nothing. He didn't seem to have the slightest clue what she was going on about.

'Oh, right. Well, I've been so busy it must have slipped my mind. I'm sure you'll have a wicked time and don't forget to make lots of memories,' he said, before kissing her on the forehead and heading upstairs to get ready for his evening shift.

Well that was weird, she thought. And then the broadest smile crept across her face. He wasn't mad or angry and he hadn't said no. In fact, he didn't seem to have any recognition of saying no in the first place. It was almost as if his memory had been wiped or altered. Little did Sue know, it had been.

Chapter 16
Commander Bartholomew

'So are you going to make us call you Miss, if you're in charge?' Austin joked at Sue as he leaned over the back of her seat on the coach. Billy, who was next to him, started laughing.

'Oh, ha ha, hilarious,' she answered and hit him on the arm with a small plastic folder she was carrying.

The bus made its way along Queen Street, past the red brick wall that separated HMS Nelson from the main road. The children crowded on the right-hand side of the bus and looked out of the window as they made their way alongside the Naval Base. The bus came to a stop as it reached the gate that led through to HMS Victory. Mr Robertson stood up and addressed the students.

'Now wait here while I report that we have arrived,' the doors on the bus opened with a *pssst* sound and Mr Robertson descended the steps and disappeared. There was lots of muttering as the children's excitement got the better of them.

'Keep the noise down,' came Miss Thompson's shrill voice from the front of the coach. The strict teacher refused to let her hair down as much as Mr Robertson had on the trip. Instead, she remained her normal, grumpy, fuss-pot self. The children sat in silence as they waited for the fun teacher to return.

Moments later Mr Robertson re-entered the bus, and everyone started chuckling. He stood there wearing a Naval cap, with his hands on his hips and a stern expression displayed on his face as he started growling at the children.

'Right you 'orrible lot. Today we are goin' be sailin' on the Navy's most famous ship. So, I hope you 'as all got your rations with you and is ready to get onboard and go 'n' sort out the French, cos we 'ates the French. Y'aaargghhhh,' he joked, causing a lot of sniggering and laughter.

'You're not a pirate, sir,' came a comment from the back.

'Oh, that reminds me,' said Mr Robertson, in his normal voice.

'Why are pirates called pirates?'

The entire bus turned silent. Another terrible joke was on the way.

'Because they arrrrrrr.'

Groans filled the coach at Mr Robertson's awful attempt at humour.

'Okay, okay. Right let's get going. Once you exit the bus, please wait in line outside of the gate and we can get you all checked off and onboard,' he said, removing the hat from his head.

'Miss Johnson. Are you ready?' he raised his eyebrows as he looked in Sue's direction.

'Yes, sir,' she answered, beaming from ear-to-ear.

'Good, let's get going,' he finished and stepped off the bus, quickly followed by the children.

******

With their passes issued, the children headed up the gangway located on the right side of the ship. Sue informed them this was the starboard side, and the left was called the port side. Waiting for them onboard was their guide for the day. He stood there looking very important in his immaculate Royal Navy uniform, which contained four medals on the left breast of his jacket. He had black hair, brown eyes, and wore a gleaming white cap with an anchor in the middle. The peak of the cap was pulled down so low that his brown eyes were only just visible beneath it. The shoes on his feet were the shiniest shoes the children had ever seen. They looked like they were made of glass. He stood, hands behind his back and his chest puffed out. As the children approached; he did not move a muscle. He looked like a statue.

Once they were all onboard, the children lined up in front of the sailor, who waited for all the jostling and movement to stop before addressing them. During school, teachers would have to shout at the children to be quiet and settle down. However, such was the demeanour of the man stood in front of them, the children soon became quiet without him having to mutter a single word.

'Good morning, children and welcome onboard HMS Victory,' he said in his thick welsh accent.

'I am Petty Officer Edwards and I will be your tour guide today,' He added, before pausing to survey the group and make sure he had their undivided attention.

'We'll start with a quick health and safety briefing before we proceed with the tour. So, if you would like to follow me, we'll get started.'

He turned on his heels and started walking away, quickly followed by the children. Some girls were swooning over him and getting flustered by all the men walking around the ship in their Naval uniforms.

******

As the children were receiving their safety brief, an excited visitor was walking through the dockyard. He approached the Mary Rose Museum with his chest out and hands clasped behind his back, looking very smart in his Naval officer's uniform. Everyone who walked past gave him a funny look or frowned, due to his diminutive size. As soon as they walked past and thought he was out of earshot, they would gossip about how funny he looked, but unbeknownst to them he could hear every single word.

'How is he in the Royal Navy? He's way too short!' Commented one.

'They shouldn't let Sea Cadets walk around the dockyard on their own,' joked another.

'Umpa lumpa doopidde dee, you are so much shorter than me,' sang a young sailor as he walked away laughing with his two shipmates. The Naval officer said nothing to them. He simply raised one hand, extended his finger skywards, and a small bolt of light shot out from the tip. Seconds later, the sailors all had seagull poo running down their faces. He chuckled as they started screaming. A quick peek behind and he saw them all searching for the toilets to clean themselves up.

'Umpa lumpa doopidde doo, ain't so funny now you're covered in poo,' he sang, as he cocked his leg and farted.

He carried on walking along the footpath which worked its way around the museum until he arrived at his destination: HMS Victory. It looked spectacular. Three large masts hung high above the ship, one in the middle and one at either end. Another mast jutted out from the front of the ship like a huge spear. Several cannons stretched the length of the ship, as if they were protecting it from any unwanted intruders.

The unusually short Naval officer started bouncing from foot to foot in his excitement, and without even realising it, started running towards the ship. But he soon remembered where he was, stopped, and started walking normally again. As he reached the vessel, he looked around. The only person he saw was a lonely guard at the top of the gangway. The officer made his way to the top and smiled at the sailor on duty. As he noticed the officer approaching, the sailor came to attention. The officer saw his expression change as he reached the top of the gangway.

'Good afternoon, young man. How are you?' The officer asked.

'Umm, I'm very well thank you, sir. Welcome onboard HMS Victory. How can I help you?' The sailor asked, with a slight frown.

'Dear boy, I am Commander Bartholomew. I'm visiting the dockyard for the day and wish to look around this fine vessel, if I may?'

As he stood there with his hands behind his back, the officer let a little fart out.

'Oh, umm, yes sir,' the sailor replied as he looked down at the officer. 'Do you have an appointment, sir?'

'One does not make an appointment. You obviously do not understand how important I am.

If you would be so kind as to allow me onboard, I will not report you to your Superior Officer,' he said in an authoritative sounding voice, as he tried to push past the guard.

'Oh, umm, okay. Well, if I could just see your identification please, sir?' The sailor asked, as he stepped in front of the visitor and swallowed hard.

'Are you deaf? Did you not hear me? You are sailing very close to the wind, if you'll pardon the pun. Now move aside and let me through.'

He made to move past the sailor again, however, the young man stood his ground.

'I'm sorry, sir. I need to see your ID,' the sailor had now become suspicious. There was no way the visitor was getting past the keen guard. As the officer stood there, he clasped his hands behind his back, extended the index finger on his right-hand and pointed it towards his left. Seconds later, the phone, which was sat above the desk to the left, began to ring. The guard glanced over at it and back to his visitor who stood there smiling. The guard once again looked at the phone as it continued to ring loudly on the gangway. He seemed unsure what to do.

'I'd answer that If I were you. It might be the Captain.'

The Sailor still did not move.

'Dear boy, answer the phone. What do you

think I'm going to do? Steal this vessel and take it to sea?' He laughed and started shaking his head. The Sailor asked him to stay where he was and went to answer the phone.

'HMS Victory,' he answered.

Nobody spoke. The line on the other end was dead. He pulled the phone away from his ear, looked at it, frowned and returned it to its cradle. The sailor turned back around to deal with his visitor, but Commander Bartholomew was gone.

Chapter 17
HMS Victory

While Commander Bartholomew was busy making the phone ring on the gangway, the children were enjoying the tour. The boys were doing boy things and getting excited by all the cannons on the gun deck. According to Sue, they were called guns on a ship, not cannons. Hence the reason they called it the gun deck, not the cannon deck. As she told the group this, several boys pulled faces and rolled their eyes at little miss know-it-all. One boy attempted to pick up a cannonball, but it proved far too heavy. The girls kept doing the girly things of showing no interest in any of the boys. With so many sailors walking up and down the ship, all dressed immaculately in their Naval uniforms, the girls seemed far more interested in looking and talking to each other about proper men, not boys.

As the tour reached its conclusion, the children visited the quarterdeck and saw the plaque that marked the spot where Lord Nelson fell after being shot by a French seaman during the battle of Trafalgar in 1805. *Here Nelson fell, 21st of Oct 1805*, the plaque read. Petty Officer Edwards told the children all about the incident. The most fascinating fact was that after being shot, they had placed Lord Nelson in a drum of Brandy to preserve his body while the ship was towed to Gibraltar after the battle.

Once the tour had finished, PO Edwards lead the children to Nelson's Great Cabin, where they were to dine for the evening. As they entered, there was a huge intake of breath from the children. The room looked spectacular. Sat in the middle of the cabin was a long mahogany table, complete with sparkling glasses, plates, and gleaming cutlery. Four candlesticks were placed at even distances through the middle of the table. There were dinner plates, stacked three high, placed in front of each chair, which were topped off with folded crisp white napkins. Red velvet covered chairs were positioned around the table and looked very elegant.

'Okay. So who is in charge of this evening's event?' Asked PO Edwards. Sue felt her stomach flipping over. She had been looking forward to this moment since she had been told about it, but now that it was here, she was frozen, and her mouth had gone dry. Billy gave her a nudge. As Sue looked at him, he nodded towards the Petty Officer.

'I...I am, PO,' she answered.

'Okay, young lady. I require you to have everybody sat and ready to receive the first course within the next five minutes. Service begins in 10 minutes, so I expect everybody to be ready. Is that clear?'

'Yes, PO, no problem,' Sue said, as she smiled at him. The dryness in her mouth seemed to have gone, thankfully.

'Good. I shall leave you to it,' he said and left the cabin. As he exited, he gave Sue a reassuring smile and a nod of the head. Sue smiled back, took a deep breath, and kicked into gear. She opened her folder and removed several small rectangular pieces of paper. The children continued chatting, checking the items in the cabin and looking out of the windows located to the rear. Sue walked around the table, placing the pieces of paper in front of each chair. When she had finished, she addressed the room.

'Right everyone, listen up.' she said, as she tried to get the children's attention. The mumbling continued as the students ignored her and carried on looking around and peering out of the vast number of windows.

'Um, excuse me, will you listen to me please?'

The children continued to ignore her. A sharp whistling sound filled the cabin and the children suddenly stopped talking. The room became quiet and everyone faced Sue. Austin removed the fingers from his mouth and smiled at Sue. She smiled back.

'Right, okay. I've placed name tags in front of your seat at the table. Boys are on one side, girls on the other. Mr Robertson and Miss Thompson, you're at either end of the table. Please find your place and sit yourself ready for service.'

The children started muttering again and smiling, as they wilfully ignored her instructions.

'NOW.' Sue shouted, causing everybody to jump. This time, the children found their seats and sat down as instructed. Before long, all the children were sat in their places, ready to enjoy the banquet. Little did they know, they would not finish their meal.

* * * * * *

Terry jumped behind a crate after he had snuck past the guard. It wasn't as difficult as he had thought. The first challenge was to get onboard without using the stone. He could not teleport in his normal manner, as he could have ended up anywhere on the ship, and if he was discovered his plan would be ruined. So he had tried to trick the guard into allowing him access onboard. But when this failed, he had to distract the guard. He laughed as he remembered making the phone ring. It created the perfect diversion. Once the guard turned his back, he ran. As he reached the ship's entrance, he looked left and right, to ensure the coast was clear. Then came the sound of the phone being dropped back into its cradle, followed by footsteps approaching. He noticed a large wooden box across from where he was standing and bolted for it. He cleared the crate just before the sailor came marching around the corner. He watched from his hiding place as the guard looked to his left and then to his right without being able to locate what he was searching for.

As the guard walked back to his post, Terry made sure there was nobody around and headed towards the rear of the ship. A quick look behind confirmed that the coast was clear. He smiled and started whistling. Then his heart stopped. The voice of the guard he had snuck past came over the main broadcast system.

'Officer of the day, please contact the gangway.'

He had a bad feeling about this and looked for somewhere else to hide. As he moved through the ship, he kept looking, but there was nowhere suitable. Then another announcement came over the main broadcast.

'Commander Bartholomew, ship's visitor, is requested to contact the gangway on extension 221.'

They were on to him. He panicked and looked around for somewhere to hide. There was a stack of crates behind some cargo netting. He moved past the netting and climbed over the crates. It was time to get changed. He removed his cap and placed it on the floor, then took off his jacket, folded it and placed it on his cap. As he was untying his shoes, there came another announcement.

'Commander Bartholomew, ship's visitor, is requested to contact the gangway on Extension 221, Immediately.'

Terry removed his shoes and placed them beside his cap and jacket. He let out a sigh as his feet returned to their normal pasty shape. Then he removed his trousers, but they got caught in his belt that he had been concealing underneath. He struggled to get them off and kept hopping around laughing as he toppled backwards and became tangled up in the netting surrounding the boxes. He freed himself, but seconds later an alarm started sounding.

'WAAAAHHH, WAAAAHHH, WAAAAHHH. Intruder alert, all visitors are requested to leave the ship by the starboard gangway, as directed by ship's staff.'

Terry couldn't let them leave yet. He wasn't ready. Suddenly, the corridor filled with people. They entered from the decks above and below. Sailors and visitors emerged from compartments throughout the ship. From his hiding spot, he grabbed the stone from his sack, held it in his hand, closed his eyes and took a deep breath. As Terry opened his eyes, the stone started spinning and then, it began to glow.

Chapter 18
Meal Time

The children were all waiting for their starters of either carrot and coriander soup with croutons and chunky bread, or prawn cocktail. Mr Robertson was at the head of the table and kept making the children laugh with his impressions and funny stories. Miss Thompson sat rigid at the opposite end, awaiting her soup. Billy and Austin were sat next to each other, with Sue opposite Billy and a single candlestick placed between them.

'Would you like me to ask PO Edwards to light that for you two. I'm guessing it's your first romantic meal as a couple?' Austin joked. Billy hit him on the arm and Sue poked her tongue out at him before laughing. Billy and Sue then looked at each other and they both went red.

The doors opened and the cabin soon became flooded with waiters and waitresses as they entered carrying trays of starters. The children were all fidgeting and rubbing their hands together, excited to taste the food that was being served up. It smelt delicious. Following the waiters and waitresses into the cabin, was a man carrying a long stick, at the end of which was an open flame. He had one hand covering the flame to avoid any accidents. As the starters were placed in front of the children, he walked around the table lighting the candles. Once all the wicks had been lit, he extinguished the flame and turned on two lamps hanging over the table. Austin lent towards Billy and whispered in his ear.

'Must have read my mind mate, don't blush... again.'

There was then an announcement over the PA system.

'Officer of the day, please contact the gangway.'

The waiters and waitresses carried on serving the food, so there was obviously nothing to worry about.

Once they had been served their food, Mr Robertson tapped the side of his glass with a spoon to get everyone's attention before standing up.

'OK, children. As this is our last day, I would like to make a toast,' he said.

'Hope it's better than your paddle-boarding, sir,' shouted one child, causing everyone to laugh.

'I told you, the board was unbalanced,' he joked. 'Anyway, I would like to say that this is the perfect way to end what has been a thoroughly enjoyable and eye-opening week. I am so proud of each and every one of you for the way you have conducted yourselves. When organising trips like this, it is imperative that you behave impeccably, treat others with respect, help each other, but above all else, enjoy yourselves. I think I am safe in saying that we have all done that.'

'Without doubt,' shouted one girl.

Mr Robertson smiled and continued.

'I think it's obvious this year has differed from previous years, and for the better I think. Some of you have excelled and proved many people wrong,' he looked at Austin and nodded. 'While others have stayed as you were last term, Miss Thompson,' he joked, and nodded at his opposite number.

This time, Miss Thompson almost broke into a smile - either that or she had a bout of wind. The children all looked her way and started chuckling.

'Anyway, we head back to school tomorrow,' he continued.

Booing echoed throughout the cabin.

'Yes, alright, alright. However, I think we head back knowing that we have all learned something on this trip. Whether it's about the history of this fine country, or maybe it's something we have tried for the first time and discovered we have a talent for. Or even that we need to get more practice in on certain activities, like paddle boarding.'

Everyone started laughing.

'The crucial thing to remember is that we all have unique talents; we all have different interests, and we all have different personalities. Yet, that is what's special about trips like this. We learn things about each other that we wouldn't learn in the classroom. So remember, when we get back to school and the arduous task of lessons and homework raise their ugly heads again, you can all help each other to get through. You can support each other, and you can encourage each other. Teamwork, and looking after each other. That's what school is all about. To friendships,' he said and raised his glass.

'To friendships,' they all chimed back. Billy and Austin stared at each other and smiled as they raised their glasses.

'Three cheers for Mr Robertson,' shouted Austin.

'Hip-hip, hooray, hip-hip, hooray, hip-hip, hooray,' they all cheered.

'Oh stop it,' the teacher joked as he pretended to wipe a tear away from his eye. The children started laughing again. Another announcement interrupted the relaxed atmosphere in the room.

'Commander Bartholomew, ship's visitor, is requested to contact the gangway on extension 221.'

'Oh, someone's in trouble,' Mr Robertson joked, sensing the children were worrying. They all laughed as they tucked into their starters. Once the children relaxed, they started talking, laughing and joking. There was a very warm feeling around the great cabin. Another announcement interrupted the talk around the table. It was a different voice and sounded more urgent this time.

'*Commander Bartholomew, ship's visitor, is requested to contact the Officer of the Day on extension 221. Immediately.*' The teachers glanced anxiously at each other, although they remained calm for the children.

'Wonder what's going on?' Billy said as he leaned towards Austin.

'I've got an awful feeling about this,' Austin whispered in his friend's ear.

'It's probably nothing. Stop worrying.

Suddenly, the sound of an alarm filled the ship.

'*WAAAAHHH, WAAAAHHH, WAAAAHHH. Intruder alert, all visitors are requested to leave the ship by the starboard gangway, as directed by ship's staff.*'

The doors burst open and all the waiters and waitresses entered and started clearing down the table, removing any rubbish and stacking the dirty plates and cutlery. PO Edwards was right on their heels.

'OK, listen up. We need to escort you off the ship while we deal with this incident. There is no need to panic. If you will follow me, we will ensure you disembark safely.'

Without saying another word, he turned on his heels and exited the cabin, quickly followed by Miss Thompson and the children. Mr Robertson was at the back, ensuring no child was left behind.

* * * * * *

As the corridor continued to fill with people, Terry remained hidden while looking around for anything he could find to create a diversion. He was not ready yet. There were boxes and crates everywhere, blocking off inaccessible compartments and out-of-bounds areas. Then came the sound of sirens from outside. The Military Police must be here.

'Oh bugger,' he thought, but he couldn't help but chuckle. He hadn't even started yet and there was already bedlam breaking loose all around him. He looked at the spinning stone, gave a nod, and a spear of light flew from it and headed for some netting on the opposite side of the ship. It shot straight through a knot at the top that secured it to the deck-head of the ship. The netting fell and brushed the shoulder of an old lady walking past. She let out a shriek and quickened her step. Terry nodded at the stone again. Another spear shot across and took out another knot. The netting remained secured to the deck-head by a single knot in the middle. Now he just had to wait. He felt a sneeze coming but held it in. The stone continued to spin, ready for its next instruction. Terry looked down the corridor. There were several police at the gangway, all with machine guns. They were looking left, then right. The one who must have been in charge was talking to a very important looking sailor, who was gesticulating with his hands and pointing to areas of the ship. The police officer nodded, before turning to his men and giving them instructions. They all made their way to different decks of the ship, with two of them standing guard on the only gangway in use. Terry continued to smile, but then, the sneeze that had threatened to escape earlier decided it wanted to pop out and see what was going on. He sneezed three times in quick succession, his head shooting forward with each sneeze. The stone took this as further instructions, and soon three bolts of light fired out and headed straight for the policemen on the gangway. He watched as they made their way over.

'Oh, double bugger,' he muttered and waited for the inevitable to happen. This was not going to plan.

* * * * * *

Sue was angry. She was not so worried about the incident onboard, unlike some children who were panicking, as she had seen much worse than this in South Africa. Sue was angry because some stupid idiot had ruined her big moment by trying to sneak onto the ship.

She was right at the back, with only Mr Robertson behind her. He had now turned back into teacher mode and was shouting instructions to the children as they made their way towards the exit. A lot of the children were flinching and screaming as the bedlam continued around them. Miss Thompson was at the front. She was walking bolt upright, completely unmoved by the surrounding carnage, and almost looked like the Terminator. Nothing would penetrate this steel beast. She led the children towards the exit, ensuring they had a safe route.

'He's here somewhere,' Billy whispered to Austin as he continued glancing from side-to-side, looking for their friend, or any strange glowing objects that might give away his location.

'You reckon it's him?' Austin asked. He had missed their old friend from the woods.

'Who else could it be?' Billy answered.

'It could be an actual intruder?' Austin answered.

One look from Billy and Austin knew that was unlikely. One thing he knew was that it was not Commander Bartholomew.

There was a shriek up ahead, and they saw an old lady half-running, half-walking away from some netting that had fallen down on one side.

Chapter 19
Carnage on the Victory

The three bolts of light remained grouped together as they continued on their journey towards the exit. As they moved through the ship, it looked like they were all heading towards the same target, but then one of them broke away and changed direction. It veered towards a stack of crates on the right side of the ship. There was an explosion as it struck the crates, and within seconds the air was filled with splintered wood. Screaming and pandemonium broke out as jagged pieces of the crates were flung around the ship. The guards all turned towards the noise with their guns held in the ready position. Passengers and guests had their hands clamped to their heads to protect themselves from debris as they fled the ship. A piece of the splintered wood hit a pole right next to the gangway and disintegrated, leading to even more screaming from those making their way off the ship. Terry watched in horror as one of the remaining bolts of light changed course, and headed towards a pile of cannonballs, stacked up in front of a gun.

'Oh, no,' Terry mumbled and put his hands over his face.

He carried on watching the carnage unfold through his fingers. The alarm sounded again, as more police arrived, but they struggled to get onboard, due to the sheer number of visitors filling the gangway as they fled the ship. They ignored the police officer at the bottom asking them to move to the side to let his men on. Hats were flying off the heads of some of the ladies, one man had his hands raised above his head as he screamed something about ghosts, while another was laughing his head off and informing everyone about an alien invasion. And then, the bolts of light went to work.

One broke off to the right and removed a blanking cover from a gun, while another shot towards a stack of cannonballs behind the guns. It picked one up and guided it towards the gun which had just had its cover removed. Terry watched as the cannonball was loaded into the gun. This did not look good. He heard screaming children approaching from behind him. He turned around and they were less than twenty feet away with the grumpy Miss Thompson at the front, leading the charge. The children were shaking, screaming, and some were even crying as they walked behind their teacher, who wasn't even flinching. More screaming came floating over from the other end of the ship. It looked like there was a sparkler behind one of the guns. Seconds later, another sparkler appeared behind the next gun, then another and another. Terry suddenly realised what was happening; the lights had loaded cannonballs into all of the guns. And now they were setting the wicks alight, ready to fire at the people gathered on the jetty.

'Oh blinkin' 'eck,' Terry said as he put his head in his hands and let a little fart out. It was a lot wetter then he wished, and he was now in trouble in more ways than one.

* * * * * *

There was absolute bedlam up ahead as the sailors and police attempted to get water across to the guns. They were eager to douse the wicks before they burnt out and fired the cannonballs towards the packed jetty. One-by-one, they were lit and came alive. Terry could do nothing about it. He needed to ensure he didn't miss Billy and Austin, or else the whole trip would have been a complete waste of time. The ship's staff continued panicking and running around with water, as they attempted to extinguish the flames behind each gun. One sailor was trying to run too fast and tripped. The bucket of water in his hands flipped up and soaked the unlucky individual. Another alarm sounded.

Wahhhhhh, Wahhhhhh, Wahhhhhh. Terry looked over to his left. A small fire had broken out in a pile of wooden crates. This caused some visitors to panic even more. One old lady, with bright ginger hair, was being particularly over dramatic, screaming and telling everyone that they were all going to die. She took off the ridiculously enormous hat perched on top of her head and tried fanning the fire away. This only increased the danger as she had now fanned the flames towards several other wooden crates. Within seconds, they started smoking, and orange flames appeared from the top of them as they also caught fire. This increased the bedlam even further. Guards escorted the silly woman, and her doddering husband, off the ship, as more sailors struggled to get to the crates with buckets of water, but they were too late. The ship filled with a loud crack as the crates exploded. This was not how it was supposed to go. Terry heard screaming and panicking from behind him. He turned again and saw the children approaching his position. They were the last visitors being led towards the exit and off the ship. Smoke had now filled the ship, and he could only just make out the target opposite him. He took aim. Some girls were crying and screaming, the boys too for that matter. He spotted Billy and Austin walking towards him. He nodded at the stone again. Another spear of light shot across and took out the last knot holding the netting up. The net fell, right on top of the children. The smoke was now engulfing the ship. It was all around them and they were trapped. Some of the ship's staff tried to help them out from underneath the netting, but another explosion sent them flying behind some crates. Bodies lay everywhere. The children started coughing as the smoke made its way down their throats and filled their lungs. Terry launched the stone. It landed in the middle of the ship. He nodded at it and the smoke suddenly had a tunnel of fresh air cut through it. Just enough to ensure the children could exit the ship free from breathing in more toxic fumes. Staff began to arrive to help the children out from under the netting. Terry nodded at the stone a second time. It started to glow and fired bright red letters out from the top of it. Children continued crawling out from under the net and made their way off the ship, helped by the tunnel of air that had penetrated the blanket of smoke. They all ran past the stone, and the invisible words that had appeared from the top of it. No need for anyone else to see them, except Billy and Austin. Terry nodded at the stone once more and then he vanished.

* * * * * *

As the children exited the cabin, led by PO Edwards, all they could see was total bedlam. There were so many people in front of them, coming out from the many compartments throughout the ship, down the ladders from the floors above and climbing up from the decks below. There was a crack up ahead and then the smell of smoke. The alarm sounded as a faint glow of orange emerged near the exit.

Wahhhhhh, Wahhhhhh, Wahhhhhh. The smoke then increased. A silly old lady up ahead was screaming about dying and fanning the flames with a huge hat. Seconds later, there was an explosion, and the smoke increased, as did the panicking and screaming. Some children started crying. Miss Thompson and Mr Robertson were trying to calm everyone down, but the children couldn't hear their voices over all the commotion. Just as it seemed they would soon be free, a large, heavy, cargo net fell and covered them, trapping them all. Billy looked at Austin.

'If this is him, he's gone too far this time,' Billy said.

Austin nodded.

Sailors and police were now hurrying over to help the children. They lifted the net up and helped them out. Some people fell over the crates, while others were knocked to the floor in the rush. It was total carnage. Austin looked up. There was a blanket of smoke ahead and he was finding it hard to see. They were in real trouble. Then, as if by magic, a tunnel of clean air appeared at head height, cutting through the smoke as if aiding the children's escape. He nudged Billy.

'There's your answer, mate. It's him alright.'

The children started heading for the exit as more and more buckets of water arrived. Then there were sizzling sounds as one-by-one, the wicks on the guns were drenched in water by sailors to make them safe and prevent them from firing.

Billy crawled out from under the net and stood there in the smoke free tunnel, reading the words hanging in the air in front of him.

'Son, keep moving. We need to get you out,' said a sailor as he gave Billy a gentle nudge towards the exit. He started walking forwards and felt Austin at his shoulder.

'Did you see that?' he whispered to him.

'Yeah, but how do we get there?' I'm not sure of the way.'

As the boys looked for the right way, the bright red words that had hung in the air seconds earlier, telling them to, *'head to the quarterdeck'*, flew over their heads. The boys continued walking forwards and as they approached a ladder to their left, there was a faint red glow overhead.

'Austin, look,' said Billy. The faint red glow of an arrow was pointing at the ladder. The letters had reformed, directing the boys towards their destination. The quarterdeck.

Austin looked around. There was nobody behind them, which seemed strange, but with the bedlam continuing, people could have easily moved past them.

'Quick, we've got to find out what the heck he's playing at,' Billy said. He moved towards the ladder and headed up, two rungs at a time. He exited onto the quarterdeck, followed by Austin. The fresh air brought some welcome relief. They both coughed to clear their lungs and then took a few deep breaths, savouring the clean air.

'Now, where is he?' Muttered an annoyed but slightly excited Billy as he looked around for the troublesome Knocker.

Chapter 20
Terry Explains

As the children stood on the quarterdeck looking for Terry, the noise rising from the jetty increased. The boys walked across and peered over the side of the ship. It looked like a scene from a disaster movie. Ambulances and fire engines now joined the police, all coming around the corner with sirens blaring and blue lights flashing. Visitors and sailors flooded out from surrounding buildings to have a good old nose. The Navy had set up a cordon at the mouth of the entrance, to control the influx of nosey onlookers. Everyone fleeing the ship tried to get as far away as possible. Sailors and police led people who needed treatment over to the ambulances gathered. More onlookers had now gathered on the jetty.

Two police officers stood guard at the bottom of the gangway, providing security as the last of the visitors disembarked. Smoke continued to exit the ship by any means possible and dissipated as it mixed with the atmosphere.

'Billy. Look,' Austin said, pointing towards a group of children all huddled next to a fire engine. Miss Thompson was standing there, looking the same as when she walked onboard two hours before. She was totally unfazed by the incident. Billy tried his hardest to spot Sue. He wanted to make sure she was alright. However, the children were all huddled together and had blankets covering them, making it difficult to identify her. As the boys watched, the authorities led their classmates away from the incident. Billy continued looking as they walked away, but he could not see Sue. She would be in there somewhere. The boys' thoughts were suddenly interrupted by a voice from behind them.

'Alright shipmates,'

Both boys spun around and there he was, standing right in front of them, bold as brass and a cheeky smirk on his face.

'Bit o' fun that, weren't it? Got a bit 'airy, be we is 'lright, ain't us?' Terry said as he started giggling. Billy marched straight over.

'What the hell are you playing at? You could have killed us, you idiot.'

Terry stopped smiling and his face dropped. He looked hurt by the comment. He had been so excited about seeing the boys again after so long, but this abrupt greeting made him realise that maybe Billy didn't feel the same.

'What on earth are you wearing?' Austin asked.

Terry stood there in another Naval uniform, he looked very strange. His attire comprised bright white trousers, which had the bottoms tucked into long white socks that ended below his knee. The jacket was far too big for him, it would not have looked out of place on an adult. There were several medals hanging on the left-hand side, just below his shoulder. His right arm was tucked into the left-hand side of the jacket and there were big gold epaulettes sat on each shoulder. Tucked under the epaulette on the right side, and running diagonally across his body, was a thick red sash. Finishing it off was a triangular hat, complete with gold trim, and a badge that sat in the middle and rose above the top.

'What d'you mean, what is I wearing? We is on HMS Vict'ry, and I is the Captain, so I as got to dress like that Nelson bloke.'

'You look ridiculous,' Billy added, sounding annoyed.

'Oh, charmin'! I 'as not seen you for monfs and that is 'ow you say 'ello,' Terry said, shaking his head.

'Well, what do you expect? You created all of this and why? Why not just come back to school and carry out a few pranks. Why did you have to do this?' Billy fumed.

Terry sighed and removed the hat from his head.

'Because I need you,' he said.

'Why? I want an explanation, Now!' Billy demanded.

'All right, Bill, calm down mate,' Austin said, feeling slightly sorry for Terry.

'What, why? Did you miss what he's done here? The small pranks in school are fine. I can handle them. They're funny, but this? It's ridiculous. He's gone too far, and you know he has,' he said, glaring at Austin.

Billy turned his attention to the people on the jetty. Their classmates were heading around the corner. He needed to get off the ship, but how?

'I'll 'xplain everyfin', but we can't 'ang 'bout, we need to get movin',' Terry said, as he looked at Billy.

'What do you mean we gotta get moving?' Austin asked.

'Back in a tick,' Terry said and then turned and headed down the ladder the boys had just climbed up. Austin watched him disappear and attempted to calm Billy down.

'Mate, I appreciate that you're worried about Sue and that's fair enough, but we need to give him a chance to explain. He wouldn't have done all this if it wasn't important. Let him talk and if we don't like what he has to say, we ask him to sort it out. That sound fair enough?'

Billy thought for a second.

'OK, I'll give him a chance, but if I don't like it, we're off. Deal?' Billy offered.

'Deal,' said Austin.

Both boys stood in silence as they waited for their Captain to return and explain himself.

* * * * * *

Terry came back up the ladder a few moments later, with the hat back on his head as he passed the stone from one hand to the other. He looked over at the boys, who had sat down next to one of the guns. He walked over and sat down between them.

'ad to nip down and pick this lil' bugger up,' he said as he held the stone up.

'Well, what's this all about, Terry?' Austin asked.

Terry once again took his hat off, gave a sigh and explained to the boys why he was there.

'Well, after everythin' that 'appened wiv you boys in the woods I 'ad to get back to normal, so as not to make Mrs T 'spicious. There was no way I wanted 'er to find out 'bout the battle wiv the Pixies and all that 'appened that night. I 'ad to keep it from 'er. So, I started minin' again, you know, lookin' for coal, an' if I found some mine gems for me old pasty scraps that would be ansum. Anyway, I found a new mine, one I 'adn't seen before, 'ad a bit of a congealed entrance.'

'A what?' Billy said.

'A congealed entrance, you know, couldn't 'ardly see it,' the boys started laughing.

'Woz matter?' Terry asked, confused by their laughter.

'You mean concealed? It's a concealed entrance if you cannot see it,' Billy said. Terry looked annoyed.

'Did you know what I meant?' he asked, frowning.

'Yeah, I did?' Billy answered, still giggling.

'Well, no need to be a pillock 'bout it is there?'

Billy's laughter stopped as he glared at Terry. Austin stepped in.

'Ok, what about this new mine?'

Terry re-focused.

'Well, woz pitch black so I used the stone to light 'en up. As it started glowin', I couldn't believe what I saw. There woz all sorts down there, minin' 'quipment, rags, bucket's of fixins, racks of old bits of machinery. I started lookin' through it all but didn't find anyfin' of any use, so I left. But as I stepped back through the door to leave, the stone started pullin' me back towards the rack. The 'arder I tried to leave, the 'arder it pulled me back.'

He looked at the boys. Billy had softened and had forgotten about how angry he was, for the time being. He was now eager to hear what Terry had to say about the new mine.

Now that Billy had calmed down, Terry needed

to distract him and Austin for the next part of his plan.

'You wanna check everyfin' down there is alright boys?'

'Why?' asked Billy.

'To be honest, I is feelin' slightly guilty and wanna make sure I as not 'urt no-one. My eyesight ain't the best, so can you boys check? Put my mind at rest?' He smiled, hoping they would buy it.

They both stood and walked over to have a quick look below at the jetty. As they stood up and turned around, Terry put his hand in his sack and removed the stone. He closed his eyes, and as the stone started spinning, he tossed it over his shoulder. It bounced on the top of a box behind him and rolled over the edge.

The jetty looked like it was ready to welcome a ship back from deployment. There were people everywhere. The boys turned around just as the stone cleared the box.

'There are still loads of people down there but it seems to be calming down,' Austin informed him. Then he and Billy sat down again and crossed their legs while they waited for the story to continue.

'Ah, that's ansum, cheers my lover. Anyway, back to the story. I 'ad no idea what was goin' on. I tried to leave once more, but the stone didn't let me go anywhere, woz pullin' so 'ard.'

At that moment, the screaming from below

started again. The three of them sat there as the ship began rocking, as if trying to break free from its shackles. Then, in the next moment, a pinging sound filled the air as one rope snapped. It flew over their heads and landed on the deck, causing the ship to rock even more violently. And then, the boys looked at each other with their eyes wide, as HMS Victory started to rise into the air. The screaming from below increased further as the gangway fell from the ship and landed in the dry-dock below. More ropes gave way. It had started.

'Oops, ship-roll,' Terry joked as the vessel rocked from side-to-side.

Pandemonium broke out and shouts of '*Oh my god, what is happening?*' came floating up from the jetty. The boys sat there watching Terry, as he looked at his finger. They knew what was coming. He had tricked them, hook, line and sinker. They were off, floating away on the most famous ship in the world. As the boys watched him, his finger drifted towards his nose. He winked and asked them a question.

'Ready my ansums?' They glared at him as he started laughing and his extended index finger disappeared up his nose.

Chapter 21
The Adventure Begins

Billy and Austin were on their feet in a flash. What was happening? The ship was suspended in the air, and the only thing keeping it in place were the final ropes securing it to the jetty. The poles, helping to support the hull of the ship, now lay at the bottom of the dry dock, along with the ship's gangway. Another rope snapped and flew high into the air. Seconds later, it came crashing down onto the quarterdeck, just missing Austin's head, causing him to jump. The ship rocked again, and this seemed to set off a chain reaction. One-by-one the ropes snapped, as the workload demanded of them was too much. The people on the jetty continued screaming, some filmed the incident, while others stood open-mouthed, unable to move. There was nothing anybody could do. They all stood there, as a ship which had been in dry dock since 1922, rose into the air, as if by magic.

Billy turned back to Terry, whose finger

remained up his nose, oblivious to the bedlam he had created.

'What the hell is going on?' he screamed at Terry, distracting him from his favourite activity.

Terry removed his finger, wiped it on his garb, looked up at Billy, and began to explain.

'There's summfin I need go 'nd get,' he said, looking at the floor. 'I need you two. I can't do it on my own. I need 'elp. Wivout you, I 'as got no chance. They know about the stone, so, if I don't go to them, they is goin' come after me and I can't put my famlie in danger, not 'gain,' he said.

'What do you need to get? Who will come?' Billy asked.

'I found this in the back of that mine,' he put his hand in his sack and removed the map.

He unfolded the sheet of paper and laid it out on the deck. The boys walked over, sat down, and cast their eyes over it.

'What on earth is that? asked Billy, almost laughing.

'Tis a map,' Terry said to Billy, who looked confused.

'A map?' Austin asked, as he stood scratching his head and frowning.

'It is, my ansum,' Terry answered, as he flattened it out. Another rope snapped and let go, leading to the screaming below to increase to an unimaginable level. Austin hurried to his feet and rushed to look over the side of the ship.

'Um, guys? You might wanna come and see this,' he said.

Billy got to his feet and ran across to see for himself. Terry picked up the map and shoved it back in his sack, then walked over and joined the boys in looking over the guardrail. The last rope gave way, and the ship continued elevating, until it was floating thirty feet above the dock. Then it stopped and started reversing. It was backing out of the dock. Billy started on Terry again.

'What are you doing? What's happening? I don't like this,' he said, looking around.

'I 'ad no choice,' Terry tried pleading. 'You is the only ones I can trust. You 'elped me before and I woz 'opin' you'd 'elp me again.'

'Guys, guys, looooooooook,' Austin had become more animated as he continued looking over the side of the ship. This time, Billy didn't turn to look. He was too busy glaring at Terry. HMS Victory was not only reversing, now it was turning. The Bowsprit mast at the front of the ship, which had been pointing inland, was now aimed at the jetty. The ship continued backing away from the dry dock as it turned. After a few minutes, the ship stopped and began moving forwards. The gasps from the jetty stopped, as Nelson's old ship floated high above their heads. The Bowsprit mast was soon pointing out to sea, as if directing them towards their destination.

There was nothing anybody on the jetty could do. They stood in silence, under the shadow of the Royal Navy's most famous ship. People pulled their phones out and captured the incident as once again, HMS Victory made its way out to sea, just like it had on its first voyage in May 1765.

* * * * * *

'This is amazing,' said Austin, loving the adventure.

Billy did not seem so pleased. Of course, he was enjoying it, but he didn't want Terry to know. After all, what 14-year-old boy wouldn't be excited about floating high above the seas on the world's most famous ship? The sounds from the jetty were now just whispers in the air, no screaming voices, no loud sirens, no hysterical screams. Nothing. The famous old ship left it all behind. It continued floating high above the sea. They passed buildings on the left and people walking below. Austin laughed at some of the amazed reactions. One lady threw her hands in the air and ran away as fast as she could. A man who was drinking from a water-bottle, started choking as the liquid sputtered out of his mouth and nostrils. Many were unable to move at the sight in front of them while others rushed out of their houses and watched, stunned. Austin saw a small boy standing as close to the sea as he could get, without swimming in it. The boy had no front teeth but was grinning from ear to ear as he frantically waved. Austin smiled and waved back.

As they moved away from the dockyard and into clear waters, a loud crack emerged from behind them. The boys spun around and saw a spear of light shoot up from a pile of boxes and float over to the middle of the ship. The light started swirling around like a bright white tornado and created a wind tunnel. Shards from the light shot off towards the rear of the ship. Seconds later, more lights shot from it and headed towards the front. Soon there were three groups of bright lights circling around. The lights headed to the top of each of the masts - the mizzenmast at the rear, the mainmast in the middle, and the foremast at the front. They positioned themselves at the top of each mast, and then, as one, they all became brighter and started circling the masts. The ship began to descend, lowering itself towards the water. A swooshing noise started filling the air as the spears of light moved faster and faster. They continued to whip up a storm as they surrounded the masts. Terry smiled at the boys, standing there looking up with their mouths agape, as they enjoyed the magic show in front of them. HMS Victory continued to descend. It was now only ten feet from the water. The lights continued working their way down, all in the same position. It was like a well-choreographed dance routine. Wind was blowing across their faces as the lights moved closer to the deck. The boys gasped as they watched the masts become covered with cotton sails. The ship continued to descend and they were now only six feet above the sea. The swirling wind seemed to increase further, probably because the lights were now just above the deck of the ship, finishing their task. Their creation was almost complete. The wind died down and the lights secured the sails to the masts in the stored position.

Billy and Austin walked across to look over the side of the ship, as the three groups of lights all joined together and hung above their heads. They could not believe what they had witnessed. The ship hovered three feet from the water. It was edging closer to its natural habitat. A look to the rear confirmed they were now miles away from the dockyard. It was a mere dot in the distance.

There was a huge splash followed by the sound of water lashing against the side as HMS Victory, once again, sailed on the open seas. Moments later, a loud flapping sound came from overhead. The boys looked up. The sails had been released from their secured positions and had fallen elegantly into place. The light hanging above their heads made its way over to the ship's wheel, weaved itself between the wooden handles and prepared to take them on a journey.

The boys looked at Terry.

'Still wish you woz sat on that there coach 'eaded 'ome? Or you wanna go on another adventure?'

The boys looked at each other and nodded.

'Ok, so what's the plan?' Asked Billy.

'That's the spirit,' Terry said, smiling.

'Right my ansums. Sit down and I'll show you.' He walked over to the boxes behind him, picked up the stone, put it in his sack and pulled the map out again.

'Right, this is woz 'appenin',' he said, flattening the map out on the deck of HMS Victory as she sailed majestically out to sea. The famous ship was about to take them on an adventure they would never forget.

Chapter 22
Finding The Map

'This is what you found in that mine?' Austin asked.

'Yep,' Terry answered, sounding smug.

'And this is the reason you've created total carnage today, is it?' Billy quizzed him as he got to his feet.

'Yep,' Terry said, sounding even more smug, as he looked up.

'Ummm, I don't want to state the obvious,' Austin said, scratching his head. 'But what on earth are you going on about?'

'What d'you mean?' Terry asked, switching his gaze to Austin.

'It's blank, Terry,' Billy said. 'This is not a map. There's nothing on it. This is by far the worst and most dangerous prank you could've played. I think you should turn this ship around and take us back. Now.' Billy stood with his hands on his hips as he glared down at Terry.

'That what you think? You not goin' let me finish the story? You wanna go back, that's fine. But unless you let me finish 'xplainin', I 'ope you 'ave got yer trunks, cos you is goin' 'ave to swim back, my cocker. I ain't goin' anywhere.'

Terry looked from Billy to Austin and back again. Sensing they had no other option, Austin nodded to Billy.

'Fine,' Billy sighed. 'But then you best get us back.'

'If you don't like what I tell you, I promise I'll take you back straight away, that ok?'

Billy sighed and nodded.

'Fine. But this had better be good,' Billy demanded.

'Ansum. You goin' sit down or no?' Terry asked.

'No, I'd rather stand to be honest,' he said as he folded his arms across his chest.

'Fair nuff, ya moody bugger. Tis yer life,' Terry said, before he chuckled, shook his head, and continued with his story.

'Ok. As I was sayin' earlier, I was 'bout to leave the mine, when the stone, which was still in me sack, started pullin'. It weren't goin' let me leave that easy. I didn't 'ave a clue what it wanted, so I let it lead me towards whatever it was after. When we got to the back of the mine, the sack started bouncin' up and down, so I took the stone out and done somfin' stupid. I started blinkin' talkin' to it.

I stood there askin' it to show me what 'e wanted, felt like a right pillock I did, talkin' to a blinkin' stone. Anyway, it started pullin' me towards the far corner. I didn't see it the first time I went there as woz pitch black and covered with an old grubby blanket. So I lifted the blanket up 'n' there, underneath, woz what the stone wanted me to find. An old box. Woz one of those made wiv long wooden twigs. Fink it's called a wicked basket.'

Austin started laughing. Terry looked at him.

'What you laughin' at?' he asked.

'You mean a wicker basket,' Austin said, laughing. Terry shook his head and tutted at him, in a *don't interrupt me* manner.

'Anyway, there woz two buckles, but one of 'em woz broke, snapped right off it 'ad. The stone was now bouncin' up 'n' down in me 'and so I put 'en down on top of the basket and it moved over to the one good buckle and started bouncin' up 'n' down 'gain. I didn't know what 'eck was goin' on, so I bent down and undone the buckle.'

Billy finally sat down next to Austin. He was now interested in what Terry had to say. He had missed the silly Knockers stories, not that he would admit it.

'Well, as I undid the buckle, the lid flew open to reveal what was inside,' he paused, allowing the boys to take everything in, and stuck his finger up his nose.

'What was inside?' Austin asked.

Billy waited, eager to hear what Terry had found.

'Nuffin'!' Terry answered, removing the finger.

'What?' Asked a confused Austin.

'What do you mean, nothing?' Billy asked, looking just as confused as his friend.

'What you think I mean? woz empty,' Terry explained.

'Empty?' Billy said.

'Yep, nuffin' in there,' Terry said as he stood, smiling.

'What the hell are you smiling at?' Billy fumed. He was getting even angrier than before with the Knocker. He sensed Terry was now making fun out of them. Billy stood and walked away before he said something he would regret.

'Well,' said Terry. 'The basket woz empty, but as I tried to close the lid, the stone jumped inside and then it 'appened.'

Billy stopped and turned back around. Austin just sat there. Terry smiled smugly at both of them.

'As I stood there, lookin' inside, the stone shone even brighter, only in one direction mind, to the back of the basket. Woz like a torch, directin' me to what it wanted me to find. Then I saw it, through the gaps in the wood. Woz attached to the back of the basket. I wouldn't 'ave seen it wivout the glow of the stone.'

Terry leaned to one side, farted and carried on, as Billy once again took his seat next to Austin, wafting away the foul stench surrounding them.

'So I closed the lid and turned it 'round. There woz an old, battered leather wallet, tied to the basket with four thin straps - one in each corner. I untied them, took the wallet off and placed it on top of the lid. On the front were some foreign words arranged in a circle around a crest. '*Quod Occultatum Regno,*' Terry said, as he raised his hands above his head and moved them in an arched motion to emphasise the mysterious words.

'Quod Occultatum Regno? What on earth does that mean?' shouted Billy.

'I dunno,' Terry answered.

'The Hidden Kingdom,' came a voice from behind them.

All three of them stopped. Billy and Austin turned and inhaled sharply as they came face-to-face with a stowaway.

Chapter 23
The Stowaway

'Does somebody want to explain to me what on earth is going on here?' Sue asked as she stood glaring at the boys.

Terry remained hidden from her. He sat behind Billy and Austin. He thought it might be better that way, while they tried to explain themselves.

'Sue?! What on earth are you doing here?' asked Billy, sounding slightly concerned, although Austin could hear the excitement in his voice too.

'How come you didn't get off with the others? We saw you all leave,' said Austin.

'Never mind that. What's going on?' she demanded.

She started walking towards the boys. She rubbed her head as she looked over the side of the ship and stopped dead in her tracks. A look of total shock covered her face.

'Oh my god, we're at sea?' she screamed.

'We're actually at sea. Sailing. What is going

on here?' she was panicking and looked like she might cry as both hands went to her face. Billy walked over to steady her.

'It's ok, don't panic. I can explain everything. Take deep breaths and try to relax.'

She looked at him, over the top of her hands. The panic was still there in her eyes, but she dropped her hands and screamed at him.

'Relax? Relax? We're on a ship that hasn't sailed for over 100 years. How do you suggest I relax?'

Terry walked over and stood beside Austin.

'Blommin' 'eck, she's lively that one ain't she? Got 'is work cut out wiv 'er,' he said, and then they both started laughing, causing Sue to look over. This made her even worse as she spotted Terry for the first time.

'Wh... Whhh... Who, or should I say what on earth is that?' she asked, pointing at the Knocker as her eyes widened in a panicked expression.

'Alright my ansum,' Terry said as he started walking towards her.

'I am Capt'n Nelson, and I am in charge of this 'ere fine vessel,' he said, placing his right hand back inside his jacket and adopting his previous pose. Sue looked him up and down, unsure what was going on. She felt her knees go weak, so she grabbed the ship's guardrail to steady herself. After a period of awkwardness, she exhaled sharply and spoke in a more controlled manner.

'Okay, will somebody please explain to me what is going on before I totally freak out?'

Billy opened his mouth to answer, but Terry beat him to it.

'We is goin' on a journey across the open seas. We is goin' fight beasts, look for treasure, and 'ave a good old adventure, goin' be a right laff. Fancy it or no?' Terry looked up at her with the biggest smile on his face as he removed his right hand from his jacket and started scratching his bum. Billy stepped in.

'Look, there's a lot to explain, so we may as well tell you everything. There's no need to freak out though. There's no need to panic and there's no need to be afraid, okay?'

Sue remained silent, as she continued staring at this odd little creature, scratching his bum with one hand and picking his nose with the other, a decidedly strange way of multitasking.

'Sue.' Billy called, disturbing her from her trance.

'Huh? What?' she said.

'Sit down and I'll explain.' He said, directing Sue to a crate as he prepared to tell her what had been going on.

Billy told Sue everything, right from the start, beginning with what had happened in the playground at the start of the school year. The whole time they were talking, Terry ambled around the ship inspecting everything and talking to himself. He started play-acting and pretending he was walking the deck during a high seas battle. He started running around pretending to shoot enemies who were attacking HMS Victory from all sides during the battle of Trafalgar. Sue and Billy watched as he removed a plate from one of the guns and put his head inside for a look.

Billy explained about the day in the woods, how they had met Terry, the scroll, the talking tree, the stone, and the adventure they had been on. He told her all about the battle over the stone with the Cornish pixies. Austin sat there. This was Billy's story and he didn't want to interrupt, so he switched his attention to Terry who was playing battleships. Running from side-to-side, front-to-back, he must have been shot over 15 times, but miraculously recovered to full health every time.

Billy finished and sat there waiting for Sue to speak. She looked around the ship, trying to process the information.

'So, you're telling me this little creature is responsible for everything, are you? Everything that's happened; he's done it?' Sue said, pointing towards Terry.

'I know it's hard to believe, but, yes,' Billy answered.

'Remember when you found that empty pasty bag in the woods and the plume of smoke you saw afterwards? That was him,' he said.

Sue looked at him, still unsure of this whole situation, but she had no choice.

A muffled scream and chuckling interrupted them. They all looked over and started laughing, Terry was back inside a gun, his jacket had bunched up and his trousers had fallen down, showing off his hairy bum.

'Does that look like something that could hurt you?' Billy said, pointing at Terry.

Sue was still dubious. She looked at the boys and thought for a moment as they walked over to rescue their captain. There was no other option. This was how she had been allowed to go on the school trip. He must have been the one who had altered the letter, signed the cheque, and erased her father's memory, so maybe she should give him a chance. She was still freaking out a bit, but she had to trust them, especially Billy. He would not allow her to be in danger. She'd had very little fun since coming back to England and she was so bored with her controlling father back home. This was out of the ordinary, unbelievable, strange, but it could be fun and exciting.

When they returned, Sue looked up at Terry while he continued to sort his jacket out and then over at the boys.

'Okay. So what's the plan?' Sue said.

They all smiled back at her and then Terry

spoke.

'That's the spirit my ansum. Let me show you,' Terry said as, once more, he removed the map and the stone from his sack.

Chapter 24
A Glimpse

Terry brought Sue up to speed with his discovery of the wicker basket and the leather wallet attached to the back of it. She stopped him a couple of times to clarify points, and ensure she understood. Once he had finished, he continued with his tale to all three of them.

'There woz a flap inserted into the top of the wallet. I opened it and put me 'and inside. I felt 'round and found this 'ere single sheet o' paper,' he said as he held up the blank map.

'As I pulled it out, the stone started glowin' different colours, red, blue, white, green, yellow. It kept changin', gettin' faster and faster. Then, it started spinnin' and before long, the old letters started firin' out. However, this time it was different.'

'What do you mean different?' asked Austin. 'In what way?'

'They gave me a glimpse,' Terry said.

They all looked at each other. What was the

crazy knocker going on about? Terry sensed their confusion.

'Wanna see?' he asked, smiling at them.

'Of course we do,' said Austin.

'See what?' asked Sue. Her previous misgivings had now disappeared. She was lost in the story, along with the boys.

'You're gonna like this,' Billy said as he smiled at her.

Terry picked up the stone and threw it across the deck of the ship. The boys watched Sue raise her hands to her face and take a sharp breath as the stone lifted from the deck, and started spinning. She shrieked through her hands, as coloured spears of light started firing out from the top of the stone and hung high above their heads. Darkness then descended as the sky turned black. It was as if they had just sailed into a tunnel. Soon the multitude of colours above them changed to pure white, bathing the ship's deck in brightness. The boys continued watching Sue. They must have looked this astounded in the woods. Billy caught sight of Austin and they smiled, they both knew exactly how she felt. The letters joined and formed words, something Billy and Austin had seen many times, but this was new to Sue. She screamed through her hands again as the excitement got the better of her, causing the boys to snigger.

Once the letters had finished moving, one of

the stone's famous poems hung in the air.

'Go on,' Billy said, nudging Sue, who turned to look at him. Her eyes looked even more beautiful under the bright glow of the letters.

'Read it out aloud,' he said, as he nodded towards the poem. Sue returned the smile, looked at the words and did as she was requested.

> *'Let's go on a journey*
> *To a magical place,*
> *Where the sights that you see*
> *Should put a smile on your face,*
> *There will be battles and conflicts*
> *Over a long-lost treasure,*
> *To help you find it*
> *Will give me great pleasure,*
> *With creatures and fighting*
> *And magic galore,*
> *The path you must take*
> *Is not quite like before,*
> *The answer you seek*
> *Is contained in your lap,*
> *Just use this old stone*
> *And follow the map.'*

Sue read and re-read the poem. Once she had finished, she looked at the boys, who were both smiling from ear-to-ear.

'I can't believe what I've just seen,' she said as she shook her head. 'That was incredible, but what does it mean?'

The boys shrugged.

'We know as much as you do,' Austin said, as he read the poem himself.

'But there's more to come,' Billy added as he glanced over to Terry. 'Isn't there?'

Terry winked and pointed skywards. All three of them returned their gaze to the words in the sky, ready for something none of them would believe possible.

As they waited, the letters transformed into shapes.

******

Huts soon filled the sky, along with several small animals. A lot of strange-looking villagers were ferrying what looked like piles of wood back and forth to a circular area, and in the background was the outline of a mountain range. The entire image had been created in the whiteness of the letters, so a lot of the detail was not clear.

Suddenly, the villagers froze and seconds later panic ensued. The animals all ran for cover and cowered behind anything they could find. The people all started darting about and some even ran into the huts and disappeared from the image. Then from over the brow of the hill came a strange-looking beast which must have been the cause of the panic. The first thing the children noticed was the long swaying tail high above it. It had three heads, but it was hard to make out what they were as the image was too fuzzy.

The beast walked down the hill towards the village and as it reached the bottom, it stopped and surveyed the area. Nobody moved. Then from overhead, a gigantic monster appeared, its enormous wings covering the entire length of the village. It was a giant dragon.

The three of them were glued to the image before them as Terry continued running around shooting imaginary pirates. One villager stepped forward and looked up at the dragon for a few seconds, then lowered his head and shook it from side-to-side. Sue noticed there was someone standing on the back of the dragon. Then another creature appeared, dragging what looked like a prisoner towards them. The villager who was stood in front of the dragon fell to his knees and raised his hands. The guard removed the prisoner from sight and seconds later the dragon expelled a white ball of fire and took to the skies. As it made its way into the distance, it faded from the image. The three-headed-beast turned and walked back through the field. It reached the top of the hill and vanished.

Villagers exited the huts, and made their way over to the villager in the middle and huddled around him. Then the strangest thing happened. They all turned to face the children. It was if they were looking directly at them. They stayed there for a moment and then the mountain range transformed into three simple but powerful words and hung above their heads. *'Please Help Us'.* The children were stunned. What did this mean? As they continued to watch, all the villagers, animals, words, and huts disappeared with a loud bang followed by a flash of light. The children closed their eyes and when they opened them, there in the sky above their heads was an item spinning around and around. It looked like a horseshoe and written on one side were three words the children had seen before: *'Quod Occultatum Regno!'*

With another flash, the image disappeared and the darkness overhead reverted back to daylight. Terry walked over, picked up the stone, put it back in his sack, and turned to face the children.

'So, wanna go on this 'ere adventure and see what that was all 'bout or no?' he asked.

The look on their faces told him they did. To everyones surprise, Sue spoke first.

'Where are we going?' She asked excitedly.

Terry smiled at her.

'Funny you should ask,' he said, sitting down next to them and pulling out the map, as HMS Victory continued its journey through the calm waters below.

Chapter 25
The Magical Map

The four of them sat there, once again, with the blank piece of parchment laid out in front of them.

'I still don't get how this is a map,' asked Sue.

She had forgotten she was at sea on a 300-year-old ship, being steered by magic and captained by a small mythical creature, who had almost killed them.

'Well, let me show you,' Terry said as he pulled the stone out of his sack and paused as he looked at the children.

'Ready my ansums?' He asked, and before they could reply, he set the stone down in the centre of the blank paper. They sat and waited, but nothing happened.

'Well, that was interesting. I'm so glad we've gone through all of this, for that. What's your next trick, Terry?' Billy asked sarcastically as he eyeballed their captain.

Terry just ignored him. He didn't understand

and scratched his head, then picked the stone up and gave it a quick once over before putting it back on the paper. The children waited. Still nothing. Then Terry started laughing. He fell backwards and grabbed his belly as tears rolled down his cheeks. Sue, Billy and Austin all stared at him, unsure what was so funny.

Terry composed himself, sat up and wiped his eyes.

'Finished?' Austin asked.

'What's the joke?' Asked Sue.

'You ain't goin' believe this, but I 'as messed up, I'm so stupid.'

'What do you mean you've messed up? Please tell me you have not forgotten the map, if it exists?' Billy asked.

'Wot? O'course I got a map. Tis right 'ere,' he said waving the blank parchment in the air. He turned it over and placed it on the deck of the ship again.

'Woz wrong way 'round,' he said as he chuckled.

Austin started sniggering, Billy and Sue shook their heads. Terry placed the stone in the middle of the paper, and they all watched as the magic unfolded. Almost immediately the stone began filling with black liquid and when it was full it emptied, soaking the cream coloured parchment with the darkest ink. Terry sat with a smug look on his face as he watched the astonishment on the children's faces as the stone continue to transform a previously blank sheet into the beginnings of a map.

The ink flowed to the top of the page and started to outline a large mountain range. Two lines ran from the middle of one mountain all the way down to a long rectangle, which had appeared on the right. More ink drifted to both sides of the paper and created, what looked like, a dense collection of trees and bushes. The last part of the sketch saw several squiggly lines drawn, one behind the other, that stretched across the full width of the map, just in front of the mountains. With no colour, it was hard to make out what they were, but that was all about to change.

As the children studied the outline of the map, the stone filled with a vibrant green colour and, just like the black, it emptied and flowed across the page. As it reached the mountains it soaked into the map, colouring them from top-to-bottom, giving the appearance of the most luscious grass. The stone filled again, light brown this time, and it soon became clear what the two lines running through the middle of the mountains had created - a path. Golden-yellow was soon emptying. It drifted over and kissed the base of the mountains before colouring the area up to the squiggly lines running across the map. The stone filled one final time. A deep, blue colour soaked into the bottom of the map adding a vast expanse of sea. The task was complete. Moments ago they were all looking at a normal plain piece of parchment paper, but now they were looking at a beautifully coloured map. Sue thought the lush green mountains looked like the fields she used to run through when she was younger. She would let her hands hang by her sides and the long blades of grass would brush through them and tickle her palms. The deep, blue sea made Austin wish he was sat beside the seaside with a nice cold ice cream, dribbling down his hand as it melted in the sun.

'Terry?' Billy asked.

'Yes, my ansum?'

'Where does that path lead?'

Their furry friend smiled before replying.

'That's wot we is goin' find out,' he said as he picked the stone up and put it back in his sack once more.

As they continued to glide through the water, Austin was looking over the guardrail, watching the sea turn into white froth as it crashed against the side of the ship. Billy and Sue were deep in conversation as they studied the fine detail of the map. Terry was attempting to climb the mizzenmast to get onto the sails, but his belt was causing him problems. He started chuckling as he tried to unhinge it from a hook that he had become snagged on.

Austin was deep in thought. Where were they going? What awaited them? Would it be dangerous? But what he wondered about more than anything was, what was the scene in the sky all about? There was no village identified on the map, no beasts, no people, no huts. So what relevance was there between the two? Was that where the path led? Not knowing what lay ahead excited him. He couldn't wait to see where they were going. He only hoped it would be as exciting as the adventure in the woods. What he didn't realise was, this would be far more exciting, yet dangerous too.

'So, how are you feeling about all of this now? Billy asked Sue.

She looked at him and gave a strained smile.

'I'm not going to lie. I'm still puzzled about what's going on. It's strange and I don't understand, but I'm trying not to think about it too much as I'll freak out. Although it is quite exciting too,' She paused, before turning away from Billy.

'What's wrong?' he asked.

She took a breath and stared back at him.

'Are you sure I won't be in trouble when I get home and my dad will never find out? I'm so worried.'

Billy looked at her, took her hand in his, and gazed into her big brown eyes.

'It's bizarre and I know how you feel, but I promise you everything will be fine. I mean, look at him, does he look like someone you can't put your trust in?' Billy said, pointing to Terry, who was on top of the mizzenmast shooting more pirates. He had discarded his belt on the hook after he had snagged it earlier. The problem with this was his trousers were now falling down and his bum was on show, once again. He kept having to hitch them up, but this did not distract him from taking on the imaginary pirates. Sue looked up at him and laughed.

'He may seem strange and look like he doesn't have a clue what's going on, but he will get you home. Your dad will never know what has happened, I promise.'

She looked at him and smiled. He smiled back before she dropped her head again.

'I don't believe it,' she said as she let go of Billy's hand.

'I'm telling you, he will.'

'What? No, not that. This,' Sue pointed at the map.

Billy thought nothing could surprise him anymore, but he was wrong.

'Terry, come here,' he shouted over his shoulder.

'Started as it? ansum,' he said, as he climbed down from the top of the mast. Austin turned around and walked over too.

As they reached Billy and Sue, they sat down.

'Whoa!' screamed Austin.

The map was the same as before, only now, the deep-blue sea was moving, it lapped against the golden sand in front of the mountains. The lines drawn earlier were now ripples of water moving towards the shore. Birds entered from one side and glided across the map before disappearing on the other side. The long grass of the mountains seemed to be swaying as the light wind blew through it. Then something tiny appeared at the bottom of the page. It was about the size of a ladybird and was a long way from the island. The white and brown item continued to bob up and down as it sailed through the water.

'What's that?' asked Austin.

Terry stood up.

'I'll show you,' he said, and walked over to a long wooden box located behind the ship's wheel, returning seconds later with a strange-looking orange gun in his hand.

The children watched as Terry cracked it open and loaded a cartridge into it. Then he pushed both ends together until there was a click. Their captain walked to the side of the ship, pointed the gun high into the air and squeezed the trigger. A plume of red smoke surrounded the barrel of the gun as the cartridge was discharged. Terry sat next to the children as the flare exploded in the sky. He pointed to the map as a series of tiny red dots appeared at the foot of the map surrounding the ladybird.

'That, my ansums...' he said as he pointed to it, '...is us. We is almost there.'

Chapter 26
The Time Jump

'How long till we arrive, Terry?' Austin shouted over to him as he was returning the flare gun.

'Eh?' Terry shouted back.

'How long till we get to the island?' Austin repeated.

'Dreckly, my ansum, we be there dreckly,' Terry said.

'What do you mean, dreckly?' Asked Sue.

'It's Cornish. It means no specific time,' Billy informed her.

'It means he doesn't know,' Austin whispered to her.

Terry came back over and sat next to them.

'I have a question,' Sue said.

'How come we are so close to this mysterious tropical island when we haven't been at sea for that long?'

'Well, you know when you woz watchin' the fing in the sky earlier?' Terry asked.

'Yeah, what about it?'

'I might have sea jumped us,' he gave a cheeky smile and giggled.

'Done what?' she asked, frowning. 'What's a sea jump?'

'Well, means take out a load of borin' sailin' and move us alon' a bit. Good, eh? Made the name up meself and everyfin',' he said, sounding proud.

'What he's trying to say, is that when we were distracted by the village scene in the sky, he used the stone to time lapse our journey and move us further along, so we reach our destination a lot quicker than we would have,' Billy answered.

'Yeah, wot 'e said,' Terry confirmed, as he nodded at Sue and pointed at Billy.

'That's impossible,' Sue said, sounding unconvinced.

'Oh, is it my ansum? Right. Stand up,' Terry stood and removed the stone.

'Might wanna hang on to something. Austin, grab the map, don't want that blowin' away,' Austin did as he was told and then joined the others in holding on to the guardrails. They all watched as Terry wasted no time in tossing the stone onto the deck of the ship, where it instantly started spinning.

'Look over the side,' Terry said.

They all did as they were told and peered into the deep, blue sea. As the ship continued on its journey, it rose out of the water and kept moving further and further away from the sea. The children had to hold on to the rails even tighter to stop them from falling over as the speed began to increase. The boys were enjoying the ride and smiling away. They glanced across at Terry, who had opened his mouth and was letting the wind enter and blow his cheeks out. He reminded Billy of a dog going along the road in a car with his head stuck out of the window. He was so childish. Sue was gripping on for dear life and screaming. After a minute of high-speed travel, the ship slowed down and once it was back to its normal sailing speed, it lowered back into the sea and carried on its way. Austin glanced at Terry who now had his mouth shut, (although there was dribble running down his chin). Sue's normally immaculate hair was wind-strewn across her face. She blew out hard to clear it from her eyes then put her hands underneath it, bent over and moved her hands back over her face and down the back of her head. The boys thought maybe Terry had gone too far and she was about to go crazy. But when she stood up straight, her eyes were alive.

'That was amazing,' she said and started laughing.

Terry nudged Billy and nodded towards Sue.

'I like 'er, my ansum. I see why you fancy 'er now.'

Billy smiled and blushed, as did Sue.

'How come we didn't feel it when we went that fast earlier?' Asked Austin. Terry chuckled.

'Cos I put us in a travel bubble, covered the whole blinkin' ship it did. You didn't see it as woz too dark. Good eh?' Austin smiled and turned his attention back to the map. They were almost at the island.

*****

The sea continued to lap against the side of the ship, as birds flew overhead. Billy and Sue were once again sat chatting, and Terry had now changed back into his normal Knocker clothing.

'So, that's what he normally looks like, is it? Sue asked, staring at him.

'Yeah, I don't know where he got that uniform from.'

'He got it wrong anyway,' said Sue.

'What do you mean? asked Billy. 'The uniform?'

'What? No. He said he dressed like the captain of the ship, Nelson. But he was not the captain at Trafalgar. That was Hardy. Nelson was onboard, but he wasn't the captain. I didn't want to say anything,' she said.

'You did way too much research for the school trip,' said Billy.

Sue laughed and poked him in the ribs.

'Guys, come here,' shouted Austin. They all ran over. In the distance, the top of a mountain range came into view. Austin turned and smiled.

'Well, we best get ready. Cos that,' Terry said pointing at the mountains, 'is Kaninjanga Island. Our destination.' He started rubbing his hands in excitement. He knew what lay ahead, to a certain degree, but he daren't tell the children about the beasts, dragons, and other dangers awaiting them. His previous visit to this island had not gone well and he had to leave in a hurry. They almost killed him, but he escaped by the skin of his teeth and now he was back to fight them and take the treasure. If he could get past the monster that lurked deep inside the cave. Whatever it was.

He couldn't wait.

Chapter 27
All Ashore

They headed for the cave. She would be back soon, and if they did not have it, she would kill another villager. The last team had once again returned with nothing. It was a recurring cycle. Janji, the head of the village, would send teams of villagers out to search, only for them to return hours later empty-handed.

The village had been working tirelessly. They had to find it, there was no other way. If they tried to fight back, she would kill them. If they found the item and hid it from her and she found out, she would kill them. If they did not find it soon, she would start killing them all, one-by-one.

Janji emerged from his hut and stood outside. They had searched most of the island, except for the one place nobody wanted to go. They had purposely left it until the end, so it must be in there, and now they had no choice but to enter.

The team received their instructions and with

a last nod of the head from Janji, they headed for the cave. He stood there and watched as they made their way along the path that lead out of the village. He knew they may never return, but there was no other option. They had to find it. He was desperate to save his village and have the prisoner she was holding released.

He headed back into his hut, as the final villagers disappeared on their way to the dark cave to try and locate the treasure that lay hidden within its network of tunnels.

******

They floated towards the shore. The water was too shallow to sail through, so they hovered 10-feet above the sea.

As they approached the long rectangular jetty, Sue looked into the sky. Birds circled around as the sun shone bright in the blue, cloudless sky. She wondered what lay ahead. She was nervous and scared, but also excited. Billy and Austin were hanging over the guardrails chatting. Sue realised how much she liked Billy. The blush earlier when he held her hand confirmed it, but that was fine. It felt nice when he took her hand in his. Was Terry joking when he said that Billy fancied her? She hoped not. A smile crept across her face at the thought.

The ship slowed as it pulled up alongside the

jetty.

'Okay my ansums, off we get,' Terry said.

Austin looked over the side. They were a long way up and there was no way of climbing down.

'How are we getting down? Expect us to jump, do you?' Billy asked.

Terry, put his fingers in his mouth and whistled. The light that was wrapped around the ship's wheel made its way over and hung above their heads.

'Okay. Stand next to each other,' Terry told them.

The children did as they were told and looked up as the light came to rest on their shoulders. They heard a light buzzing sound and seconds later, they rose into the air. They all let out a scream as their feet left the deck of the ship. Terry gave a mischievous smile, then closed his eyes as the four of them floated high into the air where they hung for few seconds. The buzzing increased, and the light intensified, causing the children to hold their breath and close their eyes. And then they were off. They screamed louder as the wind blew across their faces. Terry was belly laughing as they rose 50-feet above the water and headed out to sea. The boys opened their eyes as the light changed direction and led them back towards the ship. They were heading right at the mizzenmast, and their speed increased causing the children to panic. As they reached the mast, a swift movement to the left took them perilously close to it. Billy could almost smell the wood as they passed it. Austin felt like he was on a rollercoaster ride, changing direction and shooting around corners at speed. They reached the front of the ship and descended, flying right past the bowsprit mast as they lowered towards the water. Their feet were only inches from the sea, and they had to pull their legs up to stop them from getting wet, apart from Terry that was. He was short enough not to have to worry about his feet and besides, he was too busy laughing at the children. They turned again and headed along the port side towards the rear of the ship, still only inches from the water. They slowed as they banked to the left and started to rise again. Soon they were flying past the vast number of windows located to the rear. They came to a sudden stop, just above the path. Terry closed his eyes and seconds later their feet landed on firm ground. The light detached from their shoulders and headed back onto the ship and out of sight.

The children stood there, all panting and looking astonished.

'Enjoy that did'e?' Terry asked as he chuckled.

'That was brilliant,' said Austin.

'Could you not have just lifted us off and brought us straight down here?' Asked a breathless Sue.

'O'course I could. Bit borin' that though init and anyway we is meant t'be on an adventure?' Terry giggled.

'Right cumuson, lezz get goin',' and with that, he headed along the path towards the foot of the mountains. He did not even check to see if they were following him. They didn't have a choice and he knew it.

****

The villagers removed their weapons and made their way towards the cave entrance. As they rounded the last tree, the cave came into view. They re-grouped and readied themselves to enter. None of them wanted to advance. The dark path leading to the mouth of the cave looked cold, uninviting, and dangerous. No-one knew exactly what awaited them, but they heard it every night. The monster's warning cry would explode through every entrance to the cave, causing the inhabitants of the island to run for cover. They couldn't risk being spotted. If they were, their life would end there and then. After sending its cry out of the cave the monster would emerge and fly off to feast on whatever it wanted from the ocean. Then it would return in total darkness and settle into its cave once more.

When they reached the opening, the group stopped and savoured the daylight, potentially for the last time, before entering the dark cave. If they could sneak past the monster and work their way through the network of tunnels, they may be okay, but they didn't know where the treasure was hidden, so that was a long shot. They could almost hear the growling begin as they stood, shoulder-to-shoulder, at the mouth of cave.

With that final thought, the group leader took a deep breath and stepped inside. Just at that moment, a faint shriek came floating over from the other side of the mountains. They all turned their attention from the cave and looked towards the noise. At the sound of more screaming, the villagers headed over, all wondering what was the cause of the chaos and hysteria. They slowly walked towards a gap in the mountains and as they reached it, looked out to sea. What on earth was this? Hanging there, just above the water, was an old ship, and floating high above it, seemed to be a group of strange looking creatures. The villagers watched as they flew high into the air and circled the ship, causing the screaming to increase. They had forgotten all about the cave and their task. Who were these creatures? What were they doing on their island? And what did they want? They watched them head out to sea and moments later, spin around and come shooting back again. Their screaming seemed to get louder as they flew right over the ship before descending back towards the water. There seemed to be a bright light draped around the shoulders of the group, as if it was carrying them.

Soon they descended towards the path and once they landed, the glowing of the light decreased, before lifting from their shoulders and heading back to the ship.

The villagers continued watching their new visitors as they stood on the path chatting, until one of them, who looked like a goblin, walked off and was shortly followed by the others. A villager pointed to the overgrown wasteland behind them and they all headed towards the top of it, where they would wait for the visitors to emerge.

Their task had changed. The cave would have to wait, for now.

Chapter 28
Prisoners

The boys and Sue followed Terry as he made his way along the path, whistling and farting away.

'How cool was that?' asked Austin.

'I think you're mistaking cool for crazy,' Sue said.

Billy kept quiet. He didn't want to seem as if he was taking sides, but like Austin, he had begun to love the adventure they were on, once the initial shock had eased.

As they progressed along the path, Austin's eyes wandered around. He had never seen anything so beautiful. It was a long way from the derelict house he lived in six months ago.

'What do you reckon we're doing here?' Billy asked, shaking him from his thoughts.

'It could be anything with that nutter in charge,' Austin said as he pointed at Terry.

'I must admit it beats sitting on a coach and heading home,' said Sue, now over the shock of the journey ashore.

'Aren't you afraid?' asked Austin. 'I mean, you are a girl,' he said, trying hard not to smile as he attempted to tease her. Sue stopped dead in her tracks and glared at him.

'I beg your pardon?' she said as she folded her arms across her chest.

'Well, I mean we know how squeamish you girls are. *Oh, no a spider the size of a fly, someone come and save me,*' he said, raising his hands and pulling a scared face. Sue took a step towards him, looked into his eyes, unfolded her arms and punched him on the arm, catching him by surprise. The mischievous smile disappeared from his face as he frowned and started rubbing his arm.

'Oh, sorry, did a little girl hurt you,' Sue said as she stuck her bottom lip out, mocking him.

Billy started laughing.

'One day you'll learn to keep that mouth of yours shut, mate,' he said as he patted Austin on the back.

'It didn't hurt. She just caught me funny,' he said, trying to justify his reaction, as he continued to rub his arm while Sue and Billy smiled at him.

'Cumuson you lot, we ain't got all day,' Terry shouted at them.

They all turned and made their way towards the impatient Knocker standing with his hands on his hips. As they approached him, he turned around and led them along the path that cut through the mountains.

They reached the top and came face-to-face with an extensive area of wasteland. The path ran right through the middle of the overgrown bushes.

''Ope there's not any nasty beasts in 'ere,' Terry said as he turned to them and started laughing.

'You're not funny,' said Austin, who had now stopped rubbing his arm.

'Oh, stop bein' a wuss,' Terry said. 'Ok, 'ere we go,' he smiled, and pushed his way past the low-hanging branches, followed by Sue and the boys.

******

As Terry led them through, he kept making comments about beasts and what may lie in wait for them. Austin asked him to just keep quiet or he would throw him into the undergrowth as a snack for these so-called beasts. Terry started chuckling. Suddenly, Sue screamed out. She had caught her hand on one of the prickly bushes.

'Are you okay?' asked a concerned Billy, turning towards her.

'I'm fine, just pricked myself, that's all,' she said as she sucked on the injured finger and inspected it to make sure she did not have a splinter.

'Let me look,' said Billy, as he examined Sue's hand.

'Maybe you should kiss it better, Bill? Be her knight in shining armour,' Austin joked.

'You want another punch?' Sue asked him.

'Didn't hurt anyway,' Austin said, as he smiled.

'Oh my god, Austin. What's that behind you?' said Billy, a scared look on his face as he pointed behind his friend.

'Huh, what? Where?' Austin asked as he panicked and turned around.

'Oh, it's nothing. Just thought you'd dropped your dummy,' Billy said, and started laughing.

'If you lot 'as finished, we gotta crack on?' said a very annoyed Terry.

'Lead the way maestro,' said Billy, as he tried letting go of Sue's hand, but she tightened her grip and smiled at him. Billy smiled back.

Terry looked up ahead and noticed they were leaving the confines of the overgrown pathway.

'Almost there,' he said, as he pointed towards the opening up ahead.

'About time,' said Austin.

They left the path and stood there looking around. Sue gave Billy's hand one last squeeze and let go.

'What's that up there? Asked Billy, pointing to the left. They all turned and stared at the ominously dark opening of a cave.

'Ummm, No! No! No!' said Austin. 'There is zero chance of me going in there. I'd rather stay here and take my chances with any beasts that might lurk nearby, thank you very much.'

Suddenly, they heard a rustling and scurrying noise behind them. They all turned around and came face-to-face with the strangest creatures, all armed with spears which were now pointed at their heads. Terry and the children backed away and Billy pushed Sue behind him to protect her.

As they continued to retreat, they heard more noises from behind. They turned around and once again had spears thrust into their faces by more of the creatures. They were trapped.

******

There was nowhere for them to go. These strange creatures had surrounded them. Billy looked them up and down. He hadn't seen anything like them. They were wearing hats which had long pointy ears protruding from a hole on either side. Their expressionless faces contained pure white eyes, which were separated by a broad, flat nose. They did not have any lips and their bottom jaw jutted out and overlapped their top jaws. They all wore the same matching shirts and trousers with a twine belt fastened around their waists. The wooden knives that hung from their belts had handles bound with twine and the blades looked liked they had come from a large animal's tooth. Their feet were devoid of any shoes and on their backs, they each had a box. The weirdest thing of all about these creatures was that they were completely made of wood, from top to bottom.

One of them stepped forward and said something, but it was totally incomprehensible. Terry and the children stood, frowning and confused. The villager repeated himself, but it was no use. Terry tried talking to them.

'I 'ave somefin' 'ere that might 'elp my cocker,' he said as he reached towards his sack. But as soon as his hand touched the buckle, a creature slapped it away with his spear.

'Oi, no need for that, ya nasty git,' Terry said, rubbing his hand.

Seconds later spears were thrust in front of his face. One of them even touched the end of his fat round nose.

'Oh, bugger' Terry muttered under his breath. The villagers then talked amongst themselves. When they finished, one of them nodded and reached into the box on his back, removed something and walked behind Terry.

'What you blinkin' fink you is doin' my ansum?' Terry asked as the others watched in silence. The creature pulled Terry's hands behind his back and proceeded to tie them together. He then repeated the process on the boys and Sue. They did not move, flinch, or try to fight it. The villagers' spears were only inches from their faces, so they were not taking any chances. Once they were tied up, the leader said something else, and the villagers arranged them in single file and led them down the mountain.

'Marvellous adventure this, Terry,' Austin said, as they headed away from the cave and off to god knows where.

******

From high above the action, the Chimera had been watching the episode unfold. Those were the instructions from his master. She was the one in charge and she made sure he knew it. His task was to watch the villagers, make sure they entered the cave to look for the treasure, and then report back to her.

But the cave had been abandoned and he now watched as they marched a group of prisoner's back towards their village. What increased his intrigue even more, was that, unless his six eyes deceived him, he was sure he recognised one of the prisoner's. It couldn't be him. Could it?

He made his way back up the mountain, towards his vantage point, giving him a perfect view of the entire village. If that was really him, then it changed everything.

He reached his look-out point as they approached the village. The villagers had formed two lines, with the humans between them. The Chimera edged closer and focused on the prisoners.

It was the one at the front that interested him. Surely it wasn't him? But he could not see him clearly enough to be certain.

They entered the village and came to a stop in front of Janji's hut. The leader emerged moments later and stood in front of the prisoners. The Chimera still could not see clearly. The short one at the front was shielded by the others. Was it him? Was he stupid enough to come back? After what had happened last time?

He waited. He needed to confirm his suspicions. Moments later, the villagers lowered their spears and Janji led the prisoners into his hut. The Chimera growled. He was sure it was him. That red thing on his head gave him away. He growled once more, turned and disappeared over the top of the mountain. He had to let his master know the goblin was back and this time, he had company.

Chapter 29
Inspection Time

Their host walked around, inspecting them from head to toe. Sue and the boys continued to stare straight ahead. They did not want to give him any reason to harm them. Terry, on the other hand, was making weird popping noises and started whistling as he looked around.

'Will you be quiet.' whispered Billy.

'Why?' Terry asked.

'Because it would be nice to get out of here alive,' Billy whispered through gritted teeth.

'Ah, he won't 'urt us. If they wanted us dead we would already be strung up,' he said.

After finishing with the children, the creature moved across and stood inches from Terry's face. They were almost the same height, so he was staring straight into his eyes. Terry couldn't help himself.

'I 'ope he ain't goin' try to kiss me, 'e ain't my type,' he said as he chuckled.

'Will you shut up,' Billy demanded.

Austin was trying not to laugh. For some reason he found this all very amusing. Sue was taking deep breaths as she tried to calm herself down.

'Bet you wish you were on the coach now, don't you?' Austin joked.

'Shut up. You're not funny,' she snapped back.

Then, to their amazement, the creature stuck his head right into Terry's armpit and started sniffing.

'God, he's brave,' said Austin. 'Obviously doesn't have a sense of smell.'

After getting a lungful of Terry's unique aroma, he removed his face from sweat-pit-city, put his hands inside Terry's garb and started rummaging around inside, causing him to giggle and let a little fart out.

'Nervous, Terry?' Austin joked.

As he moved his hands around inside the garb, searching for any hidden weapons, Terry burst out laughing. Nevertheless, the creature continued, unabated, sniffing and searching all over the laughing Knocker. When he finished his search, he walked around to the rear. Terry had now regained control, but he lost it again when a nose touched his bum and started sniffing.

'Ere, take it easy, don't be so disgustin'. I ain't a dog, my ansum,' he said, through his giggling.

'He likes you,' Austin joked, again.

'Will you two be quiet,' said an annoyed Sue.

'Thats' easy for you to say, you ain't got a nose creeping its way up your butt-crack,' Terry quipped back as he continued to giggle.

With the inspection complete he walked back around to face them. There was no inspection of the children, much to their delight. He turned around and nodded to one of his men standing guard at the door who then walked over and cut their restraining ties. All four of them stood there, rubbing their wrists, relieved they were no longer in any immediate danger. The villager pointed to a pile of large cushions in the middle of the hut and motioned for them to sit down. They all did as requested and moved over to sit down. Billy, Austin, and Sue sat, but there was no room for Terry, so he stood in front of them. Austin smiled and patted his knee.

'Come on fella, snuggle up,' he looked up at Terry as he laughed. Terry frowned at him.

'You 'spect me to sit on yer lap? Fat chance my ansum,' Terry said.

'Oh, come on, let's have a little cooch, big-man,' Austin said as his laughing increased.

'Just sit down,' said Billy.

Austin leaned towards him.

'You know, you're a lot more fun when your wife ain't around,' Billy elbowed him in the ribs, leading to a *humph* sound escaping Austin.

Terry squeezed between the boys, pushing Billy closer to Sue. They looked at each other and smiled as the redness in their cheeks returned.

'Well, this is cosy. Who's reading the bedtime story tonight,' joked Austin.

They all ignored him. The creature was over in the corner, with his back to the children. Soon steam started to appear above his head and after a few seconds he turned and walked over to them, carrying a tray that contained four cups and a teapot made with what looked like tightly bound leaves.

'Ansum, can't beat a nice cup of tea, I is chackin,' said Terry as he smiled.

'You're what?' asked Sue.

'Chackin',' Terry repeated. 'You know, throat's dryer than that there Sahara Desert place.'

Sue frowned at him, baffled.

'What he's trying to say is he is thirsty and would love a cup of tea,' explained Billy. Sue continued looking confused, as Terry sat there licking his lips and rubbing his hands.

'He has some weird sayings,' she said.

'Damn right he does,' said Billy.

As the tray was placed down on a small tree-stump table in front of them, Terry's eyes widened as he waited for his cup of tea, but he was not expecting what happened next. The creature picked up the pot of bound leaves and filled up the four cups. But it was not tea in the pot. In fact, it was hard to make out what it was at all. Terry stood there frowning as he watched the cups fill up.

'What the blinkin' 'eck is this?' he exclaimed as he picked up his cup and peered inside. The children leaned forwards and looked into their own cups. Bright coloured liquids sat there. Red, yellow, green, purple, silver and blue. But unlike normal colours that mix when poured into a container, these remained separated. Austin took a wooden stick that was lying on the tray next to the cups and gave his a stir. The colours in his cup started mixing together, but once he stopped moving his spoon around, they returned to the individual colours they were before.

'Oh my god, this is crazy,' said Sue, looking in her cup.

Austin glanced at her cup and saw that it was the same as his. He started moving the stick again and without Sue stirring hers, the colours moved around in the same direction. Billy's and Terry's were doing exactly the same, moving in the same way, the same pattern, and at the same speed. As they looked at each other, smiles crept across their faces. What they had witnessed was nothing short of magical.

'That's nice, but I'd rather 'ave a cup of blinkin' tea?' A very grumpy Terry moaned.

When they had finished being mesmerised by what they had seen, they looked up at the creature in front of them. He nodded and pointed to their cups. They knew what he wanted them to do, but despite the magical show they had just seen, none of them were keen to drink the liquid staring up at them. He repeated the action, but they simply stared back at him. They didn't want to offend their host, but they also didn't want to drink the contents of their cups. He shook his head, and poured himself a cup of the strange liquid. He closed his eyes and a swirling pocket of air circled around his cup. Terry lent forward and let a little squeak out of his bottom, but nobody noticed. They were all watching as their host kept his eyes closed, lowered his head and took a sniff from the cup.

What happened next amazed them all.

Chapter 30
It's Time

The Chimera could not understand why he had returned. He must be stupid. They had him cornered and almost killed him the last time he was here. But the echoes and lava filling the ravine had distracted him and the little goblin managed to creep underneath him and escape. But now he was back, and the Chimera would make him pay. He would retrieve the stone and his master would forgive him.

As he entered her den, he found his master attending the fire. She heard his footsteps approaching and turned to face him. The beast stopped in front of her as she put down the poker and picked up the cane lying next to it.

'Well, do they have it?' She asked.

'No master, not yet. However, they do have something that will interest you,' he said. He sensed her unhappiness at the treasure still not being located.

'What?' She demanded.

'He's back, master.'

'Who?' She asked, edging closer.

'The one with the stone.'

As she looked at the beast, her curious expression changed to a devilish smile.

'Excellent. Excellent. I knew he would come back. He is too stupid to stay away,' she walked around the den, head held high, chest puffed out, slapping the palm of her left hand with the cane.

'This time, we will finish him. He will not escape. You will not let him escape again,' she glared down at the beast, as he lowered his gaze.

'Yes master.'

'There's something else, master.'

'Which is?' She asked.

'He is not alone. There are others,' his eyes remained locked on the floor.

'What do you mean, others?' She asked.

'Other creatures, master. They came via the sea. Janji has them captive in his hut,' the Chimera risked a glance towards his master.

She paced around, the devilish smile seemed to have become even darker.

'Well, that makes it even better. Now he's back, we can pinpoint the exact location of the treasure. The stone and the map will show us where, and the fastachees will retrieve it. We will make him relinquish the stone and then they will all die, along with the pathetic fastachees. We will have the treasure and the stone in one foul-swoop. It's perfect.'

As she explained her plan, she circled the beast.

'Prepare the troops,' she went on. 'We travel tonight, in the darkness. They will not expect us. We must catch them off guard and attack. There is no time to waste,' she added.

'Yes master,' the beast answered.

She did not hear him she was already heading inside the mouth of the den, her laughter echoing as she disappeared from view.

The Chimera turned and headed off to inform the others.

It was time to finish this.

******

The children watched as the colours in the cup rose and started circling around above their heads.

'Whoa,' shouted Sue.

The four of them sat there mesmerised, but silent. Even Terry was being quiet for once. The creature blew into the colours above his head causing them to mix and swirl around. They were moving one way and then the other, shooting left-to-right, up-and-down. Their host watched his visitors. They were smiling as the magic show continued above their heads.

The colours then separated and moved in opposite directions. The children and Terry tried to follow them, turning their heads one way and the other, as the colours flew over their heads, through their legs, and over their shoulders. The streaming colours crackled and fizzed as they moved at speed around them. Then, as quick as a flash, they all shot back to the middle of the hut and combined once again. The show was not over yet. The best part was yet to come.

The colours slowed and transformed. They increased in size as they took on the size and shape of a bowling ball. All the while, Terry was partaking in his favourite activity - digging for green nuggets. Sue nudged Billy and whispered in his ear.

'This is so exciting,' she said as she continued to watch the transformation above them.

Austin glanced sideways, smiled, and gave Terry a shove. He slipped forwards and his finger disappeared further up his nose, causing him to cry out.

'Owww, that blinkin' 'urt, ya idgit,' he said, rubbing the side of his nose, as his eyes watered.

'Sorry mate, I slipped.'

'Shuusssh,' Sue demanded, as she frowned at them.

They directed their gaze back above their heads and watched as the colours finished their creation. When it was over, their mouths were completely agape. They were looking into the bright eyes of a large, colourful, holographic face that was now hanging above their heads.

******

As he ambled towards his den, the Chimera thought about the newcomers. He was glad the stupid creature had come back. There would be time for redemption. Last time, he had let him escape, which proved a massive mistake and something he would not repeat. Now that he was back, he would finish him once and for all. However, there was something niggling him, but he didn't know what.

The animals were gathered in the gully below his den. Previously it had only been him living here, which was fine. No-one to bother him and no-one to answer to, just the way he liked it. But that all changed when he saved her. The creatures had grown in numbers as they followed her plan, building an army of the island's inhabitants as they prepared to find the treasure that she so desperately needed.

He stood there and cast an eye over the surroundings. There were many creatures gathered, all prowling around, waiting for their mission to start. He stood on the rock overlooking them and gave a loud, fearsome cry to get their attention. All heads turned to face him. He waited for the last creatures to stop moving and then gave them the news they had been waiting for.

'It's time,' he announced.

Growls, excited battle-cries, and howling filled

the air.

'Silence!' the Chimera demanded, as the serpent's head swayed and hissed in their direction. After a few seconds, stillness returned and he had their undivided attention again.

'They do not have it. They have not found it. It's still missing.'

The creatures down below looked at each other, confused and unsure what was happening. Their sole purpose was to kill the fastachees once they located the treasure. But if they had not found it, why attack? Had their master's patience worn thin? Was she sending them into the cave to find it instead?

'He's back, the funny little goblin,' the Chimera informed them. Growling sounds followed as their confused looks were replaced with angry grimaces.

'Now is our time. We will kill him, take the stone, and complete our mission. That is why we must be ready. Our master has spoken. We will prepare and attack at dusk. We must not fail this time. We will not fail this time. Prepare to fight!'

With that, the Chimera turned and disappeared into the darkness of his den as the howls and growling from below began once more.

Chapter 31
The Holographic Face

The holographic face glaring down at them slowly moved from side-to-side. As it did, it glimmered, giving the impression of being made of glitter. Long wavy hair, which fell to his shoulders, was blue on the left-hand side and red on the right. Bushy green eyebrows, that looked like they were crawling across the top of his face, hung above his eyes, which, like his hair, were different colours. His left one was gold and his right was silver. As Austin looked closer, he realised the irises inside the eyes were spinning around in a clockwise direction. A thin yellow moustache ran across his top lip, curled upwards, and became bushy at the ends. A thin line of purple hair ran down the centre of his chin and, as it reached the bottom, led back up his cheeks and finished at the earlobes.

The face continued to stare at the four visitors sat in front of him, eyeballing each of them without saying a word. Then, he lowered his face to within inches of Terry's. The Knocker couldn't keep quiet. He just had to say something.

'Feels like I is in trouble wiv the missus and gettin' told off this does,' Terry joked under his breath.

'I bet your missus would love to hear you have compared her to a grumpy, multi-coloured, oversized head. Mind you, she already gets the grumpy part,' Austin said.

They both started sniggering as the glittery face continued to move amongst them. He stopped in front of Austin, who winked at him.

'Alright beautiful. What's your name?' Austin joked, causing Terry to giggle again. They were like naughty schoolchildren. The face frowned at him and moved to Billy who did not say a word. He was trying to show how mature he was. Finally, he drifted over and finished his inspection with Sue. She stared back and gave a nervous wave.

'Hi,' she said, as she smiled. Trying to show she was friendly.

The face frowned at her as she spoke before returning to his previous position in front of all of them.

He closed his eyes and shouted, 'Hallal graft falack torsq tac.' His eyes rolled and he gradually shrunk in size, getting smaller and smaller. Before long it was the size of a golf ball. He hung in the air for a moment and then moved amongst the children and Terry, passing at speed over their shoulders, past their heads, and through their legs. The children did not move. The mysterious object slowed as it floated over them before finally stopping on Terry's left shoulder. Terry saw it out of the corner of his eye as it moved up to his ear. Then it whispered something in its native tongue, causing Terry to frown. Before he could do anything, the golf ball shot straight into his ear. Terry let out a scream which caused the children to scream too. The face had disappeared. It was now bouncing around inside of Terry's head. The Knocker continued screaming as he stood up, turned his head to one side and started slapping his right ear to try and remove the invader from inside his head. The others looked around. There was nothing they could do but watch Terry frantically smack his ear.

He bounced against the wall as he danced his way around the hut, frantically shaking his head from side-to-side. He barged into the village leader and almost knocked him over. Terry toppled forward and ran straight into the table, spilling the contents of the cups all over the floor. He was screaming and trying to do anything to get this intruder out of his head. The children were now getting worried. Was this going to happen to all of them? Terry bounded around the hut, crashing into everything in sight, before the ball finally shot out of his ear and landed on the carpet in front of them. Terry cradled his head in his hands as he gingerly got up from the floor and sat down on the cushions. He looked at the face that was hanging above them again as it grew back into the size of a bowling ball.

'What the blinkin' 'eck was that all 'bout?' Terry asked, as he continued cradling his head.

'You okay, mate? Asked Austin as he placed his hand on his shoulder.

'Better than I was 30 seconds ago, my ansum,' he answered.

They all looked back up at the face, worried and confused about what had just happened. Little did they know what was about to occur.

The face was now back to its original size and in its previous position above their heads with its eyes closed. As they studied his face he slowly opened his eyes and spoke to them in a tone they would all recognise.

'Alright my ansums, wasson?' he said, as he smiled at them for the first time.

The holographic face had turned Cornish.

Chapter 32
The Surprise Visitor

'Well, don't just sit lookin' so blinkin' stupid,' the face asked in his new accent. But they did not move, none of them. They sat there staring at him, mouths wide open. He tutted before speaking again.

'Very well, you rude buggers. I 'spose you want an explanation as to woz goin' on? You is all lookin' a bit discombobulated,' he said as he chuckled.

'Well, old Janji here could not communicate wiv' you, so he summoned me to conjure up a bit of magic,' he said as his eyes widened.

'What do you mean, magic?' Sue finally asked.

'Well, I can transform,' he informed them.

'Transform?' Billy said, frowning, looking very confused. 'Into what?' he added.

'Anyfin',' the face said. 'Depends on what's needed. I as the ability to change into people, shapes, animals. I 'as 'ad some fun over the years,' he said as he chuckled.

'All Janji 'ere 'as to do is summon me and tell me what 'e wants, been 'ere for years I 'as,' he explained.

'So, I 'ad to get into yer memory bank, see what you woz 'bout, where you woz from, and 'ow you spoke, so we could communicate. I tell 'e what my ansum,' he said looking at Terry, 'you 'as got some weird stuff inside that there 'ead o' yours. You is a bit keen on them there pasties ain't you. I mean, you 'as two lovely little children, but does yer wife know you wanted to call one of 'em large steak and the other medium steak? I mean, cumuson, woz that all 'bout, eh?'

The children sat there and started sniggering. Terry giggled too.

'I do love a good pasty, my ansum,' he said.

'Like you need to tell us that mate,' laughed Austin.

'Anyway, after bouncin' 'round in yer 'ead, I discovered a few fings. You 'ave been on this 'ere island before and we both know what you want. I can't believe you came back, knowing what awaits you. She's pure evil, but you already know that after last time.'

The children turned to face Terry, confused with what they had discovered.

'What does he mean you've been here before and you know how dangerous it is, Terry?' Billy demanded, as he glared at the sheepish-looking Knocker.

'Must 'ave me mistaken wiv someone else,' Terry said, as he looked away.

'Terry?' Austin demanded.

'Okay, okay. Well, when I went missing for a few monfs, I might of, kind of, come 'ere on me own,' he said, still looking very sheepish, but smiling.

'You mean you have already been here? You knew the danger but you brought us all anyway?' fumed Billy.

'I did kind o' tell 'e, my ansum,' Terry tried pleading.

'You told us we were going on an adventure. You said nothing about danger or the fact that we might get killed!' Billy raged.

Terry looked up at him and, as usual, could not contain himself.

'Looks like we got two girls and one boy on this 'ere adventure, you big baby,' he said, as he giggled once more.

'This is not funny!' Billy was fuming.

''Tis a little funny though, if you fink 'bout it, init?' Terry joked.

Billy made a move for the Knocker, but to his surprise, Sue stepped in between them.

'Let's calm this down. We're here now and there's nothing we can do about it,' she explained.

'So, why did we have to go through that whole

drama with stealing the ship? Why couldn't we teleport like we did in the woods?' Asked Austin.

'Cos it's too far. On me own tis fine as does not ask too much work of the stone, because I is so small. But three of us all this way? Stone would lose its power over the ocean and then we would be swimming with the fishes,' Terry explained. 'The ship was the best option as it's supported by the water. Help's to reduce the work needed by the stone.'

'We might be dead by the morning anyway now because of your selfish actions,' said Billy.

The conversation was then interrupted by the sound of commotion outside, as a mixture of shouting and screaming drifted into the hut. The children heard a voice and looked at each other in disbelief. Oh no. They all turned around and made their way out of the hut to confirm their suspicions.

They gathered outside and stood shoulder-to-shoulder as they realised this adventure had now taken another twist. There were several villagers huddled around a new prisoner who, like the children, had been led into the village with his hands tied behind his back. He was remonstrating with his captors when he looked up and spotted the children. He stopped pleading his innocence and frowned as he registered who they were. Everybody stood staring at each other, nobody knowing quite what to say. The new prisoner broke the silence surrounding them all.

'Billy, Austin, Sue? Where on earth are we? And what is going on?' Panic and confusion was clear in his tone.

'Mr Robertson?' Sue asked. 'What are you doing here?'

'I could ask you the same question, young lady?' Their angry teacher replied.

Chapter 33
The Chimera

The beast lay at the mouth of his cave. The excited noises drifting up to him from the army of creatures gathered below confirmed that it was time to end this. It had been building to this moment, the long search and countless battles had all been leading them here. It started out with just the two of them, but over time, they had built up their army. The goal was to find the treasure and retrieve the sacred ring. However, that all changed after her encounter with the short furry goblin and the magical stone. His mind wondered to what she had told him at the start. Was it true that the stone worked with the ring to form a greater power? She did not know for certain, but she was desperate to find out. Tonight, they would end this. Janji and his tribe would retrieve the treasure from the cave, the mere thought of which made the Chimera shudder. He would not risk his army by sending them into the cave. He would use the fastachees. There was no-way Janji would say no, not if he wanted to save *her*. She was all they needed to ensure he and his tribe would follow orders.

The Chimera stood and walked to the back of his cave. Sat there, looking forlorn, their prisoner looked helpless. They removed her weeks before from the fastachees, ripping her from Janji's grasp. Now she sat here in the same position she had been in since arriving. Her hands were chained together and attached to a longer chain, which was wrapped around her ankles. Both chains were then fixed to a ring bolted to the cave wall. There was no chance of escaping. A bowl of food sat next to her, untouched. Her head was bowed, staring at the cold floor.

'You must eat. We travel tonight and you need your strength. This will all be over soon,' he informed her, but she didn't move, or acknowledge him. He turned and made his way back to the mouth of his cave and stood watching the creatures below.

They had cleared out the other creatures on the island. The fastachee tribe was all that remained. They had been left as the last tribe on the island for a purpose. They were weak, and they would carry out any task asked of them with no remonstrating or questioning.

The Chimera stretched. He could not relax.

They were so close to ending this and he was restless. He paced around, thinking about what the future held. Would his master stay true to her word? Or would she dispose of him? Just as she had culled the others who would not stand by her side, and as she was planning to do with the fastachees once the mission ended? He stayed ferociously loyal to her. Throughout everything, he had remained dedicated to the cause.

After the disastrous attempt at finding the treasure with her team, she almost died, but he saved her, removed her from danger, and protected her. He brought her here, under the cover of darkness, taking the long trek around the back of the island. An island full of dangerous inhabitants. He took the longer route to ensure he got her back without being seen. That was what had saved her. Once back in his cave, he got the help he needed and they nursed her back to full health, ensuring she ate, drank and rested. At night he would hunt for her, so she could build her strength back up, and he did not let her leave the cave until the time was right.

It would have been easy to kill her as soon as he found her, but she was unconscious, lying at the foot of the tree. So where would the fun have been in that? He liked to hunt. Killing something so defenceless was not an option. He liked to see the fear in his victim's eyes before the kill. So, he planned to help her back to full health, and when she was strong enough, she could leave and then the hunt would begin.

However, little did he know that once back to full health, she would be untouchable. She had protection and her guardian would not allow any harm to come to her. The Chimera realised that he should have killed her when he had the chance, after she landed on the island three years ago, but it was too late now.

Chapter 34
Professor Thomas

She sat there, looking out of the window, as the plane continued its journey through the clear blue sky. This was it. They were almost there. After five years of hard work, the end was in sight. They had jumped so many hurdles, gathered and processed so much information and completed endless hours of research. But it had all been worth it. Finally, it was time.

She took the job for one reason. Professor Thomas. His expedition work was amongst the best in the world. He had climbed Mount Everest on more than one occasion, walked to both the North and South Poles, and even sailed non-stop across the Atlantic. Professor Thomas was a remarkable man who was always looking for weird and wonderful challenges to attempt. The more dangerous, the better. His only weakness was being told that something was impossible, or that he couldn't or shouldn't do it. Those were the words that always drove him to succeed on every challenge. So one night, while talking to a colleague over a drink, the subject came up about a long-lost treasure on a remote tropical island. Well, his ears pricked up immediately. According to his friend, Professor Rushforth, there had been many attempts to locate this treasure, but they all ended in disaster. Each expedition ended with the entire team being killed on the island. Numerous expeditions had been undertaken from all around the world, but none had ever returned. Well, except one. The one team that did escape had never been the same again. The only thing they returned with were dreadful memories that led to traumatic flashbacks on a regular basis. The sights they saw on the island had a major impact on them and they never took on another expedition ever again.

Professor Thomas sat there listening intently to his friend as he described the failed attempts in significant detail. As he listened, he started grinning from ear to ear. The seed for his next adventure was being planted.

Professor Thomas started researching the failed attempts the very next day, gaining as much information as possible. There was never any proof of the treasure existing on the island because, as he already knew, none of the expeditions had been successful. The only team that returned had found no evidence of it, but that only made it even more enticing.

The Professor dug up all the information from that returning team. He found a report written by the leader and the daily log kept during the expedition, detailing their findings and encounters. He found their old map, showing the route taken, places of interest, location markings of inhabitants and areas to avoid. There were detailed drawings of creatures, and notes on their behaviour patterns. He read the report from cover to cover, making notes, taking photos and highlighting areas visited in the search for the treasure that proved fruitless. Through his resources, he obtained a fresh copy of a map of the island and, armed with the wealth of information he had uncovered, marked it with past routes planned, colonies of inhabitants, and places where the treasure may be located. As he did so, he continued grinning and getting more and more excited at the thought of his next challenge. Every expedition to the island had left with the same aim, the same mission and the same mindset - to retrieve the treasure at whatever cost. But once they stepped onto the plane and set off, they were never heard from again. Except that one team, whose members were now all dead. It seemed the treasure on Kaninjanga island was cursed.

******

What drove Professor Thomas more than anything was being told that he would not find it. And as for being warned that it would probably lead to his death, well, that just made it even more intriguing, not to mention exciting.

Once he finished the planning phase, he assembled his team. A team of dedicated explorers, all with abilities that would be essential in locating the treasure. Each one of them needed to be fearless, bold, and daring. He informed them of the dangers that lay ahead and that they may never see their families again. He reiterated that this may prove to be their last ever expedition and he could not guarantee their safe return. But it did not phase any of them. They were Professor Thomas's type of people; determined, driven, hungry and brave. They wanted the same thing that he did, to find the treasure. The rewards it offered would be life-changing.

That was why she pushed so hard for the opportunity to join them. Her eagerness to work with his team was clear to see. She was the first woman to take part in an expedition of this magnitude, and the first female explorer to accompany the Professor on one of his challenges. There was no way she was missing this opportunity. She had proven to him what an asset she would be to his team and that she was just as strong and determined as the men. After much deliberating, he agreed and allowed her to join them.

The Professor had a fantastic reputation. He had been on so many dangerous and terrifying missions over the years, but this was different. This was not an expedition for the university, or for some big organisation who had offered to pay him handsomely to locate and retrieve the treasure. No, this was purely for his enjoyment.

She sat back, closed her eyes, and tried to get some rest, before the plane landed and left them to complete their mission on the island of Kaninjanga.

If only she knew what lay ahead.

******

An hour later the seaplane landed on the calm blue waters and glided towards the coastline. Professor Thomas and his team jumped into the water, only a few feet from the shore. They waded towards the golden sands as the seaplane sped through the water and was soon making its way through the clear blue sky once more. They stood there looking around as their leader readied himself to brief them all.

'Okay team. Here we are,' he said, rubbing his hands together.

'Welcome to Kaninjanga,' he was smiling from

ear to ear, eager to get started.

'Now, we all know the history of this island and the failure of the previous expeditions attempted. However, there's one thing they didn't have, that we do,' he observed.

The others stood in silence, unsure what he meant.

'Me,' he said, smiling and throwing his hands out to the side. His team all laughed and nodded in agreement. He reached into the side pocket of his backpack and removed a piece of paper.

'Okay, gather around,' he said as he unfolded it.

'Jan, Sebastian, if you would, please,' he said offering the map to two burly Swedish men. They held the map out so that the Professor could go over their route once again.

'So, we are here,' he informed them as he placed his finger on an area marked on the map with a small red dot.

'Now, after studying the previous attempts, it seems they all favoured this route,' he said.

They watched as the Professor traced his finger from their current position all the way along a thin red line drawn on the map. It led through the mountains, along a path, and into the heart of the island.

'However, we will take a different route. It will take much longer and be far more arduous, however, after doing some research, it seems a far safer route. We'll need to camp overnight, so I've sourced all the equipment we'll need. I like to travel light, but we need to ensure we're prepared for every eventuality. We also have a bit of a climb, so I hope you've all been working on your fitness levels,' he said, looking up at them and grinning.

They all smiled, back.

'So, we will head along the face of the mountains to this point, here,' he dropped his index finger on the other side of the map. A blue dot marked the checkpoint.

'We will then work our way up through here,' he traced his finger along the map. 'Then approach this mountain and enter the cave from this position.' He stopped his finger on a black X, a mile or so inland from the top of the mountain they planned to climb.

'I believe this will be the best entrance point to start the search, as it's the furthest point from where the previous expeditions began. Understood?' he looked up at his team, who were all frowning, but nodding in agreement. Their eyes were fixed on the thick black X that marked the cave entrance.

'X marks the spot,' she said.

'Precisely, Clara,' the Professor said.

'Now, we don't know what lies within the heart of this island, so remain vigilant, watch each other's backs, and be careful. I'll take the lead,

Sebastian, you take the back,' he said, turning to the strapping 6ft 4in Scandinavian man to his left, who was still holding the map. Sebastian nodded in agreement.

'Okay. Grab some water and let's get moving,' he told them. As his team re-hydrated, he folded up the map and placed it back in his rucksack.

'Right, are we all ready? Here we go. Good luck, stay focused, and let's find this treasure,' he then gave them all a reassuring smile and led his team away. They had no idea that they would all soon be dead. All except one.

Chapter 35
The Expedition Begins

Clara found herself in the middle of the group, eyes darting from side-to-side, looking for any predators that may be lurking in the deep overgrown jungle. She always saw herself as brave, fearless, and robust, yet here she was almost panicking as the sounds of the island swept through the trees and echoed around them.

The expedition was now real. The excitement was, for the moment, on hold. She was not thinking about the treasure and what it meant, or about how this could change her life, or the exhilaration she would feel if they retrieved it. There was only one thing on her mind right now and that was surviving.

******

They had been walking for six hours and the light was fast disappearing. Exhaustion was also starting to set in. They came upon a large clearing and Professor Thomas decided this would be their base for the night.

'Right, that's enough ground covered for one day. We shall setup camp for the night, grab something to eat, and head off to get some well-earned rest. Frederick, Liam, would you be so kind as to get a fire up and running?' They knelt down and removed some items from the back of their rucksacks as the professor turned to the remaining members of the team.

'Clara, Sebastian, Jan, could you setup the tents please?'

They all nodded and walked off to do as requested.

Thirty minutes later they were all sat around a roaring fire, cooking their ration packs and telling each other stories, laughing and joking. After a couple of hours, they all headed off to their tents, eager to get some shut-eye before they set off again at dawn.

Clara settled herself down and tried her hardest to get to sleep, but it was proving hard. She continued tossing and turning inside her tent, wrestling with her sleeping bag, as her mind grappled with the task ahead.

Her mind wondered back to the reasons why she wanted to become an explorer. It was because of her mother. Clara would always show an interest in what her mother had been doing at work.

Instead of the normal bedtime stories children would be told, Clara liked her mum to tell her about what she had been doing in the museum that day. As Clara grew she took more and more interest in these subjects and even worked at the museum during work experience. It was all she ever wanted to do. She was seen as a bit of a geek when she was at school. She never really mixed with any of the other children. Except Toby. He was into the same things that Clara was; fossils, artefacts, dinosaurs. They would talk about excavations and things that had been discovered over the years. They grew up a couple of miles away from one another. He was the first boy she ever liked and the only boy she had ever kissed. She never saw herself as pretty, but Toby told her differently. He would run his hand through her long brown hair as he stared into her piercing green eyes and tell her how special she was. They were good together. Two geeks who were going to conquer the world. Everything was going well, until one night. He went out with a couple of friends from college. The three of them got set on whilst leaving a bar because they were different. Toby stepped in to try to appease the situation, which proved a mistake. There was a scuffle and Toby ended up falling and hitting his head on the pavement. He never regained consciousness after that. He was in a comma for months, but he was never going to come out of it. She had lost the love of her life. That was the moment that changed her. She threw herself into her work and this expedition was the perfect opportunity to escape. That was why she pushed so hard for it and that was why she had to come, no matter what.

Prior to leaving Sweden, Professor Thomas had given them all an itinerary of the expedition. She leaned over, reached into her bag, and removed hers. With sleep proving elusive, she opened the itinerary and flicked through to the final few pages. She knew this wasn't the best idea given that she was already anxious, but she wanted to familiarise herself with the most dangerous part of the expedition.

She read the title and her heart skipped a beat.

The Inhabitants of Kaninjanga Island

Fastachee Tribe
- Short wooden figures.
- Friendly.
- Never venture from their own village.
- Located at the back of the Island.
- Threat level - VERY LOW.

Korrigans

- Short dwarf-like creatures.
- Long hair and beards with bells attached.
- Have the ability to transform into shapes.
- Draw enemies in with hypnotic singing.
- Lightning fast.
- Arm-guard spikes used to slay their prey.
- THREAT LEVEL - VERY HIGH.

Cave Monster

- Never seen.
- Heard every night as it comes to feed.
- Immediately find cover when you hear the scream.
- Lives in the cave under the island.
- THREAT LEVEL - VERY HIGH.

Clara shuddered, closed the itinerary, and placed it back inside her rucksack. She lay there thinking about what may lie in wait for them tomorrow. After a further twenty minutes of tossing and turning, exhaustion finally got the better of her and she drifted off.

As she eased into a deep sleep, the beady eyes that had been watching for the past hour, retreated into the jungle and were gone once more.

******

The following day, they got up early, ate breakfast and packed their rucksacks, ready for a full day of walking and climbing. Clara's feet were still aching from the previous day and she had the first signs of blisters. She forgot to tape them up as the Professor had informed them. *'Don't forget to protect your feet with Zinc Oxide tape, unless you want some very nasty blisters. You have been warned!'*. Clara didn't make a fuss or say anything as he would be most annoyed. He was a stickler for ensuring his instructions were followed. Clara taped her feet as best she could and gingerly put her boots on.

Once they were all ready, they set off. Little did they know today would be their last day trekking together.

******

After three hours of walking, fighting through wasteland, going up and down the perilous terrain of the cliff face, the Professor stopped, as did his team. He reached into his rucksack, removed the map, and gathered his bearings.

'Here we are. That's the easy bit out of the way,' he pointed up the mountainside. It looked very treacherous and not at all safe to Clara.

'This is where we climb. It will take a fair while and use a lot of energy, so shout if you need to stop. You know me, I'll keep climbing until we get to the top if you don't stop me,' he said as he smiled at them. The man was a nutter, but they knew he was true to his word. He nodded and began climbing.

******

Three-and-a-half hours later they reached the top of the climb, thankfully without incident, and decided to take a break for food and water. Standing ominously in front of them was the dense jungle. They found an area of rocks in amongst the long grass and set themselves down. Clara used the opportunity to remove her boots and check on her feet. They were in a much better state than she thought they would be after the climb. She applied cream and was putting her socks back on when the Professor noticed a beautiful fountain to their left, on the other side of the long grass. He did not say a word. He stood, picked up his rucksack and started heading towards it, as did the rest of the team. Clara shouted for them to wait for her, but they kept walking. It was as if they were either ignoring her or did not hear. She finished putting her socks and boots on and was kneeling down to tie her laces when she heard the faintest singing coming from the fountain. She looked up just as her team reached it. Colourful water was shooting from the top and beautiful fish were jumping out of the water before landing with a splash. It was the most amazing display she had ever seen. She caught herself smiling at it and could not tie her laces quick enough to run across and take a closer look. As her team approached, it happened. The fountain vanished and was replaced by several short dwarf-like creatures, with long wavy hair and beards which had small golden bells attached to the ends. Arm-guards covered both forearms, with four spikes sitting proudly on the top of each one. Two fangs jutted out from their bottom gums and ended just below the enormous fat nose that occupied most of their grumpy-looking faces. They were devoid of any footwear and each of them wore a red and green tartan skirt which stopped above their knobbly knees. They were the Korrigans; fairy-like creatures that possess an evil spirit and can change shape, sing beautifully to lure victims, and move at lightning speeds.

As quick as a flash the Korrigan tribe drew their arms back, attacked and killed her entire team, the bells on their long beards jingling with each ferocious strike. Professor Thomas and the others did not stand a chance. Clara put her hands over her mouth to stifle her screams as she backed away, keeping low and using the long grass as camouflage.

As she slowly retreated, a Korrigan raised his head and began sniffing the air. He had picked up her scent. He glanced over and caught sight of the top of her head poking out of the long grass. She turned to run as he started growling, his long beard now covered in fresh blood. She was 20-feet from the mountain's edge and the grass was proving hard to run through. Her eyes were wide and her lungs felt like they were about to burst. She could hear the Korrigan fast approaching through the grass. He was quick. She reached the edge and suddenly felt his hand around her forearm. Instinctively, she turned and lashed out, her fist connecting with his nose. She felt it explode under the force of the impact and as she toppled over the edge, her last image was his gnarled expression and blood-soaked face - partly from his nose, but mainly from whichever member of her team he had been devouring before he spotted her.

As she disappeared from view, the Korrigan wiped the blood from his face with the back of his arm, turned around and headed back to finish his meal.

Present day...

Chapter 36
Mr Robertson

'Will someone please explain what no earth is going on?' A very confused Mr Robertson asked.

They were now inside the hut. Austin and Billy sat on the cushions, as their teacher paced around. Mr Robertson's eyes darted from one to the other, as the holographic face hung above them.

'It's a long story, sir,' said Billy.

'Well, I don't think we have anything better to do, do you ?' said their teacher.

Billy sighed and told the entire tale. The others sat in silence. Terry smiled throughout and looked proud as punch at some of the things he had done. Mr Robertson did not make a sound or ask questions. He sat down and listened, just as a teacher would sit and listen to a student reading aloud to the class.

When Billy had finished, Mr Robertson just sat there, looking shocked and confused. Once he processed the wealth of information he had been given, he let out a long sigh and put his head in his hands. The children glanced at each other, unsure how this was going to go. Their teacher then raised his head, puffed out his cheeks, stood and started walking around the hut again, looking at the floor as if deep in thought.

After a few moments of silence, Sue spoke.

'Sir, are you okay?'

Mr Robertson carried on walking around, ignoring her question. Then he stopped, and looked at them for a few seconds before replying.

'Well, this is nothing like a normal school trip, I'll give you that much,' he said as he shook his head from side-to-side.

'So what happened to you, sir? How come you didn't get off the ship with the rest of the children and Miss Thompson?' asked Austin.

'Simple, I got knocked out. I was helping everyone out from under the netting, and the next thing I remember was waking up at the bottom of a ladder. I must have tripped, hit my head and passed out as I toppled down. When I woke up, I wondered what happened and where I was. After sorting myself out I climbed back up the ladder and came face-to-face with a deserted ship. There was nobody around, so I made my way up another ladder which lead me out onto the quarterdeck. As I stood there, I was even more confused. The scene that greeted me looked nothing like Portsmouth dockyard, although it smelt far better,' he joked, before continuing. 'When I looked over the side of the ship, I couldn't believe what I saw. The ship wasn't on the water, but suspended above it. I heard whirring and fizzing sounds behind me, so I spun around, but there was nothing there. I started searching for a way of getting down to dry land, and then I heard another noise behind me. Suddenly something landed on my shoulders and I was lifted high into the air. It was as if someone had grabbed me and pulled me off the deck of the ship.'

Terry started giggling, as did the holographic face.

'Did you leave it on the ship?' The face giggled as he looked at Terry, who nodded to confirm he had.

'Terry, you is a cheeky little bugger-lugs,' the face said with a giggle.

'I know, what am I like, my ansum? I forgot all about it, left it on the ship I did. Tis funny though.'

'It certainly is, my cocker,' the face replied.

The others watched as the two Cornishmen sat there giggling.

'Anyway,' Mr Robertson interrupted, bringing the attention back to his story. 'As I was saying, it took me around the ship and then flew me out to sea. God I went so high, I wondered where I was going. I tried to glance over my shoulder but all I could see was the brightest light, pulling me one way and then the other. After I had gone around the ship, twice - and screamed, a lot - I got dropped on a path. I turned around and saw a ray of light head back onto the ship and disappear. The path lead into wasteland and I didn't know what was on the other side, but it was the only route. So I took a few moments to compose myself and headed along the path. As I left the wasteland, those guys apprehended me,' he said as he pointed towards the hut doorway. 'And they brought me here.'

Mr Robertson looked around the hut, but it had once again fallen silent. Nobody was sure what to say. Then, to everyone's surprise, the holographic face broke the silence.

'Well, that was some bleedin' story, my cocker. Now tis my turn. I 'spose I should tell you all 'bout this 'ere island and the secret that it 'olds?'

Everyone nodded in agreement.

'Janji,' he called to the leader, 'stick kettle on willie. Goin' need some of that there magic drink o' yours,' he announced. They all frowned as they looked up at the face.

'I didn't think he understood English?' asked Sue.

The face chuckled.

''E can't my cocker, but when I speak to you it gets translated to a language 'e will understand, so 'e can follow everyfin that is goin' on. It still sounds English to you, though. Clever, eh?' The face smiled but did not wait for an answer.

As Janji walked over to the stove, the holographic face told the tale of the island and what lay hidden inside the deep dark cave.

******

This was it, the day she never thought she would see. After all these years. From that first meeting with the Professor, this was the aim. Clara was walking around her den, packing everything she needed and discarding anything she didn't. She had been on the island for three years now. There had been many battles, many failed attempts at locating it, and many missed opportunities, but none of that mattered now. It had been eight years since she first met the brilliant Professor Thomas and he told her all about the treasure. Clara could not leave empty-handed. This was the reason they came to the island. She owed it to him, to his memory, and to those members of her team viciously slain in front of her by the Korrigan tribe. They had paid for what they done to her team. She made sure of that. They were the first tribe to die.

Over the years she had erased the inhabitants of the island one by one. There were so many colonies, so many creatures, and so many living things that she had eradicated. She was never a vicious or vengeful person, but that changed after the attack. Seeing her team torn apart and eaten unlocked something inside of her. When she recovered, she swore vengeance. At first it was only against the Korrigans, but once she wiped them out, she came up with a plan to work her way through every species on the island. She gave them a choice, to either stand with her and find the treasure, or go on their way. They did not have to join her cause. It was their choice. She led away those that said they were with her, and those that declined to join the cause were free to leave. But within 24 hours of turning their backs on her, they were dead. As they made their way back to the safety of their colony, they were followed and killed when they were least expecting it.

She recruited as many inhabitants of the island as she could. They were all needed if what the Professor told her was true. If it existed. The cave that reached deep underground was, according to legend, home to the most vicious monster alive. It had never been seen, but it was heard. Every night, a thunderous roar echoed from the cave, causing every other living thing on the island to run for cover. No creature that ever faced the monster lived to tell the tale of what lived inside the cave. She stood there, thinking of what she had been through, the sacrifices she had made, the battles she had fought and the patience she had shown. But the time to attack and take what was hers from the monster in the cave was here. Ever since that first meeting with the Chimera that saved her life, this was all she wanted, all she needed, and nothing would stop her.

Chapter 37
Clara

Clara spent a long time recovering after the attack. In fact, she was lucky to survive at all. After she escaped the clutches of the Korrigan, she fell down the mountainside and almost died. If it wasn't for her backpack, she would have. She had probably broken the Korrigan's nose. After turning and lashing out, her fist had connected with it and she felt the nose explode on impact. Then she was hurtling towards the ground at breakneck speed, heading to meet her death. She kept tumbling down and seconds later was thrown clear as the sloping mountainside ended in a sheer drop to the ground eighty feet below. She was launched into the air and hit a group of trees sixty feet above the ground, winding herself as she bounced from branch to branch. She was in total free fall and took more hits to the ribs, and a few to the head, on her way down as there was no way of controlling or stopping the descent.

The ground was now fast approaching. Just as it looked like this was the end, Clara's backpack caught on a thick branch, suspending her 15-feet from the ground. Dazed and confused, she hung there, struggling to breathe after the impact of the fall. Her head was throbbing and her sight was blurry. Moments later, the branch she was hanging on gave way and she landed awkwardly on a rock and heard a crack as her ankle buckled under the weight of the fall. Clara screamed in pain and met total darkness as she blacked out.

The next thing she remembered was waking up in a cave with no idea what had happened. She tried to move, but it felt like someone had thrust a red-hot poker into her ankle. Her ribs hurt like mad too, which made breathing difficult. She lifted her top up to check. There was a large slice along her belly and she knew she had broken some ribs. It felt the same as a netball injury she had suffered two years previously. She lay down and took small breaths, once again wincing at the sharp pain in her chest as her lungs filled with oxygen, causing her broken ribs to move.

Clara lay there on a bed of leaves and looked around the cave. There was a small fire crackling away in the corner. The orange and blue flames danced away and gave a false warmth, but ultimate eerie feeling to the cave. She could see the entrance 20-feet from her and once again she attempted to move, but the pain in her ankle and chest let her know that she was not going anywhere, anytime soon. She lay back down and tried her hardest to remember what had happened. Where were the rest of them? And then it all started coming back to her. They were dead. They had killed her entire team. She remembered rolling down the mountainside and being flung into the air before... *what was that?*

The sound of movement outside interrupted her thoughts. She held her breath as best she could. Loud footsteps were approaching the mouth of the cave, causing the ground to vibrate. Her heart rate increased at the sight of a shadow covering the entrance. Seconds later, a shape she recognised appeared above the shadow - the head of a snake.

The sound of the fire crackling away in the corner was soon joined by another noise, as the shadow entered the cave and the snake began to hiss.

******

Clara gasped, ignoring the pain screaming through her body as she stared into the eyes of the Chimera. The long serpent tail continued to hiss at her as it swayed from side-to-side.

Clara lay there, unable to move because of the pain, and also the fear of not knowing what the beast was going to do to her. This was it, this was the end, and there was nothing she could do. The lion head edged closer and the serpent lowered to within inches of her face.

Just as she thought it was about to attack and kill her, she heard a shuffling noise coming from behind the beast, followed by the sound of a voice.

'Are you goin' get out of the way, you hairy freak?' said whoever was behind the creature. There was the sound of a slap as whoever or whatever was trying to get through, smacked the beast's bum.

'Move, you big lump!' The Chimera growled as it moved to the side. A tiny green hand slipped between the beast and the wall, followed by the top of a bald head. The long pointy end of a spear emerged, and before long, a small creature slipped through and fell onto the floor, right in front of her. He stood up and thrust his spear at the beast. The snake lowered and hissed at him, but the small creature did not care, he batted it away with the spear.

'Thanks for being so helpful, and moving,' he said, before brushing himself down. She had seen nothing like it before. He was emerald green, from head to toe, with long pointy ears that had one big, hoop earring hanging from each lobe. Piercing green eyes and a mouth full of razor-sharp teeth, give him an evil look. He wore a necklace that looked like it was comprised of small animal's teeth, and on his upper body, running along his chest, were three black straps. Another collection of animal teeth were inserted into the straps. Around the top of his arms he had three gold rings, so tightly fitted it looked like they were part of his body. He was wearing brown shorts that looked like they were made of tree bark, and around his lower legs there were more black straps from his kneecaps to his ankles.

The creature looked up and saw her staring at the tooth collection on his chest. He huffed and pointed to them. Her gaze switched to his eyes.

'Took these from my victims. Nice little souvenir,' he said, looking proud of his accomplishments, as he gave her a toothy-grin.

'I got loads more, but can't wear all of them as I would look stupid.' He exclaimed.

Clara moved slightly and flinched as her hand reached for her injured ribs. The creature pointed at her chest with his spear.

'Best get that sorted out now you is awake,' he said, then turned and walked over to the small fire in the corner. Clara turned her attention back to the beast who had not moved his eyes from her. The snake continued to sway and hiss. It was as if it was waiting for its moment to attack.

The small green creature was making some noise over in the corner. He started whistling as he busied himself with whatever it was he was doing. He picked up a bowl, dropped a few leaves into it and started grinding them up. Grunting noises were escaping him as he worked away. Steam then started to rise above his head. He picked up a steel pan that was hanging over the fire and poured some liquid into the bowl. It made a hissing sound as it covered the crushed leaves. There was another bowl on the floor next to him. He picked it up and sprinkled what looked like powder into the first bowl. There was a *bang* and then coloured steam rose towards the roof of the cave. He blew it away and placed the bowl on a tray next to him. Next he reached out and grabbed a handful of fresh leaves that were lying beside the fire and placed them on the tray next to the bowl. The creature walked over and placed the tray next to her, while the three-headed-beast relaxed and lay down. It looked like a strange, oversized dog, lying beside an open fire in its front room. The snake lowered its head and curled itself around the beast. The hissing had stopped for now.

'So what are you?' She asked.

'Me? Why, can't you tell?' The creature asked as he knelt down next to her.

'I'm a doctor,' he said as he chuckled.

She watched him as he picked up a wooden stick, gave the mixture a stir, and tapped it on the bowl before placing it back on the tray. He placed both hands around the bottom of the bowl and passed it to her. She stared into his eyes. He was even uglier up close. Some teeth around his chest had dried blood on them and he was also missing three of his own. More than likely lost in battle.

'Drink up,' he said, moving his eyes towards the bowl and back to Clara.

She stared at him, frowning.

'Tis ok, nothing to worry about. If we wanted to hurt you, we've already had our chance. Don't you think?' He asked. She stared at him for a second longer and then glanced down into the bowl. What she saw made her wonder what was in there. A bright red liquid sat in the bowl. The steam rising from it seemed to be dancing as it swirled around. She frowned and looked back towards the creature, who was now smiling and nodding at the bowl expectantly.

'Will make you feel better, trust me,' he said, gently placing his hand under the bowl and guiding it towards her mouth. She had nothing to lose. This funny little creature was right, if he wanted her dead, she would be.

She edged the bowl towards her lips and took a sip. She almost spat it out straight away, not because of the taste, but out of surprise. The liquid inside the bowl was ice cold. Her throat almost froze as it made its way down towards her stomach. She could feel it start to pulse as it entered her bloodstream and then the strangest thing happened. As the liquid worked its way through her body, it started warming up and began moving in different directions. She could feel it separate and start to travel through her veins. Some shot past her stomach and seconds later, entered the top of her injured leg, while the second pool of liquid headed over to the injured side of her chest. She lay there, still unable to move, and looked up at the little creature, wondering what was going on. He smiled at her.

'Warmed up has it?' he asked and smiled. 'Wait for this bit.'

As she lay there, the two pools of warm liquid continued to flow towards their destinations, getting warmer and warmer. The one in her leg had travelled underneath her kneecap and made its way down her calf muscle on the way to her broken ankle. The other was now flowing around her badly injured ribs. She lifted her top to expose her broken, disfigured bones. As she did, she gasped and looked up at the funny little green figure, with her mouth agape. He smiled back at her.

'Cool innit?' he said.

Her ribs now had a bright orange colour circling around them, her skin had become transparent and she could see the ribs as they knitted back together. She lowered her top, but she could still feel the warm liquid flowing around the injury.

Her ankle became warm too as the liquid worked its magic. She didn't bend down to see what was happening. It would still be painful, and she already knew what was happening underneath her thick sock. The creature was rubbing his hands together and grinning from ear to ear. Maybe he was a doctor, she thought to herself.

As the liquid continued to swirl around her injuries, the temperature of it increased further. And then, for the first time since the attack, Clara smiled.

******

Within minutes of the liquid reaching Clara's injuries, the pain had subsided. She could breathe a little easier, although she still did not want to move too much. The little creature was keeping himself busy, ripping leaves apart and inspecting them. He discarded some, and placed them to one side, while the rest were all placed on the tray. Once he had sorted through the leaves, he picked up the discarded ones and threw them towards the beast who devoured them, giving Clara a glimpse of its ferocious blood-stained teeth. The goblin-like-figure picked up the good leaves, walked back to the fire and dropped them into the steel pan. When he removed them, they were soaking wet, but once again, something strange happened. He walked back over to Clara and shook the excess water off. As he knelt down beside her, she noticed the leaves had already dried. Who was this creature? Was he a witch doctor? Why was he trying to fix her while the beast looked like she was going to be his next meal? After he had separated the leaves into two piles, he turned his attention back to her.

'Okay, I need to dress those injuries now. The medicine will help, but it won't fix them completely. Ribs first,' he said, nodding at her chest as he knelt down beside her.

'Do you have to tie them in place?' She asked, looking concerned. 'I don't think I can move.'

He smiled at her.

'You'll see, pull it up,' he nodded again.

She pulled her top up to expose her injuries. The skin was no longer transparent, it was back to its normal pinkish colour. She noticed that the deep cut on her stomach was already healing. He picked up a handful of leaves and covered her ribs, causing Clara to wince as they came into contact with her skin. Once he had arranged them as he wanted, he applied gentle pressure to the leaves, Clara had to bite her lip. She knew he was trying to help, but her body was screaming with pain.

'I know it's uncomfortable, but we're almost done, just gotta do this bit,' he reassured her.

He removed his hands and left the leaves lying loose.

'Now, watch,' he said, not even looking at her.

She frowned as he extended his index finger and placed it on the edge of the leaves. He traced it along the outside of the leaves, and as he did, a gold line appeared, as if he was drawing it on. The gold line followed the finger all the way around the leaves until he completed the circle. As he lifted his finger, the outline started to glow and pulse a bright gold colour. Within seconds, the leaves shrank and clung to her skin. They became tighter around the injury. Before long it was as if she had a tight casing around her ribcage. Once they had finished shrinking, the gold line faded and disappeared. She reached a hand down to touch the leaves and they were rock solid. She could not have removed them even if she wanted to. While she was inspecting the dressing on her injury, the little creature picked up the second batch of leaves. Clara pulled her top back down, to cover them, and continued to watch. She knew what he wanted without him having to say a word. She bent down to lift her trouser leg up, but he scolded her and slapped her hand.

'No you don't. I'll do that. I 'as just dressed those ribs, and I can do this on my own.'

He placed a hand two inches above her ankle and without even touching her leg it rose into the air. He moved his hand from her ankle towards her knee and her trouser leg instantly rose up. Clara watched in amazement as the laces of her boot undid themselves and it eased itself off, followed by her sock, exposing her broken and disfigured ankle. The pain was excruciating, and it made her cry out, but she knew it needed to be done. The creature grabbed the second pile of leaves and wrapped them around her ankle, as it remained suspended in the air. He traced around the leaves again and then turned to Clara.

'This one is gonna hurt a lil bit, but it needs doing,' she nodded at him to confirm she understood. Once again, as the gold outline around the leaves faded, they wrapped themselves around her ankle, encasing it. The leaves started tightening and the air filled with a cracking and popping sound as they pulled and adjusted her ankle to re-align it. Clara screamed out as the pain in her ankle exploded. As soon as the scream left her mouth, the snake reared its ugly head and hissed, but the creature picked up its spear and batted it away again. Once the pain had eased, her ankle lowered to the floor and moments later felt better. The loose leaves had now tightly wrapped themselves around it, giving it the support it needed to mend.

'Now, this is gonna take a while to fix. These will help,' he said, pointing at the leaves. 'But you still gotta take it easy, your ankle was in a hell-of-a-mess and is gonna take time. Now, try to get some rest, old Sinka here will keep an eye out tonight, so no need to worry. He brought you here, so he has no intention of hurting you, okay?' He nodded at her, stood, picked the tray up and returned it to the fire. Then he picked his spear up, walked over to the beast, patted the lion's head and left.

Clara lay down as everything became hazy. Before long, she drifted off to sleep, leaving the leaves and the liquid to repair her bruised and battered body.

Sinka lay there, watching their visitor. He knew why she was here. She was just like the others. However, before long he would discover that she was nothing like the others, far from it in fact.

As she drifted off to sleep, he closed his eyes and relaxed in front of the warmth of the glowing, crackling-fire.

Chapter 38
Clara Recovers

The following morning, Clara awoke feeling disorientated. Where was she? How did she get here? Where were her team? As she tried to sit up, a sharp pain in her chest jolted her memory. She lifted her top up to inspect the dressing on her wound. It was no longer rock hard, but had softened overnight. After pulling her top down, she looked up and noticed there was no one else in the cave. Sinka was not lying by the open doorway guarding her, and the green creature was not there either.

She lay back down and closed her eyes again. As she was drifting back off to sleep a screeching noise and what sounded like the flapping of wings startled her. She opened her eyes and sat bolt upright, but her ribs quickly let her know they were not fixed yet and she let out a scream. Outside, the shadow from the day before was back. Sinka had returned. He entered with a small animal clenched in his mouth. Clara couldn't make it out at first, but as he got closer, she saw what it was. He dropped it in front of her and spoke for the first time.

'Eat,' he said.

Clara looked shocked, both at what had been dropped on the floor and also the fact that he could talk. She frowned at him but didn't move. He bowed his head and pushed the thing at his feet towards her.

'Eat,' he demanded.

Clara looked down at the animal flapping around at her feet. It was slightly bigger than a chicken and had small wings, one of which looked injured as it was not moving. It lay still on the ground as the good wing continued frantically flapping around. The animal began squawking as it looked around the cave. No wonder it was frightened after being stuck in Sinka's mouth.

Sinka looked at her again.

'I told you to eat.' Clara looked into the dark black eyes of her supposed breakfast. It looked so defenceless. She glared up at Sinka.

'No.' She replied angrily. The serpent flew around and stopped inches from her face, but Clara didn't even flinch.

At that moment, the green creature bimbled into the cave.

'How is my patient doing today?' He asked,

smiling. His eyes wandered towards the animal withering around and laughed as Clara picked it up and sat it on her lap.

'What the blinking heck is that thing?' He asked.

'Breakfast, apparently,' Clara said, a sharp tone attached to the statement.

Sinka growled at her as the snake continued to hiss.

'I'll tell you what Sinka, if that blinking thing keeps swaying around hissing, I'm gonna cut it off,' he said smacking the snake's head with his spear.

'Now get some proper food, coconuts, plants, nuts, there's plenty out there. Not this stupid thing,' he said as he pointed at the animal. Clara smiled at the sight of Sinka exiting the cave with his snake tail tucked between his legs.

'Now, let's have a look at those injuries,' he said, kneeling down beside her.

Clara lay down and placed the animal on her uninjured side. It snuggled in and stopped flapping around as it felt the warmness of Clara's body. As the creature inspected her wounds, she looked at the broken wing. It needed attention.

'Where did he find this?' She asked, stroking the wing.

'Probably found it lying out in the jungle. Told him you won't eat that stuff, but he's too stupid to understand,' he explained as he gently removed the dressing.

Clara lay there comforting the animal as the creature prepared more leaves and a drink for her. He passed her the bowl and this time she did not hesitate. She drunk it in one gulp. It was still ice cold and caused her to gasp, but not as much as it did the previous day. The liquid warmed and travelled through her body as the creature dressed her wounds, once again discarding the unwanted leaves. Her ankle did not crack this time; yesterday's treatment had rectified the break and it was now on the mend. Once he had finished, Clara placed the animal down and it munched on the discarded leaves as she spoke to her doctor.

'Why are you looking after me?' Clara asked in her softest voice.

'Because that's what I do,' he said without looking at her. 'I 'elp people. Tis my job,' he smiled as he caught her gaze.

'Thank you, you're very kind. I keep thinking Sinka will kill me.'

The creature looked at her, shocked.

'What, that hairy lump? He couldn't hurt anyone. Scared of his own shadow, that one. He won't hurt you. He's the reason you're still alive.'

'What, how?' She asked, surprised.

'He found you lying at the bottom of that tree

and brought you back here. You is lucky he found you when he did. Another couple of hours and you would have made a delightful meal for someone. He took the long route back to ensure you didn't get discovered.'

'Really?' The disbelief was clear in her tone.

'Yes. So you've got nothing to worry about with that one,' the creature gave her a toothy-grin, picked up the tray and went to leave, until Clara stopped him.

'Wait,' she said.

He turned around, frowning at her.

'What's your name?' she asked. 'If you are looking after me, I would like to know your name.'

He smiled at her.

'Jeremy. My name is Jeremy.'

Clara looked shocked and almost started laughing.

'Jeremy?' she said, frowning.

'Don't ask. Tis a long story,' he laughed and made to walk away, until she stopped him again.

'Can you fix this?' She said, picking the animal up again and holding the broken wing out.

'Why you wanna do that? His family will be dead and left him on his own,' Jeremy explained.

'I don't care. You saved me and I'm on my own.'

Jeremy stared at her but seemed reluctant to help.

'He can keep me company while I recover.

Please Jeremy, help him,' she begged.

He sighed and rubbed his forehead. Then he walked back over to get more leaves and medicine and did as requested. Once he had finished dressing the wing he headed towards the exit.

'Thank you, Jeremy,' Clara said.

Before walking outside, he looked over his shoulder. Clara was lying down, with the baby dragon asleep in her arms.

Chapter 39
Denzel

Janji finished making the drinks as everyone else sat in silence waiting for him.

'Hope you is all ready for a bit of a story?' Asked the face.

Billy looked up at him.

'So, what do we call you?' He asked.

The face thought for a moment and smiled before answering.

'I don't 'ave a name, I'm just, The face. I only come 'ere when I is demanded, see, so I ain't got one,' he informed them.

'Well, we is goin' 'ave to sort that out my ansum,' said Terry.

'Can't'ave you walking 'round calling yourself 'The face', sounds stupid.'

'Hmmm, let me fink. I know, wiv' that accent, there is only one name you can 'ave,' Terry added.

They all looked at him as he started chuckling to himself.

'Denzel. You shall henceforth be known as Denzel. A good old Cornish name,' Terry said as he smiled.

'What are you going on about?' Asked Billy.

'You could have picked any name and you go for Denzel?' said Austin

'And what is wrong wiv' that? Tis an ansum name,' said Terry.

'Denzel. Denzel,' said the face.

They all turned to look at him, he was nodding up and down as he smiled.

'I like it, Terry. Sounds proper important, that does. Cheers my cocker.' Terry smugly smiled at Billy and the others.

'No problem my ansum, umm, I mean, Denzel,' said Terry and once again, they both started chuckling. The group looked at them both and shook their heads.

'Are we going to be in trouble when we get home, sir?' Asked an anxious-looking Sue. Mr Robertson sighed and looked at her.

'And what do I tell everyone? You'll never guess what, during our visit onboard HMS Victory some children and a Cornish goblin stole the ship,' he replied sarcastically.

Terry frowned and raised his hand, but Austin nudged him and shook his head. The mischievous Knocker pulled his hand back down and started picking his nose instead, as Mr Robertson continued.

'We all went on a little adventure and ended up on some tropical island. I was flown out to sea under the guidance of a magical ray of light. The light then dropped me on dry land, and I walked through an overgrown wasteland, where a tribe of wooden people with no eyes took me prisoner. Once in their village I met a large holographic face who spoke with a Cornish accent, and was called Denzel, apparently,' Mr Robertson said as he flashed a look at Terry.

Everyone remained silent until Terry spoke.

'You sound like a bit of a nutter my ansum. They is goin' lock you up if you say that,' he said before smiling up at Denzel. They both started chuckling yet again.

Janji walked over with the tray of drinks, interrupting the conversation, and placed it on the tree-stump-table. Mr Robertson reached out to pick up his cup.

'What on earth is this?' he asked as he looked inside at the liquid.

'What d'you mean, what's this? Tis ansum my lover,' said Denzel.

'Have you guys tried it?' Mr Robertson asked the children.

'No, none of us have,' said Sue. They all took their cups and looked at them dubiously.

'Well, this has been a strange day, so let's see

what this does shall we,' said Mr Robertson. 'Any volunteers to go first?'

The children all sat in silence. None of them were eager to be the guinea pig.

'Oh, gizzit 'ere,' said Terry, holding out his hand.

'Really?' Asked Billy.

'Well, you gaet sissies ain't gonna do it, are you?'

Mr Robertson passed him the cup. Terry paused, took a deep breath and drank the liquid in the cup.

Nothing happened.

'Well?' Asked Sue. 'Do you feel anything?'

'Nope. Nothing. It don't taste nice, thou—'

'Look!' Shouted Billy.

Blue smoke suddenly rose from under Terry's bandana. Seconds later, gold smoke flowed out from his ears, green smoke poured out of his nostrils, and as brown smoke appeared from the back of his trousers. Terry giggled.

'You don't wanna know where that smoke has come from, but let's just say it tickled,' he said.

They all sat there, watching as more and more colours poured out from different areas of the Knocker; his feet, his sack, his fingers, and even his eyeballs.

Once the smoke stopped emptying from him, the colours all sat in the air above his head and started mixing. As they all watched the colours merge, an image appeared above them. It was blurry at first, but then it became clear. In the middle of the picture were three Knockers. Billy and Austin recognised them straightaway from their day in the woods. It was Terry's family, standing in front of an enormous house, but this was no ordinary house. It was in the shape of a Cornish pasty, golden brown with steam rising from the top of it. It looked delicious. Terry was behind his family, next to the house, munching away on the side of it, sinking his teeth into the wall and taking bite after bite. However, within seconds of biting into the house, it would grow back. This was not the only weird thing in the picture. Terry's garden fence and his path were made of strips of steak. Hot, cooked potatoes and onions were also growing in his garden. Terry had his own everlasting Cornish pasty.

Terry looked like he was in a trance; saliva was running down his chin and dripping onto the floor.

Seconds later, the image vanished and their furry friend started wiping his mouth.

'What was that all about?' Asked Austin.

'Dream juice,' said Denzel.

'What?' Asked Billy.

'Dream juice. When you drink it, it shows one of your most desired fantasies. Tis quite something, wouldn't believe some o' the things we 'ave seen over the years,' said Denzel.

'Really?' Asked a very dubious looking Austin.

'Try it if you don't believe me,' Denzel challenged

him.

Austin stared at him before replying.

'Okay,' he said leaning forwards.

Before anyone could protest, he picked his cup up and drank the entire contents. Seconds later, the smoke started emanating from everywhere and then an image appeared above his head. Billy recognised it immediately. It was his bedroom. He and Austin were sat with their eyes wide and PlayStation controllers in their hands. Seconds later, Austin was jumping around, while Billy sat on his bed with his head in his hands as his best friend ridiculed him. They were playing FIFA and the scoreboard said it all: Manchester United 5, Liverpool 0. He had not only beaten Billy at FIFA, but he had thrashed him. Moments later, the image disappeared.

'Keep dreaming, mate,' Billy said as he smiled at Austin.

'One day, buddy. Your turn,' Austin said, passing Billy a cup.

'No, I'm okay. Thanks mate. I'm not thirsty,' Billy said, as he pushed the cup away.

'Oh, this ain't about being thirsty. Let's see what your deepest fantasy is,' Austin said, laughing as he teased Billy.

He offered the cup back to him. Billy sighed, closed his eyes and drank the juice. He sat there with his eyes closed as the smoke made another appearance. When he opened them, there in the air in front of him, was the image of a man and a woman, walking down the street, hand-in-hand. In front of them were two young children, one boy and one girl, twins, about five years old. Both were smiling and riding scooters. The adults looked familiar, but a lot older. There was no mistaking them. It was Billy and Sue, blissfully happy as they watched their cute little children zooming up and down the path in front of them. The image disappeared and Billy felt himself blush as he bowed his head and stared at the floor in embarrassment. Then something touch his hand, which made him look up. It was Sue and she was smiling.

Mr Robertson and Sue refused to drink their juice. There were more pressing matters that needed addressing, rather than seeing everyone's thoughts laid bare for all to see, according to Mr Robertson.

Terry looked at him and frowned. Mr Robertson quickly diverted the attention away from the drinks.

'So, Denzel ,what's the story of this island?' He asked.

'Ah yes. I suppose I better tell you why this place is so dangerous,' said Denzel. 'Okay, sit back, relax, and get ready to learn about the cursed treasure that lies hidden on Kaninjanga island.'

Chapter 40
The Cursed Treasure

'It all started over 300 years ago when a group of pirates set out on a lengthy journey in search of a lost treasure. Now, the treasure they sought was not located here, but on an island nearby, Barikaga. It ended up here after a fierce storm resulted in the pirates being shipwrecked some 500 miles to the west of Kaninjanga. They were on their way home when their ship was destroyed and the treasure washed up here, where it 'as remained ever since. Some say the weather that caused the shipwreck was a brief storm. Whilst others believe it was conjured up by the evil spirits of Barikaga to stop the pirates escaping with the loot.' Denzel looked around the room. They were all transfixed, so he continued.

'The pirates journey had taken them two years to complete, ending with them arriving on the island of Barikaga, over 1,000 miles to the west of Kaninjanga. The skies were clear and the seas calm as they made their approach to the island. Upon arrival, they unloaded their large, empty chests and prepared for the two-day trek to where their captain believed the treasure lay. After trekking for almost three days, they found it and wasted no time in filling their chests to the brim. However, one item should not have been taken from the island - a ring. It was the big prize - *The Holy Grail, the Jewel in the crown.* Unfortunately, it should never have left Barikaga. It is said that the ring was placed there many years before by the tribe who used to inhabit the island. It was a gift from the Tribal Chief of Barikaga as a memorial to his late wife. The ring signified his undying love for her and was to remain on the island to signify their lives together. A powerful spell was cast so that any person or creature who removed the ring would have hell unleashed on them. The ring was inserted into the face of a sacred rock, and it was to never be disturbed. The rock even displayed a warning underneath it: *quod sacris circulum autem Barikaga, quod decorum sun vigilabo.'* Denzel said, in a dramatic, soft tone, to add mystery to the phrase. Denzel paused and looked around, awaiting the question that would inevitably follow, but no question came. Instead, Sue gave the answer.

'The Sacred ring of Barikaga, The gods are watching,' Sue translated. Everyone turned to look at her, stunned.

'What? So I used to be a geek and studied Latin when I was in South Africa, that okay with you lot?' She said, frowning.

'No you didn't,' replied Austin.

'Um, excuse me? Sue said, turning her frown on him.

'I don't believe you,' he said, trying not to smile as he wound her up.

'Oh, I'm sorry, pulled that off the top of my head, did I?' She said, getting even more irate.

'No, I meant you said you used to be a geek. You still are one, you mean,' he said.

'Idiot.'

'Finished 'ave you?' Asked an impatient Denzel.

'Please, carry on,' said an excited Mr Robertson. He was loving the tale more than anyone. Denzel nodded and continued.

'The captain did not take heed of the warning, and despite the protestations of his crew, he prised the ring out of the rock and ordered them to load it.

Once they arrived back at the ship the crew stored the treasure in the hold, and prepared to set sail. As they reached open waters, the celebrations started. After years of sailing, they had located the treasure, so the captain thought it only fair to reward his loyal and dedicated crew with a sailor's favourite tipple - rum. As the ship made its voyage home, the rum flowed and the party began. But as they sailed further away from Barikaga, the sea became choppy and the wind increased. It was nothin' major at first, but this was only the start of the storm. The further they sailed, the worst it became. The party ended and the captain looked skywards as he ordered the crew to prepare the ship for the imminent storm approaching. Little did they know this would be a storm like none of them had ever experienced before. What the ship's crew didn't realise is that *they* had been summoned, all because of the pirates greed and their captain's failure to take heed of the warning.'

Denzel paused, his audience sat there in total silence. After a few seconds, Billy spoke.

'Who was summoned?' His eyes widened.

'The gods 'ad been summoned, Poseidon, Zeus and the Anemoi,' he informed him.

'Who are they? Asked a confused looking Austin. Before Denzel could reply, Mr Robertson jumped in.

'Poseidon is the god of the sea, Zeus is the god of the sky and the Anemoi are the four gods of the winds. North, South, East and West,' he said.

'They created the storm, didn't they?' He said.

Denzel nodded, looking impressed.

'That's right, my cocker,' he replied.

'God, you is some clever. You should become a

teacher or summfin,' said a chuckling Terry who was leaning back, pulling fluff out of his hairy belly button.

Denzel giggled before continuing with the rest of the tale.

'As they sailed away from the island, the seas became rough and before long the ship was being thrown around more violently,' Denzel became more animated as he described the incident.

'Water poured onto the ship's deck and overhead the skies became darker and then the rain came. It was torrential and battered the ship from all sides. Moments later the first clap of thunder echoed around them, followed by a bolt of lightnin' that crackled overhead. The thunder and lightnin' continued as the rough seas crashed onto the deck of the ship. It ripped the sails from their riggin' and the masts creaked louder as the ship rocked ferociously from side-to-side. The hull twisted one way and then the other. Sailors tried their hardest to stay onboard and save the ship, but before long, the sea took its first victim. A wave rose high above the ship and crashed down on the crew who were hangin' on for dear life. One pirate was not holdin' on tight enough though, and he got swept away. His shipmates could do nuffin' to help him as the sea swallowed his screams. Wave upon wave continued crashin' against the ship. The sea was relentless, enterin' the ship on one side and then exitin' on the other with a pirate in its clutches, draggin' them to their deaths. The fierce lighnin' that was explodin' overhead would momentarily break the darkness of the sky. The only 'fing keepin' the sailors safe was their own determination not to be taken by the sea. But it was no use, the wind increased, it howled across the bows of the ship as the sea continued to batter it from both sides. A gigantic bolt of lightnin' struck the ship's wheel and it obliterated on impact, sendin' splintered wood and shrapnel everywhere, some of which ended up embedded in several crew members. Their screams of pain joined the panickin' cries of the rest of the crew. Navigation was now impossible. They were at the mercy of the sea. The winds continued to howl, the thunder and lightnin' became more fierce and the rain continued to beat down on them. It was now a matter of survival until the storm passed. The ship's direction altered. There was no way of stoppin' it. It was headin' on its last journey. A cruel endin' for the captain and what remained of his crew. Then the grand finale. As they held on, the wind blew the ship towards some huge rocks juttin' out of the water. White foam was frothin' up over the rocks as the sea battered against them. They could do nothin' but hold on and watch their final moments unfold. The biggest wave yet attacked them and forced them closer.

The ship hit the rocks with such force that its hull split in two. The remainin' members of the crew tried their hardest to grab anyfin' that would help to keep them afloat. Some even tried gettin' onto the rocks, but it was no use. One-by-one it dragged them under the sea, and before long only one pirate remained - the captain. He was hangin' onto a broken piece of the ship's hull, to keep himself afloat. Suddenly, and out of nowhere, the rain stopped, the winds died down and the black skies cleared. The thunder and lightnin' stopped, and the previously stormy seas had calmed. The captain was all alone in the middle of the ocean, still hangin' on to a broken part of his now stricken vessel, as the sun, once again, shone. Just then, bubbles appeared ten feet in front of him. As he lay there, watchin', the bubbles increased. More and more rose to the surface and popped. Seconds later, three chests, full of treasure, shot up from below, piercin' the calm waters, before gently bobbin' up and down on the surface, as if tauntin' him. This was what he came for, but he had no ship, no crew, and no way of gettin' home. As a cruel final act, the chests slowly drifted away from him. He reached out a hand, as if tryin' to grab them, but he would never lay his hands on the treasure again. The captain watched as the chests, that contained a small fortune, ebbed away from him. All he could do was lie and wait for his life to end, however long that might take. It looked like it would be sooner rather than later. In the distance, several shark fins emerged from the water and headed in his direction.'

The hut fell silent as they all sat and thought about the curse that now lay hidden in the deep, dark cave on Kaninjanga island.

Chapter 41
Revenge

'So, this treasure,' said Mr Robertson. 'Has anybody else tried to retrieve it?' Denzel started laughing.

'O' course people 'ave tried to retrieve it. There 'ave been so many visitors over the years, from all corners of the earth. All thought they woz goin' be the ones to find it and take it 'ome. But, one way or another they fled the island or were killed. All except one,' he said.

'Who was the one?' Asked Sue. 'What happened to him?'

'Her,' said Denzel, correcting Sue.

They all looked up at him, surprised.

'She came here in search of the treasure, with a team of explorers, only, like every other expedition, it ended in disaster. A tribe attacked them and she was the only one to survive.'

'But surely, if it's only one woman she will be easy to defeat?' Asked a puzzled Billy.

'On her own, yes, but she wasn't alone.'

'What do you mean?' Asked Mr Robertson. 'I thought they killed her entire team?'

'Well, where do I begin? To cut a long story short, every member of her team was killed, slain by the Korrigans. Evil fings they is, yet she somehow survived and escaped. They searched for her but never found her. It was as if she had disappeared. Then, months later, she returned, only this time, she had protection. We only knew she was back when one night, screamin' could be heard comin' from the Korrigan village. We went to inspect and found somethin' disturbin'. Now, the Korrigans were a nasty bunch. They would entice you into their trap and then rip you apart, limb from limb, before devourin' your body. They liked to eat you when you was still warm. However, what we found in that there village would turn anyone's stomach. That night, the Korrigans had received a taste of their own medicine. As we entered the village, pieces of the tribe lay everywhere, someone had torn them apart, slaughtered every last one of them, men, women, even children. Animals lay gutted, all the huts had been burned to the ground, and as a pleasant finishin' touch, one word had been written on the wall in six-foot high letters. The most disturbin' 'fing about it was, it had been written in the Korrigans blood. A callous and vicious attack,' Denzel let them take everything in.

Sue was feeling a little queasy and was thankful that the Korrigan tribe no longer existed. Although, whoever had slaughtered them must be one evil person.

'What was written?' Asked Austin.

They all looked goggle-eyed at Denzel, who answered slowly.

'Revenge!'

'Well, the entire island did not know what had happened, we thought it may be a battle with another village. Only...' he paused.

'Only what?' Sue asked.

'...only, nobody took on the Korrigan tribe. They is the most evil, vicious and despicable creatures you could ever wish to meet. If they woz on yer side, you woz in luck, but if they woz yer enemy, well, you better watch out. So it woz obvious whoever had attacked and tortured the Korrigans would be a very nasty piece of work.'

Denzel continued to tell them all about Clara, the Chimera, and the dragon. He explained how villages had been emptied, one-by-one and how attacking her directly was not an option because the dragon would protect her from everyone. He gave them details on all the creatures wiped out from the island: *Korrigans, Kappas, Maskasores, Grifalores,* and many more.

'See she 'as been usin' the fastachees 'ere to

search for the treasure. They 'ave searched the entire island and now there is only one place left – the cave. But nobody wants to go in there because of what lies hidden within its network of tunnels,' he said.

The children's ears pricked up when he explained about the prisoner that she had taken from the village.

'That's what we saw in the sky on the way here, remember?' Austin shouted out.

'Yes, on the dragon, a glimpse into the past. That right, Terry?' Billy asked. 'That's why they asked us to help them. And that spinning item, that was the sacred ring, wasn't it?' He looked expectantly at the Knocker.

'Certainly was,' Terry confirmed.

'So, that is what this island is all about, and now there's a huge problem,' Denzel continued. 'She will know Terry is back and the stone will 'elp her to pinpoint the exact location of the treasure. She no longer needs to wait, she'll come, take the stone, and find the treasure. She'll kill us all if she has to. There's no reason for her to wait any longer. She'll be here soon to fight and take the stone.'

The hut fell silent again.

'Well,' said a determined looking Mr Robertson as he stood up. 'We had better be prepared.'

Chapter 42
The Magic Begins

They had to move fast, time was of the essence, and they could not waste another minute.

'What weapons do you have?' Asked Mr Robertson.

Denzel had a brief conversation with Janji and turned back to him.

'They only 'as a few spears. They need little else these days.'

'A few spears won't be enough to take on an army,' Mr Robertson said and started rubbing his forehead.

The children stood, listening, unsure what to do or say. Janji then said something else to Denzel.

'There is something that may help, but it's going to be almost impossible,' said Denzel.

'Explain?' Asked Mr Robertson.

'Some of the plants in the jungle. If we collect them, we can use them to make weapons. They 'ave got certain powers, like the one you drank,'

Denzel said.

'Sounds great. But what's the issue?' Asked Mr Robertson, now sounding slightly more upbeat.

'They're scattered throughout the entire jungle, and to find 'em would take ages if you don't know what you is lookin' for. There is not enough time to identify them and get them back here to prepare the potions for battle. If only we 'ad more time,' Denzel said, sounding disappointed.

'I can 'elp,' Terry said, as he stood there scratching his bum.

'What, how?' Asked Billy.

Terry did not say a word. He smiled, walked in between them and put his hand in his sack. He pulled out the map and put it on the floor. Then he reached into his sack again, removed the stone and placed it next to the map.

'This 'ere can 'elp,' he said, pointing to the map. The children looked down and realised it had changed from earlier. It was no longer a far off map of the sea and the island, it was a closeup of the village. The huts, the fields, the little fastachees walking around were all populated throughout. And slap bang in the middle, there they all were; Billy, Austin, Sue, Terry, and Mr Robertson. All identified by different coloured markers, with their names displayed above. It reminded Billy of a map in one of his computer games. They all gasped. Mr Robertson more than the children. It was the first time he had seen it in action.

'Watch this,' Terry said and started rubbing his hands together. He placed the index fingers from both of his hands in opposite corners of the map and drew them towards the middle. There were sharp intakes of breath from everyone as the image zoomed out, showing a much larger area of the entire island.

'You ain't seen nuffin yet, my ansum's,' Terry said as he chuckled.

He picked up the stone and placed it in the middle of the map. At first nothing happened, but he nodded at it and then it filled with several colours; purple, red, blue, and finally gold. It reminded Austin of a knickerbocker glory, causing his mouth to fill with saliva. Everyone was glued to the map, nobody dared to even blink as the magic show continued. The colours, like before, started emptying from the stone. Once they had emptied, individual pools of coloured ink sat in the middle of the map, looking like spilt pots of paint. And then, something magical happened. All of the colours floated over the map, moving away from the village and heading in different directions. Each time they reached a location, they would glow bright for a second and then move on, leaving a drop of ink to mark the area. The map was becoming covered in tiny dots of blue, red, purple, and gold ink. Once all the locations had been marked, the dots all transformed into spinning circular markers. Terry looked up at Mr Robertson.

'That 'elp 'e out does it, my ansum?'

'What are they?' Sue asked, looking excited.

'They is the location of the plants. Just gotta pick 'em now. Easy,' said a smug looking Terry.

But Mr Robertson brought them all back down to earth with a bang.

'There's a problem, Terry,' he said, as he stood there stroking his chin.

'What's that?' Terry asked.

'Well, this is good, but you're forgetting something important?'

'Like what? We knows where all the plants is, so I see no problem. We just 'as to follow the map and collect 'em all. Tis that simple.'

'Does nobody else get it?' Mr Robertson asked the group, but nobody answered.

'OK, well the colours on the map are great and would be a massive help. But there's only one map and we'll need to split up into teams and spread ourselves over a vast area to collect as many plants as possible. We also have a limited timeframe as the light will disappear in the next couple of hours. So with that in mind, how is it going to work? One map, between four teams going in different directions. It's not possible.'

The group looked deflated. Mr Robertson was

right, there was no way they could remember where all the plants were without having their own map. Everyone looked beaten. Everyone except Terry. He just smiled as he stared at Mr Robertson.

'You got no faith in me at all 'ave you my lover? Come wiv me,' he said, as he headed towards the middle of the village. Everyone was frowning and looking confused as they followed Terry. Billy and Austin shook their heads and shrugged at each other. Once they were all gathered around him, he pointed towards the jungle.

'Now, watch,' he said.

'Watch what?' Asked Mr Robertson.

'Stop bein' so blikin' impatient,' said an annoyed Terry. They all stood waiting, and then it started.

'Look!' Screamed Billy, pointing towards a red, circular beam of light that had started to emerge in front of them, soft at first, but soon it was glowing a deeper, brighter colour.

'There's another one,' screamed Austin, pointing towards a purple glow to the left of the red one.

The group all stood, motionless, as more and more lights appeared. The spinning beams were marking the areas highlighted on the map - the location of the plants.

'That is amazing,' said Sue as her eyes darted

around following the lights.

'It ain't over yet,' said Terry.

'What do you mean?' Asked Mr Robertson.

'Ave I not just told you to be patient?' Terry said, sounding even more annoyed. 'Just Watch.'

Then it started, the spinning discs on the ground rose into the air. There were mumblings around the group as they watch the lights continue to rise. Mr Robertson stood with his mouth open and his eyes wide.

The beams climbed higher and higher. Before long, they reached the top of the trees where they burst through and headed towards the sky. In the distance, light after light pierced the jungle canopy. Sue shrieked with excitement, but no-one else made a sound. The lights continued to appear from inside the jungle. The plants, identified on the map, were now all lit up like Christmas trees. The sky was soon full of red, blue, purple and gold beams, spinning around and shining bright.

Terry sidled up next to Mr Robertson. The locations of all the plants were now unmissable.

'That's 'ow you'll know, my ansum' Terry said as he looked up at the teacher, whose expression was like that of a kid in a sweet shop, trying to decide which of his favourite treats to buy.

'Won't they see the lights and wonder what's happening?' Asked a concerned Billy. 'They may come now if they do.'

'No chance,' said Terry. 'I can make 'em as high and as bright as I want. I can make them sound alarms with bells on and she won't have a clue.'

'How come?' Asked Austin.

'Because, my ansum, only you can see 'em, if you 'as seen 'em on the map. So she won't 'ave a blinkin' clue. I does love a bit of magic,' he said, as he started giggling, cocked his leg, farted and walked away. Everyone else stood there, mesmerised by the magic show, as his unique fragrance filled their nostrils.

Chapter 43
The Hibknibs

Billy, Austin, and Sue were emptying the sacks that were to be used to collect the plants, whilst Janji was over with his villagers, telling them everything that had happened, and explaining how the strange-looking people were here to help them. Terry was sitting with Mr Robertson, looking at the map as they discussed the action plan. Once everyone had finished what they were doing, they walked back over to them.

'Right, we need to split up into teams. We can't mix the plants up. You 'ave to keep 'em separate. One type of plant per sack. This 'ere needs to be done quickly. So, we is goin' split you up into four groups and then give you the colour of the plants you is to pick. Do not pick any other colour, even if you finks you is 'elpin',' Terry said, as he looked around to make sure they were all listening. 'If the wrong plants go in the wrong sacks they will be lost forever.'

'You in charge now are you, Terry?' Austin joked.

'Oh, I'm sorry, you wanna take charge does 'e, my ansum? Ere you go,' he said, offering the map and the stone to Austin, who blushed.

'U...u...umm, no you're okay mate,' he managed to spit out.

'Thought so,' Terry joked.

'Once you 'as got a sack full of plants, bring 'em back 'ere and we can get everyfin' ready, okay?' He didn't wait for a reply.

'Teams!' Terry announced.

'As we 'ave 'already said, there are four types of plants, so we is goin' need four teams,' he nodded at each of them. 'Billy, purple. Sue, red. Robbie, gold,' he said to Mr Robertson, who corrected him.

'Um, I prefer Mr Robertson if you don't mind.'

'Oh, I'm sorry my ansum, was I rude there? I do apologise. What was your name again?' Terry asked, as he started rubbing his chin and frowning, as if he had forgotten the teacher's name.

'Mr Robertson, you know that?'

'I tell you what I do know. I know I is not in your classroom my ansum, so I is not goin' be calling you Mr Robertson, that clear, Robbie?' He joked, the children all sniggered. Their teacher opened his mouth to reply, but thought better of it. Terry continued detailing them.

'And last but not least, Austin, you're to collect

blue. Happy?' They all nodded. 'Good. Okay everyone, grab a sack and we can get goin'.'

'Are you not coming into the jungle with us, Terry?' Asked Sue.

'No my ansum, I as got work to do 'ere.'

'What work?' Asked Billy.

'You'll see,' Terry smirked.

They all picked up a sack and headed towards the jungle.

'We're you lot goin'?' asked Denzel.

'To collect the plants,' said Billy.

'If you is goin' walk, it'll take you forever,' Denzel laughed.

'How else are we meant to collect them?' Mr Robertson asked, throwing his hands in the air. 'Got speed bikes have you?'

'Not exactly, but we 'as got summin' you can use,' said Denzel. He turned and nodded at Janji, who returned the nod and shouted something over to four villagers gathered behind him. They turned and walked between two of the huts, returning moments later with the strangest animals the children had ever seen. They were the same size as a Shetland pony and had the head of an anteater, the body of a zebra, and what looked like the legs of an ostrich.

'What on earth are those?' asked Billy.

'They is hibknibs,' said Denzel, 'ansum ain't they? Wait until you ride 'em,' he said, sounding excited.

'Ride them?' asked a panicking Austin.

'That's right, my cocker, be quicker than walkin', that's for sure. The key is to ride 'em like you stole 'em,' Denzel said as he chuckled.

'Don't worry, these 'ere fastachees are goin' be in charge, you just 'ave to enjoy the ride. All you gotta do is 'old on tight. Once you reach the plants, jump off, ease them out of the ground and put 'em in yer sacks. That's it, easy. Now, when you pull the plants out, make sure you don't squash any of the roots. They is the most important part and what gives the plants their powers. So if you squash 'em, they is no good to anyone.'

Billy walked over and held one hand under a hibknib's mouth whilst stroking its head with his other hand. The animal started licking his palm, which tickled and caused Billy to giggle.

'It's just like a little pony,' he said over his shoulder.

They all followed him and stroked their own creature.

After being patted for a few minutes, the animals ambled over to eat some leaves lying on the ground. Billy wondered how these slow-moving animals could possibly help them retrieve the magical plants scattered throughout the jungle? The way they were sauntering about like a group of sloths made him think they may have been better off walking. However, they were about to discover these creatures were not what they seemed; the children were about to embark on the ride of their lives.

'Right, we all clear on what we 'ave to do?' asked Terry.

'Too right. This could be fun,' said Sue.

The others were all in agreement. They walked over, picked up their sacks and made their way over to the edge of the village. They stood, shoulder-to-shoulder, looking into the dark jungle stretched out in front of them, illuminated by beams of light piercing the trees and spinning high in the sky.

'Good luck my ansums. We'll be 'ere waiting,' shouted Denzel.

'Remember, only pick your own plants, can't be gettin' 'em mixed up,' said Terry.

'In fact,' he said as he started to chuckle. 'This reminds me of a story.'

'I don't think we have time for a story, Terry,' said Mr Robertson.

'Is only a quick one. Make you laugh it will.'

'Fine, okay, whatever makes you happy.'

'Ansum. Well, once, I was walking past Old Farmer Penberthy's strawberry field, and he had a sign up sayin' 'Pick your own strawberries'. I was blinkin' starvin', so I jumped in the field and started pickin' the biggest, juiciest red strawberries I could find. I popped one in my mouth and crushed it between me teeth. It tasted delicious. Well, as I stood there with the juice runnin' down my chin —

'You mean chins,' chuckled Austin, causing Terry to glare at him before continuing.

'As the juice ran down my chin, old farmer Penberthy came out pointin' his shotgun at me. What are you doin'? He shouted. Well, I dropped all the strawberries I 'ad picked and smiled at him. It says pick your own strawberries, my ansum, I told him. He glared at me. Yes, pick your own strawberries, leave mine alone! Now get lost.'

Terry stood there laughing at his ridiculous bad joke.

'Well, that was hilarious,' said a sarcastic looking Mr Robertson.

Terry continued chuckling as he took the stone from his sack and held it in the palm of his hand.

'Only one thing left to do before you leave,' Terry said.

'Which is?' Asked Sue.

'Watch.'

He wrapped his fingers around the stone, uncurled his index finger and pointed at the sacks, one-by-one. The children watched as a swirling wind appeared at the bottom of their sacks and started circling around them. As the wind engulfed the sacks, they started changing colour. From the bottom all the way to the top. Billy's turned a bright purple, Sue's was soon scarlet red, Mr Robertson's was glowing gold, and Austin's was deep-blue.

'No excuses for gettin' mixed up now is there,' said Terry.

The children, and Mr Robertson, all smiled, before throwing a leg over their hibknibs and settling behind their chauffeurs. The fastachees looked at each other, nodded, raised the ropes in their hands a few inches and pulled them down against the necks of the creatures. They took off like horses being released from their traps at the start of a race. The children, and in fact Mr Robertson too, all screamed as they headed away from the village. Denzel and Terry stood there, watching and giggling, as the four of them bounced up and down, while holding on for dear life. Seconds later, they disappeared from view and headed into the heart of the jungle.

'Okay my ansum, I suppose I best get to work. So, where can I find some sturdy wood?' Terry asked, rubbing his hands as he stared up at his fellow Cornishman.

Chapter 44
Beware of the Plants

The creatures travelled so fast and changed direction without losing speed as they weaved in and out of the trees. They flew so close that Billy could almost smell the bark. The fastachees all kept their heads down, as if whispering into the ears of the hibknibs. Once they entered the jungle, Austin's headed towards the left, Billy's to the right, whilst Sue and Mr Robertson's continued going straight ahead, one behind the other. Seconds later, Mr Robertson's branched off to the left, as Sue's carried on ahead. They may have been heading in different directions, but they all had the same plan, the same task - collect the plants. Billy could see the first beam appearing in the distance. They were going so fast, and the beams were so far away that the colour wasn't clear. He tried to focus, but the wind caused his eyes to water, making identifying the colour even more difficult. The fastachee shifted the animal to the left, flying only inches past another tree. Once they had passed it, he pulled them back to the right. Billy gripped the animal with his legs and his hands were wrapped around his driver. As they got closer to the beam, Billy noticed something appear in the air next to it, which seemed to bob up and down. He tried to focus harder. It looked like some sort of symbol - 70M. Then it changed - 65M. They shot to the left, Billy lost sight of the symbol for a few seconds as they jumped over a fallen log. But as they landed, he spotted it again - 60M this time, then 55M, 50M. The wind was blowing through his hair and he had to squint as the water ran from his eyes. Then, Billy realised what it was, the distance in metres to the plant. The colour was becoming clearer too, it could have been blue or purple. Now it was just 45M away. He was getting closer and would know the colour soon enough. They seemed to be going even faster. 30M. Billy could now make out the colour. Purple. *Yes*, he thought. They headed straight for the plant. Almost there. The marker was right in front of them. The number counted down metre by metre, 20M...19M...18M. Billy's heart started beating faster. He loosened his grip as he prepared to dismount, which proved to be a mistake. Almost there. 9M...8M. Just as the number reached 5M, the hibknib came to an abrupt halt. Billy was now only holding on with one hand and was thrown into a bush. He climbed out and brushed himself down.

'Thanks for the warning,' he muttered as he looked at the driver.

They had been travelling at top speed for well over a minute and yet this animal stood, not panting or out of breath at all. The creature looked the same as when Billy first saw it in the village. He shook his head, then refocused. They were right next to the circular beam, which was spinning around and around, as if protecting the plant sat in the middle of it. After taking a deep breath, Billy stepped into the beam with his eyes closed, looking like he was afraid of receiving an electric shock, but nothing happened. He bent down and inspected the plant. It looked more like a flower, with bright, glowing purple leaves. He placed his hands under the leaves and let them fan out into his palms. A noise to the left made Billy look across. The fastachee was giving hand signals that he knew very well. Hurry-up! He reached out and placed his hands around the base of the stem and gave the plant a gentle tug. The plant left the ground with little effort. As it did, the purple beam of light descended from above the tree tops. Billy stood there and watched as it headed back towards the ground and then disappeared for good. Billy switched his attention back to the plant. At first he thought he was seeing things. He brought the plant closer to his face. The leaves continued to pulse that deep purple colour, but Billy felt his eyes being drawn to the roots. Sat in the middle was one small face. As Billy watched, it started to multiply, one after the other. Soon there was a face attached to every root of the plant. The faces started spinning around and were trying to bite each other. Billy moved the plant closer. As he did, one face gnarled at him, opened its mouth to show several razor-sharp teeth and tried to bite him. He pulled away just in time, much to the annoyance of the grumpy little face.

Billy walked over to his sack, attached to the saddle, and placed the plant inside. What happened next filled him with horror. As soon as the plant entered the sack, there was a loud *puff*, followed by a plume of purple smoke. Billy wafted it away and looked into the sack. The plant was gone. He searched inside the sack, on the floor, under the saddle, but it was nowhere. He walked back over to where he'd picked the plant from, hoping that a fresh one may have grown back, like the food on the trees in Terry's village. But the only thing there was the disturbed earth left by the freshly picked plant. The fastachee motioned for him to jump back on. Billy could not understand what had happened. He picked the correct colour, as Terry had instructed him, and yet his plant had disappeared into thin air. He could do nothing about it now, he had to move on to the next one. Billy climbed back onto his hibknib and held on tight. Just as before, his transportation took off at lightning speed towards the next target. Leaving Billy to wonder what had happened to the plant?

******

Austin reached his first target, and just like Billy, went flying through the air as his animal came to a sudden stop. After brushing himself down and shaking his head in annoyance at the fastachee, he walked over and gently removed the plant from the ground. He stood there, shocked at what he was looking at. Attached to the roots of the plant were tiny fingers, all stretching and moving in the air. Austin pulled the plant up to his face for a closer look and as he did, the fingers all lunged for him.

'Arrgh,' he screamed, as he recoiled.

'I think it's best you boys go to bed,' he muttered.

He walked over, opened the sack, and attempted to place the plant inside, but the fingers all grabbed the edge and held on tight, saving themselves from the darkness. Austin gently prised the fingers off as they tried to pinch him, and lowered the plant into the sack. There was soon a puff of blue smoke and the plant, once again, disappeared. *That's weird,* he muttered to himself. After searching for the plant and coming up with no explanation, he thought it best to forget it and head to his next target. *Must have been a bad plant. I mean, what were those fingers all about?* he thought. Austin climbed back on his animal and was soon racing through the jungle.

****

Sue was already at her second plant. She hoped that this would end better than her first one. At least she had stayed on her animal when it came to a sudden stop this time. She only hoped that the roots were better on this one. She dismounted and walked straight up to the plant, grabbed the bottom of the stem and eased it out of the ground. As the red beam vanished, she checked the roots again. Nope, they were exactly the same. Attached to the ends of the roots were many faces, all of which had blindfolds over their eyes so they couldn't see a thing. They were just dangling from the roots. This is weird, Sue thought. She placed the plant inside her sack and just as before, the disappearing trick happened again in a puff of red smoke. What on earth was going on?

******

Mr Robertson felt like he was a boy again horse riding with his dad. He was enjoying himself. Four plants down, and none in his sack though. Maybe the plants were dead? There must be an explanation.

He reached the fifth plant, dismounted, walked

over to the plant, picked it clean, and placed it in his sack. Those weird roots were something else. What sort of roots had bums attached to them? When he inspected the first one, he held it out in front of him and, one bum let off a stinker which made his eyes water it was that bad. The stench made Terry's bottom burps smell like the latest aftershave scent, it was so revolting. Once again, it disappeared in a cloud of gold smoke when he put it in his sack. He tried not to think about it too much as he jumped on the hibknib and headed off to his next target, he couldn't help but wonder what was wrong with his plants. He only hoped that the children were having better luck. If only he knew they were having the same luck as him.

Things did not look good at all.

Chapter 45
Someone's Missing

Terry walked back over to the map to check on their progress. They set off 35 minutes ago and most of the plants had now been picked. There was a key on the left hand side of the map, showing how many plants each of them had remaining. It looked like Sue would be the first one back, she only had two plants left, Billy had four, and once Austin picked the one at his current location he would have five. Mr Robertson was taking his time, he still had seven remaining.

The beams of light that had been littered throughout the jungle at the start were vanishing from the sky, as well as from the map. Terry had watched the map eagerly as they started out on the task. It took them a while to arrive and even leave their first location, which was understandable. However, they were now in the flow, especially Sue. She wasted no time at all in moving with speed between targets. Her key on the map had just changed, showing she was heading towards her final plant.

'Denzel, they be 'ere in a minute, how we doin?,' Terry shouted over his shoulder.

'We is crackin' on, should be finished in time' he replied.

'Good. I only 'ope we is goin' be 'lright, I can't let anyfin' 'appen to 'em. I got 'em in this 'ere mess,' Terry said.

'It'll be fine, don't worry,' Denzel said.

'Yeah, 'spose yer right.' Terry looked back at the map. There were no more red locations, only one purple, two blue and two gold. Thankfully Mr Robertson had pulled his finger out, he was only 25m away from his next target. Terry stood up and switched his gaze towards the jungle. His heart started beating faster as he rubbed his sweaty palms on the front of his garb. He wondered if parents felt like this as they stood waiting for their children to return from their first ever school camp?

He took a deep breath and blew out hard, then the sound of rustling leaves made him look up, and seconds later a hibknib burst out of the jungle, expertly ridden by the fastachee. Sue was sat behind him with both hands wrapped around his waist, as her hair blew out wildly behind her. They reached Terry and once again came to a sudden stop. In one movement, Sue dismounted and removed the sack from the creature. She walked to the front of her animal and held something under its mouth, some wild flowers. The hibknib ate them as she patted his head. She placed a hand on the fastachee's knee, and, as he looked at her, she smiled and gave a simple nod of the head. The villager reciprocated the gesture.

'That was awesome fun,' she said with a giggle. 'There's one problem thou—,'

'ang on a sec my ansum,' Terry interrupted, as he held up a hand. Sue turned around and beamed as she saw Billy heading their way, with Austin right behind him, one hand raised in the air as he screamed from the top of his lungs. Both Terry and Sue started laughing.

Sue walked over to see them as they dismounted, whilst Terry returned his attention to the map. There were still two gold plants left, which seemed odd. Mr Robertson should be on his last one by now. The three children all stood there, hugging each other and talking excitedly. Terry's eyes remained fixed on the map, almost willing the situation displayed on it to change. But no matter how hard he stared it remained the same, this did not look good. The children finished talking and realised they were missing one member.

'Where's Mr Robertson? Asked Sue. Terry didn't answer, he was glued to the map. Still no change.

'Umm, he ain't back yet, won't be long though,'

he said as he tried smiling.

'Well, where is he?' asked a concerned Austin.

'Two targets left,' Terry said.

'Oh well, that's okay. He'll be back soon,' said an upbeat Austin.

Terry slowly nodded up and down.

'What is it Terry? What's wrong?' Asked Sue, sensing the unease in his body language. Terry puffed out hard before looking at her and giving her the news.

'He's not moved for a while,' he said.

'What?' The children all chimed together. They rushed over and checked the map. It was the same as it had been for the past few minutes. Two gold locations remained, one had a 25m marker slowly bouncing up and down next to it.

'Well, where is his marker, you know, like we all had earlier? We're still on there, look,' said Billy, pointing to the coloured cursors denoting their position in the village.

'Cause, when you is in the jungle your markers change for the distance markers. Then, once you exit the jungle they change back to individual markers, like yours have, but it won't change until then. Nuffin I can do,' Terry explained with a shrug of the shoulders.

'So you're telling us there is no way of knowing where Mr Robertson is?' Asked Austin.

Terry shook his head as he continued to study

the map, willing the 25M marker to start counting down.

The children stood there, unable to move, Mr Robertson was not back, his distance marker was not moving, and they did not know where he was.

It seemed their teacher was lost in the jungle.

Chapter 46
The Search for Mr Robertson

'I'm going back in,' shouted Austin.

They all spun to face him as he moved towards one of the hibknibs.

'What? you can't go back in there. What if something bad has happened to him? What if someone or something has got him? They might grab you too? It's too dangerous,' said Billy.

'So? We're going to leave him in there to deal with it on his own are we? No chance. You guys stay here. I'll be back soon,' Austin explained. Billy looked up at his best friend, he had never seen him act like this before. When they first met and ended up lost in the woods, Austin seemed scared of his own shadow. The darkness brought out a panic that made him look like a baby. Yet here he was, about to risk his life and enter the jungle to search for a man he never used to like. Billy understood why Austin wanted to find him, and he nodded in agreement.

'Then I'm coming with you,' Billy said defiantly.

'What, No!' Screamed Sue. 'You can't, neither of you can,' she begged, looking from Billy to Austin and back again. The pleading clear in her expression.

'No, you stay here, Bill. You need to get ready. I'm sure Terry has some stuff for you to be getting on with,' Austin said nodding at Terry, who confirmed he had.

'That can wait,' Billy replied. 'I'm coming with you. You're not going back in there on your own.'

Before Austin said another word, Billy had turned around, grabbed his own animal, and climbed onboard. Austin looked at Billy. The steeliness in his eyes told Austin that he would be wasting his time objecting. Instead, he gave Billy a nod that said, *Let's do this*. Sue stood there with her hands held up to her face, looking worried. Billy smiled at her.

'We'll be back before you know it,' he said in a reassuring voice.

'Ready?' Austin said.

'As I'll ever be.'

Both boys sat side-by-side on their creatures, facing the jungle. They raised their hands and both shouted '*Haaa*' as they brought the ropes down simultaneously and gripped on for dear life. The hibknibs understood the command and took off at breakneck speed.

Seconds later, the boys headed into the jungle to search for their missing schoolteacher.

He could be in serious trouble so they needed to find him, quick.

******

They entered the jungle and continued straight ahead for a while before veering off to the left. Austin was in front, with Billy following close behind. They moved from left to right as they continued slaloming between the enormous trees. Austin was keeping an eye out for the gold beams of light, but no luck so far. They were approaching a fallen trunk up ahead, but it was too high to jump. Trees and undergrowth surrounded them. They could not get past. Why had they come this way? Austin closed his eyes tight. Unbeknownst to him, Billy had done exactly the same. Suddenly, Austin's hibknib sent out a piercing scream, and seconds later Billy's animal returned the cry. They were communicating with each other. The boys opened their eyes and as they approached the log, their animals bent so low that their chins almost touched the ground. The boys held on tight as the wind continued blowing into their eyes. They were squinting and struggling to see what was in front of them as their eyes filled with water. Austin continued at speed, with Billy staying right on his tail. As they reached the fallen trunk, Austin's animal bent his knees, moving closer to the ground. Surely it wasn't going to try to go under the trunk, was it? Just as Austin thought he was going to meet a messy end, his hibknib let out another high-pitched scream and exploded up from the ground, causing Austin to close his eyes again. He heard Billy's animal cry out and then he felt the full force of the jump as they flew skywards. Almost instantly, he was being smacked on the head by the branches of the trees. Once he had stopped being attacked, he opened his eyes, and when he did, he gasped at the sight that greeted him. He was staring, not into the jungle like before, but into the clear sky that stretched out for miles in front of them. Their speed had reduced, allowing Austin to open his eyes fully. He looked down at the top of the trees as they soared high above them. Then he looked behind. Billy had an expression that mirrored his own. The boys smiled at each other. This was incredible. They had both jumped not only the fallen trunk, but the entire jungle. Then, just as they thought they would start heading back to the jungle, something grazed the boys legs, causing them to look down again. Billy's animal drew up alongside Austin's. The boys looked at each other and their smiles grew even wider. Both of them could not believe what was happening. They were flying high above the jungle, aided by the 10-foot-long-wings that had just unfurled from underneath their hibknibs.

'This is amazing,' shouted Austin.

'Look!' Screamed Billy, raising a finger and pointing towards something in the distance. There they were, shooting up through the treetops, two gold beams of light, one of which had something bouncing up and down next to it. The boys could not make out what it was because of the trees obstructing their view, but they already knew it was the 25m marker.

'Let's go find our teacher,' said a determined Austin.

Billy nodded in agreement.

The boys raised their hands together, and for the second time that day, gave a joint '*Haaa*' as they whipped the ropes back down again, giving the '*go*' command. The animals responded by shrieking into the sky and flapping their enormous wings as they bolted forwards, descending back towards the heart of the jungle.

******

Back in the clearing, Sue continued pacing around, unable to take her mind off the boys and Mr Robertson. She hoped they would be back soon. But what if they didn't come back? What then?

'Don't worry my ansum. They goin' be 'lright. Tough as old bricks them two.'

She looked down at Terry, who had walked over and stood beside her.

'But what if they don't come back? What if they're gone forever? I mean, Mr Robertson has gone missing, so there's no reason to believe the boys will find him, or even return themselves, is there?'

Terry stayed silent, he could offer some comforting words, but he knew Sue was right. They may not return at all.

'Well, we'll 'ave to wait and see. 'Tis no good walkin' 'round worryin' 'bout it. We will 'ave to prepare like they is goin' be back soon. So, cumuson over 'ere and give us a 'and. We as got so much to do,' he turned and walked over to where four small campfires had been built. As they approached, Sue noticed the fires were being tended to by a team of fastachees. Denzel hovered above them, whilst Janji walked from fire-to-fire, giving them instructions, inspecting their work and patting them on the back in a show of appreciation. Over each fire hung a steel pan. Water was bubbling away inside and hissing as it dripped over the sides onto the flames. As Sue looked around, it occurred to her that each fire had a pile of plants lying next to it. There was one colour for each fire – red, purple, blue and gold.

Next to one fire, there were piles of balls all tied together with twine. The balls were encased in a bright blue aura. At the next station, there was a pile of different foods - coconuts, bananas, dates, avocados, all being filled with a powder that had been extracted from the plants. Once the powder was poured inside, the fruits were sealed and would pulse a bright red colour. The third team worked with Y-shaped pieces of wood. Twine had been fixed to the widest parts at the top and once securely fixed in place, the twine of the catapults started glowing gold. Finally, Sue noticed something that both excited and terrified her - arrows. She walked over, picked one up and let it run through her fingers. Her heart rate and excitement increased. The arrows brought back happy memories of being back in South Africa before the incident that had changed her family's lives, back when everything was fine. But it also worried her. The sight of these weapons reinforced how dangerous the task ahead of them would be. She passed the arrow through her fingers, stopping and gently caressing the fletching at the rear which was glowing a deep purple colour, Billy's colour. She smiled as she placed the arrow back on the pile by her feet.

She suddenly realised what had been happening when they picked the plants earlier.

'Terry?'

'Yes, my ansum.'

'You made these with the plants we picked, didn't you?'

Terry smiled up at her.

'Certainly did. These little buggers bein' workin' their blinkin' socks off they 'as,' he said, motioning towards the villagers and smiling.

'That's why the plants disappeared when we put them in our sacks, they got teleported straight back here, didn't they?' She said.

Terry winked at her.

'Yep, 'ad to get em back 'ere and get started on this lot,' he said, gesturing towards their newly created stash of weapons.

'So, when you used the stone to light up our sacks, in case we forgot our colours, it was more like you put a spell on our sacks. So that once we put the plants inside, they transported straight back here for you to start making the weapons?'

'Smart 'lil lady ain't you my lover? Very impressive. You could be one o' them detectives or summfin',' he chuckled.

Sue smiled.

Suddenly a shriek filled the sky, forcing them both to look towards it. They could not believe what they were seeing. In the distance, it looked like there were two animals flying through the sky. They had huge wings and Sue was sure she saw a person sat on the back of each one. They were only there for a few moments before they dived back towards the jungle.

It couldn't be, could it?

Chapter 47
Sue's Present

The boys re-entered the jungle and were standing at the gold beam with the 25m symbol bouncing up and down above their heads.

'Where is he?' Asked Austin, looking around for any sign of Mr Robertson.

'He has to be here somewhere, unless someone or something has taken him?' Added Billy.

'Well, we knew he wouldn't be at the tree, as the marker says he's still 25 metres away. So, we work out 25 metres from the tree and start our search from there. Agreed?' Austin said.

'Yeah, good plan, Batman,' Billy joked.

'Does that make you boy wonder? Cause I do often wonder if you are actually a boy, especially when you keep staring all gooey eyed at your new missus,' Austin jested.

'Funny you, ain't ya?'

'Almost as funny as your face,' Austin said. 'Anyway, enough of this jovial conversation, you're boring me now. We need to find Mr Robertson.'

Billy walked to the centre of the tree, turned and took big strides from the centre, counting out loud with each step.

'What are you doing?' asked Austin, frowning.

Billy ignored him and continued striding forwards and counting.

'15, 16, 17, 18, 19,' Billy shouted out. Austin thought he had lost the plot. His friend was heading further and further away from the tree.

'22, 23, 24, annnnd 25!' he stopped when he reached the number matching the spinning marker.

'Twenty-five metres, roughly,' he shouted. Austin tied their hibknibs to a nearby tree and ran over to him. Billy stood there looking pleased with himself.

'I've seen my dad do that before, it's only a rough guide to the distance - one metre per step, give or take. Now, we will have to be careful and listen for any noises. There is a possibility he's in here somewhere and we can't afford to miss him, okay?' Billy asked.

'You're in charge.'

The boys walked around the tree in a circular motion, Billy in front and Austin close behind him. They were trying as hard as they could to listen for the slightest sound which would give them a clue as to their teacher's location. After a few minutes, Billy stopped dead.

'What is it?' Asked Austin.

'Look,' said Billy, pointing to the ground.

There were some disturbed leaves next to a gap between two bushes and, right next to them, the partial imprint of a shoe.

******

'How on earth have you made all of this?' Sue asked Terry.

'We 'as been working since you entered the jungle. The stone did most of it. But all this, 'the magic,' well, that needs to be done by hand,' he explained.

'I can't believe it. It's amazing, but I take it we will be firing the arrows and not throwing them?' Asked Sue, as she searched around for the bows.

'Yep, we is goin' be firin' 'em,' Terry said, as he bent down and picked up three arrows from the pile lying by his feet.

'How?' She asked, sounding confused as there were no bows anywhere. Terry winked at her and beckoned for her to follow him.

'Come with me,' he said.

Sue took one last look at the villagers, who continued to make and stockpile the weapons, before following Terry.

As they walked out of the village, he headed towards a stack of large logs.

'Wanna see sommfin' cool?' Terry asked, with a cheeky look on his face. Sue wondered what he was up to this time.

'Okay,' she said, sounding dubious.

'Watch this,' he replied.

He put his hand into his sack and removed the stone. He was about to close his eyes when he stopped himself and looked up at Sue.

'What is it?' She quizzed him. 'What's wrong?'

'Nuffin's wrong. It's just I do this loads, but you ain't 'ad a go yet 'ave you? 'old 'em out,' Terry said as he nodded at Sue's hands.

'What, why?' She asked.

'Just blinkin' 'old 'em out you nosey so-'n'- so,' Terry insisted.

Sue did as she was told and held her hands out. Terry gently placed the stone inside.

'Now, we is almost ready for tonight. But you is right, we 'as not got any bows yet for our arrows and I don't fink we is goin' do very well wivout 'em. I mean, unless the fastachees can 'frow like those there javelin people,' he said as he chuckled. 'So, you is goin' make 'em for us, okay?'

'What do you mean, I'm making them? How am I supposed to do that?' Sue asked, unsure what he expected from her.

'Magic,' Terry said, smiling. 'Now, all you gotta do is 'old the stone and it'll do the rest. Close yer eyes, and imagine how you want the bows to look, open your eyes, and nod at the stone to transfer the image. Once you 'as done that, it'll go to work. Easy,' Terry said.

Sue stood with the cold stone sat in her hands. She seemed unsure what to do, even with the instructions Terry had given her.

'Face the logs and do what I told you, tis goin' be 'lright. Don't worry,' he said, trying to reassure her.

Sue nodded at him and turned to face the logs. She thought of the bow she used back home. It was so beautiful. She loved it. When she held it in her hands, it felt like an extension to her arm. She missed it so much, she hadn't realised how much until now. As Sue thought about the bow, she remembered the last time she had fired it, the day before her father had come home in a trance, burdened by whatever it was he had experienced that day.

Once she had the image of that bow, her bow, in her mind, she closed her eyes and seconds later, opened them and nodded at the stone. Terry stood, watching, as it filled with colour. Sue gasped as the logs lying on the floor raised into the air, one-by-one, until they were all bobbing up and down, as if they were suspended on a piece of string. Then the colours contained in the stone poured from the top of it and headed over to the logs. Sue was holding her breath, as if exhaling would stop the magic show that had begun in front of her. The logs started spinning, slowly at first, but soon their speed increased. The colours began to circle around them. Drilling sounds soon filled the air as the lights moved up and down the huge logs. Chunks of wood lay littered all over the floor, as the lights continued with their creation. Sue was glued to the magical sight. She could not believe what she was seeing. Every log was being shaped in exactly the same way. Slithers of light headed towards the village. Sue ducked as they flew past her head and shot between two huts and out of sight.

The spinning logs started slowing down, the brightness of the lights reduced and before long they came to a stop. Shards of wood covered the floor. It looked like a carpenter's workshop that had not been swept for weeks. Sue looked across at Terry. He was smiling away. She was flabbergasted, yet excited.

'You is lookin' a lil bit discombobulated, if you don't mind me sayin' so,' he said, as he took the stone from Sue and put it back in his sack.

'I can't believe what I've just seen. Was that real?'

Before Terry could answer, the slivers of light which had disappeared into the village moments earlier returned carrying lengths of twine. They went back to the logs and completed the creation.

When they had finished, Terry walked over and picked up one of the items that was suspended in the air. Sue looked down at him as he approached and held it towards her.

'Ere you go, my lover,' Terry said nodding at it.

'Really?'

'Yes, tis yours, if you want it? Go on, take it,' he instructed her as he nodded at it. Sue smiled and took the item from him. It was just as she remembered, only this bow was even more beautiful. She started running her hands up and down it, as if reacquainting herself with a long-lost possession. It looked stunning. A deep red colour ran from the top of the upper limb, to the base of the lower limb. The handle was jet-black and smooth to the touch. Gold twine was pulled so tightly that the tension held within it would give her ample distance over which to fire the arrows. As she wrapped her fingers around the handle and took ownership of it, she gasped and raised one hand to cover her mouth. A gold dot had appeared on the bow and began to glow as it wrote her name in calligraphic lettering along the lower limb of the bow. Once it had finished, she looked at Terry with her mouth wide open and her eyes like saucers.

'Let's see how good you is, shall us,' Terry said, waking her from her daydreaming. She looked at him, not understanding what he meant. Then, the lights hanging in the air transformed into perfect circles, each one slightly smaller than the one preceding it. They were all different colours; white, black, blue, red and gold. As each circle surrounded the previous one, Sue smiled as she realised what was happening. Terry handed over the arrows he had picked up earlier and pointed towards the colourful target, which the lights had just created. Sue took the arrows from him and stabbed them into the ground next to her, making them easy to pick up and feed into the bow. She gently gripped the handle of the bow, glanced over at the target, which had moved 50 metres away, and retrieved the first arrow. She gently placed it on the rest with the arrowhead pointing towards the ground. Next, she inserted the nock of the arrow into the nocking point of the string and held it in place with her index and middle fingers. She took two breaths to calm herself, brought the bow up and looked down the shaft of the arrow towards the target. She adjusted her aim, allowing for a slight change in trajectory, regulated her breathing, and then released the arrow, sending it flying towards its target. It shot straight through the red section, left of centre, and disappeared. Terry watched in amazement as a big red 'eight' appeared above the target. Sue was beaming from ear-to-ear. She missed this feeling so much.

'Well, what are you waiting for?' Terry asked

her. The excitement clear in his voice. 'You got two more yet. Let's see if that was luck,' he said as he started bouncing up and down.

Sue repeated the process. She did not need asking twice. This time she adjusted her aim, and when she was ready, she released the arrow. It pierced the air and struck its target. She had over-corrected her aim, and a blue 'six' appeared. Terry stopped bouncing around and put his hands on his hips.

'Guess it was beginners' luck, after all,' he said sarcastically.

Sue removed the final arrow, placed it on the arrow rest and prepared to fire again. She closed her eyes, took five slow breaths to relax and then opened them again. She adjusted her aim and seconds later, when she was completely focused, she sent it on its way. The arrow made a swooshing sound as it left the bow. It seemed to take forever to reach the target, but in fact, it was there in less than two seconds. Her heart seemed to be trying to jump out of her chest as she waited for the score. The arrow pierced the target and sparks started to explode from the gold 10 that was now bouncing up and down above it. Bullseye. She turned to Terry.

'Better?' She asked, mocking his sarcasm.

'That'll do for me, my ansum. I got a bit excited there, and I fink a lil bit of wee came out,' he said as he started giggling. 'Anyway, you is missin' summfin.'

'Missing something? What?'

'What 'as I told you about bein' patient?' He joked.

Then he nodded at the lights, that were still hanging in the air, and they started working on a log.

Within minutes, Sue was standing there looking like a complete archer, with a bow hanging from her hand, wrist guards on both forearms, and a beautiful wooden quiver strapped diagonally across her back.

'Now, that's more like it,' Terry said to her.

Sue couldn't speak. She just kept staring at her arm guards and her personalised bow. She looked at Terry, with tears in her eyes and just nodded up and down in a thank you gesture.

'You're welcome, my lover. Now, let's see if the boys are back with your naughty school teacher shall we,' he said with a wink, before heading back to the village, closely followed by Sue.

Chapter 48
What's Going On?

'You reckon it's Mr Robertson's?' Austin asked Billy as they stood there inspecting the shoe print.

'Well, who else's could it be?' Billy replied.

'Well, he must be around here somewhere, but where's the fastachee and the hibknib?' Asked Austin, as he surveyed the floor around them.

'Here's another one,' he said, moving more leaves aside to expose a fresh print. The boys edged forwards. There seemed to be a trail of disturbed leaves, and a few more prints. Billy lead the way, with Austin following him, checking behind to ensure nobody was lurking, ready to attack them.

After a few minutes, Billy heard some movement up ahead of them and stopped, holding his hand up and gesturing for Austin to do the same.

'Shush. Listen,' Billy whispered.

Both boys went quiet, and there it was again. The sound of rustling leaves up ahead. Billy crouched as low as he could get and edged himself closer. He could feel Austin's breath on the back of his neck as they crept behind a tall bush separating them from the noise. The movement and rustling seemed to get louder as they approached. The boys' hearts began beating faster as the unmistakable sound of a voice floated towards them. Billy continued to move forwards at a snail's pace. He was now right behind the bush that separated them from whatever lay on the other side. Austin crept closer and positioned himself right next to Billy. He motioned at a slight gap in the middle of the bush. Billy nodded in agreement and the boys both edged towards it. They placed their hands inside the bush and moved them apart to create viewing holes. They both peered through the gap and saw what was on the other side making all the noise.

'What the hell is this?' Asked Billy, as he looked at Austin.

******

Sue stood in front of the map. She could not take her eyes off of it. The 25M symbol continued bouncing up and down next to the gold beam of light. The boys had made no progress since entering the jungle. Billy and Austin's markers were there, right next to the beam. Billy's marker moved towards the tree and instantly started moving away. Austin's marker did not move.

What on earth was happening? Had someone attacked them? Had they injured Austin? She stood there biting her nails, wishing she was with them. Billy's marker stopped moving and then Austin's started towards him. He wasn't injured. Thank goodness. Once Austin reached Billy, both markers started moving together. Soon they stopped again. Sue had an idea. She placed her fingers in the middle of the map and dragged them out to opposite corners. The map zoomed in on the boys. They seemed to be hiding behind a bush. Had they spotted something? She looked across at a stray hibknib. It would be easy to jump on and head into the jungle. It wasn't that she didn't trust the boys, she just wondered what was going on. But she decided against it. Instead, she stayed and watched the events unfold on the map as Billy and Austin moved through the jungle, continuing their search for Mr Robertson. She turned her attention back to the map just as their markers started moving again. If only she knew the sight they now faced. She would know their task had become even more challenging.

Chapter 49
Crazy Mr Robertson

Billy and Austin remained crouched behind the bush. They had been watching the confrontation for the past five minutes and time was ticking away.

'This is no use. We have to go in there and sort it out. It's getting dark and we need to get back,' said Austin.

'So what are you suggesting?' Whispered Billy.

'I'm not sure, but we have to try something.'

The boys stood and looked over the top of the bush. Standing there, right in the middle, was Mr Robertson. A tie was wrapped around his head, his shirt was unbuttoned, and his trousers were torn and dirty. His eyes were wide and he was running around, shouting obscenities into the air. Their teacher kept hiding behind a tree and jumping back out before pretending to shoot someone with his make-believe gun. He raised the gun and fired across at something on the other side.

From behind another tree, on the opposite side, emerged another figure, who, until this point, stood camouflaged against the brown bark of the tree. The fastachee danced around and dodged the imaginary bullets, but as the ammunition continued its assault, he grabbed his chest and stumbled around as if he had been shot.

'Bang, bang, you're dead. I got you. Can't hide now, hahahaha, hehehehe, you're not as good a shot as me,' sang Mr Robertson.

The fastachee dropped to his knees, before lying prone on the ground.

'Yesssss! Get down. You're gone, no coming back now,' he said, fist pumping the air. To his surprise, the victim recovered to full health and danced around whilst he pointed his own imaginary gun at Mr Robertson.

'No, I got you. You're dead. Stop cheating. I can't believe you're cheating. You're dead. Dead as a dodo,' he shouted as he pointed angrily at the enemy.

Billy and Austin moved around to the front of the bush. They needed to get this over and done with.

Mr Robertson spotted them and ran over in a panic.

'Hey—hey—hey you, are you here to help me?' He asked, talking so fast that they could only just understand what he was saying. Austin noticed his eyes were wide and there was an unmistakable desperation in his voice.

'Have you come to help fight this reprobate? He's a cheat, ya'know. I killed him,' he looked over at his opponent. 'I killed you,' he shouted before turning back to the boys.

'He's only come here to steal from me, but I shot him, and he won't die. He ain't having the treasure. I'm telling you now. I found it and no one is getting their hands on it, except me. I found it, it's mine, mine, I'm telling you,' he said as he poked himself in the chest with his index finger. 'He won't get past me and take my treasure, no chance. You've no chance, you hear me? Nooooo chance,' he shouted across. But the perpetrator seemed unmoved. He stood there, raised his hands, placed his thumbs on the side of his head and wiggled his fingers, mocking Mr Robertson. This incensed their teacher even further.

'Right, that's it, I'm not playing games anymore, I've had enough. I know. I'll lash him, see how he likes that,' he seemed to be having a conversation with himself.

The boys needed to intervene. This was ridiculous. What on earth was going on? They stood there frowning as their crazy teacher reached down and undid the belt from his trousers. As it slipped out of the last loop, he raised it above his head and charged at his opponent, but as he ran his trousers slid down. This did not deter him at all, and he carried on regardless. His opponent started pointing at him and laughing. Before long, Mr Robertson's trousers were around his ankles and he was now waddling forwards like a penguin, with his big white pants on show. Then he lost his balance and face-planted into the ground, with his opponent stood in front of him in hysterics. Austin stepped in to help.

'Hey, hey. Listen. How about we put him in jail for being a thief? Come with us and tell the police what happened and they'll lock him up for good. Then you could come back here and your treasure will be safe?'

The crazy man listened but would not take his eyes off his rival. His eyes were wide-open and unblinking. He must have taken something.

'Jail?' Mr Robertson said, as he stood and awkwardly pulled his trousers up before refastening the belt, without threading it through the loopholes.

'For how long?'

Austin could sense the eagerness to have his enemy locked up.

'Well, he's a thief, and he's after all your treasure. So long enough for you to move it to a new location, far away from here. And he would never ever find you,' Austin said.

Mr Robertson was staring right through him,

deep in thought.

'Forever?' He muttered and then started nodding. 'Yes, that would be lovely,' he agreed.

'Okay, well, come with me and we'll get it sorted,' Austin looked at Billy and nodded across to the fastachee.

'You grab him and I'll take Robbie,' Austin said.

'Yeah, okay mate,' Billy agreed.

'Who's Robbie? Are we picking him up on the way? He better not be a thief too, or I'll kill him,' Mr Robertson said as he wrung his hands.

Austin looked at Billy and rolled his eyes. Billy smiled and walked over to grab the other crazy fool in the jungle.

Austin grabbed the hibknib that was stood by the tree and Billy took the fastachee back to his own animal.

Austin jumped on and his teacher climbed up behind him.

'Hold on tight.'

As the man grabbed on to his waist, Austin gave the 'go' command. They took off at lightning speed, with Austin and a deranged Mr Robertson heading back to the village. Followed by Billy and his own crazy passenger.

Chapter 50
Rescuing Mr Robertson

The excitement was almost too much to bear. She knew what needed to be done, and when it was all over, she would wipe out the entire island. She had made assurances to the creatures that they would be spared, but that was not the case. Once she had the ring in her possession, she would destroy them and flee.

Clara looked around the cave that had been her home for the past three years. The enormous rug made of Korrigan fur, the warm fireplace, the bed in the far corner, which was made with bones from the creatures she had killed. It had served her well, but now she had to retrieve the treasure and leave.

She walked out of the cave and headed towards the assembled creatures awaiting the rallying cry before heading into the last battle. She made her way along the path and looked skywards. A full moon appeared in the otherwise clear sky. She smiled at the sight. I hope it doesn't bring out all those nasty creatures, she thought, raising her head and giving a devilish laugh to nobody but herself. Her army were around the corner and her smile was quickly replaced with an evil grin as she focused on the speech she was about to deliver to rally her troops before they went into battle for the last time.

******

'It's moving,' Sue shouted across to Terry, who was talking to Denzel. He turned and ran over to join Sue staring at the map. The gold 25M had disappeared from the map, along with the accompanying gold beam marking the location of the plant. A 75M symbol appeared next to the last target. Sue watched as the marker started counting down, 70M, 60M, 55M. Her heart was racing again. The boys were on their way back. They must have found Mr Robertson. Sue's attention turned towards a loud fizzing sound that came from the team making the catapults. Sue inhaled sharply as a gold dot appeared next to the campfire and increased in size as it started spinning. The fizzing noise continued as the light expanded, and with a flash of light, a plant with bright gold leaves appeared through the portal. The spinning portal slowly reduced back to a dot and with a quick flash, it vanished.

'That's 'ow they come 'ere,' said Terry.

Sue stood in silence as the teams continued to work with the plants and build their arsenal, before turning her attention back to the map. There were no more beams above the treetops or on the map. They must have picked the last plant. Sue turned towards the jungle and stood there waiting for the boys and Mr Robertson to return as a fizzing sound started behind her.

******

Austin jumped down and removed the last plant. Mr Robertson had calmed down now, although he was still going on about hiding his treasure and killing the thief if he came back. Austin had made sure that Billy stayed out of sight, he did not want to risk antagonising Mr Robertson. However, he needed to stay close enough so they could look after each other if anything happened. Austin placed the plant into the sack and watched as it vanished yet again. The light and the marker disappeared, just like all the other beams throughout the jungle. Austin climbed onto his hibknib and instructed Mr Robertson to hold on tight again. Then he looked over his shoulder, as if confirming they had completed the task. Daylight was now starting to fade and there were no signs of any beams. He already knew this, but wanted to double-check just in case. Austin only hoped they could find out what on earth had happened to Mr Robertson. Hopefully Denzel would know.

The boys both raised their hands, whipped the ropes down and hung on as their delusional teacher continued blabbing on about his invisible treasure.

Chapter 51
The Battle Plan

While Sue stood waiting for the boys to return from the jungle, Terry sat contemplating what lay ahead. When he first came to the island after finding out about the treasure, he knew he would be okay. He had the stone and could quickly disappear if needed. However, he was now having second thoughts about involving Billy and Austin. He had put them in massive danger without consulting them. He realised how selfish he had been in hijacking their school trip and bringing them here with no explanation. And now, what made matters worse, was Sue and Robbie were involved. They may have ended up here by pure bad luck, but it was still caused by his actions.

Terry knew it would be dangerous coming here, but he needed the ring. He needed to find it first, then it would all be worth it. However, his mind kept reflecting on everything. The shipwrecked pirates, the treasure being washed up on these shores, the Chimera, the dragon, Clara, and the monster in the cave. The plan to retrieve the ring should work, but if not, he had created a back-up that would kick-in and save the day.

Or so he hoped.

'Here they come,' Sue shouted over, disturbing him from his thoughts. Terry walked over and stood beside her. Austin was heading towards them, with Mr Robertson tucked in behind. Billy emerged seconds later causing Sue to sigh happily as she felt a smile creep across her face.

Austin and Billy both came to a stop in front of them. Mr Robertson jumped off and started mumbling something about the thief that needed locking up in jail because he tried stealing his treasure. Sue stood there looking flummoxed at what he was saying. Terry noticed and called Denzel over.

'Think you need to look at this crazy old git,' Terry explained, as he laughed.

'Blinkin' 'eck taste good did it my cocker?' He asked Mr Robertson.

'What?' He replied.

Denzel called over to Janji, who walked over, shook his head and led Mr Robertson into his hut, while Denzel explained to everyone.

'He's gonna be fine, just eaten somefin' in the jungle he shouldn't 'ave. Some plants make you go crazy for a short period. That's why we only wanted the ones we highlighted. Janji will sort 'im out. Bit of medicine and a little sleep and he'll be right on,' Denzel said.

The villagers led the fastachee away to another hut to receive the same treatment.

'Speakin' of eatin',' Denzel said.

Moments later, everyone was sat on logs around a campfire with a warm bowl of what looked like stew in front of them. Billy let his eyes wander around the fastachee tribe. There were a high number of them, but would it be enough to take on what their enemy would bring? Fearsome monsters, beasts and creatures that would all have the killer instinct. Billy couldn't help but think these guys would struggle to kill anything.

'Nice arm-guards,' Billy said, as he looked at Sue's latest addition.

'Oh, thanks, like the bow too?' She said as she picked it up from beside a log and passed it to him. He looked it up and down. She liked it when he rolled his thumb over the gold lettering of her name.

'Very snazzy,' he said, passing it back to her. 'Can I get one?'

'Can you fire a bow?' She asked, sounding keen.

'Nope, but I wouldn't mind giving it a go,' he explained.

'Well, I can show you if you like?'

'Yeah, when this is all over, we should go,' he

said, blushing.

'Yeah, I'd like that,' she said, joining him in blushing. 'I only hope we get out of this okay,' she said, as her face took on a worried expression.

'We'll be fine, everyone knows the plan and what they need to do. You'll see. It'll be okay,' he reassured her as he smiled. Although inside he was as worried and as scared as Sue.

'What's been going on here? You lot been busy,' Austin said through a mouthful of food as he pointed around the clearing with his spoon and sat beside Billy. Sue told them both about the plants, and the teleportation from the sacks via the portal. She told them all about the weapons and how they were prepared and manufactured for the battle. Her eyes lit up as she explained about the entire episode with the creation of the bow and her target practice. However, she did not tell them about her little secret. Nobody needed to be told. Sue had promised Terry she would not say a word, and she never broke a promise.

After eating, they discussed their plans for the impending confrontation. Clara knew Terry was back here with the stone so it would only be a matter of time. Darkness was fast approaching now and Janji was certain she would attack at night. He told them she had always planned on entering the cave when the monster left to feed. That would be the easiest time to retrieve the treasure.

They went through the battle plan. There would be several teams scattered around the clearing, positioned in such a way as to ensure the best execution of the plan. Janji felt the best thing to do was to pair everyone up in a buddy system. Billy and Sue would be in the team covering the right-hand side of the village. Mr Robertson and Austin would be with the group protecting the left-hand side, and Janji would guard Terry at the bottom of the village. Terry had the stone and that was what they were coming for. They must protect him and keep him deep inside the village and out of sight for as long as possible. Janji hoped this would lure them in and once there, the ambush would begin. It was a bold plan, but one that everybody agreed with and understood.

Janji walked into his hut and returned a few moments later with a very weary looking Mr Robertson. Thankfully, he was now back to his old self and not the crazy person he was two hours ago.

'What happened to me?' He asked as he rubbed his head and inspected his torn trousers.

'You fell and banged your head again, that's all,' Billy said.

Everyone smiled at his sharp thinking. They did not need Mr Robertson having a panic attack, not right now.

Austin and Terry sat down next to him and explained the plan, as he took some fluid and food onboard. He nodded as they covered every aspect of the impending battle.

The crackling of the fire and the chatting around the village clearing was interrupted by a loud shriek in the distance. Howling sounds penetrated the air and entered the clearing. Denzel looked at Terry. Their panicked expressions said it all.

They're coming.

Chapter 52
The Decoy

They remained silent, but alert, as they waited for their visitors to come and invade. The campfire, surrounded by the seats they had been sat on moments before, continued to burn away. The odd crackle and hiss joined the howling creatures that were now fast approaching. Billy and Sue were together on one side, with Mr Robertson and Austin positioned opposite them.

'Everything will be okay. As long as we can reduce their numbers, Terry can finish it with the stone,' Billy assured Sue.

Sue turned and smiled. However, her growing panic was not because of the battle ahead, it was because of what Terry had tasked her with if things did not go as planned.

Suddenly, the noise grew louder and the trees around the top of the village started rustling. Seconds later, an army of vicious creatures came bursting through and landed in the middle of the clearing. Sue covered her mouth to suppress the scream that threatened to explode. They began snarling and growling as they searched the clearing. A group at the front all had one huge horn positioned in the centre of their foreheads. They were covered in brown slime that dribbled onto the floor as they prowled around, turning one way and then the other. Several hairy beasts, with long swaying tails started sniffing around the fire pit and licking the discarded bowls of food. Their four eyes were darting around and making sure nobody went for their food. And then there were the giant frog like creatures. Green in colour with eight arms and four sets of eyes. They had a scaly texture and as they hissed their long lizard-like tongues reached out three feet in front of them. Saliva was dripping from their mouths, snot was running from their noses, and their eyes were wide as they looked around for anything to kill.

The creatures all searched around with purpose, eager to find what they were looking for. In their excitement, they even started attacking each other. Their boisterous behaviour came to an abrupt halt as a loud roar exploded overhead, followed by the sound of flapping wings. Even though there was a large fire in the middle of the village, there was soon a chill in the air, as an enormous shadow descended from above. The huge dragon only just managed to land, and as it did, they saw their adversary standing proudly on top of the beast. She held a chain in one hand, which was wrapped around the dragon's neck, and the staff she held in the other was resting on its back.

Sue felt her grip around the bow increase as she reached up and drew an arrow from her quiver. She loaded it into the arrow-rest and pulled the nock of it into the nocking point on the string, just as she had earlier in the day. The fletchings at the rear of the arrow were a still purple colour. She took two deep breaths as she began to focus, with the arrow loaded but pointing at the ground. Her heart continued racing, her palms were sweating, and her breathing was deeper than she would have liked, but she was ready. Sue took one final breath, raised her bow, and looked down the shaft of the arrow. Then, as she took aim and pulled the string back, the purple fletchings started to glow.

******

Clara heard the creatures roaring and growling as they searched the village and caught herself smiling. They would soon have the stone. She pulled on the chain, causing the dragon to bellow as it descended into the village. She stood tall on the back of the beast, her usual intimidating and formidable stance during an attack. The dragon extended its wings to their full span as it prepared to land. Clara jumped off and surveyed the area she had visited so many times before.

There was a large fire burning away in the centre, with huge logs spaced around it. Bowls, spoons and cups lay scattered all around. Food that would have been sat in the bowls before she arrived, now lay on the ground in front of the logs. She looked up and switched her gaze towards the huts. Each one looked the same. No lights, no sign of life, and no movement. There were some sheets, and items of clothing leading from one of the huts into the jungle. Clara followed the trail and spotted a piece of material that had caught on a tree branch and had been left hanging there. She took a look around the rest of the village. Apart from the fire crackling away and the odd growl from her army, there was not a single sound.

The village was empty.

******

They watched them all enter. Everyone was ready. As soon as they heard the growls approaching and knew they were on the way, they had taken up their positions. The villagers had moved the weapons, ammunition, and animals earlier in the day, to prepare for the battle. The tribe gutted the huts, all lights were extinguished, and belongings moved. Terry could not believe how efficient the villagers had been. It was as if they had a new lease of life since he had turned up with the stone, as if they knew this was a chance they had not had before. The stone would save their village.

Terry lay there in his hiding place as the creatures burst through the jungle and started growling at nothing but a large campfire. They started turning one way and then the other, looking for something, anything to attack. But apart from the empty dishes they had strategically placed around the fire before leaving, there was nothing there. The scene of the abandoned bowls, cups and spoons would make it look like they had not been expecting company. That was all part of their strategy. Janji had planned it all meticulously. Everything had to look as if they were unprepared, and that they had abandoned the village in a hurry, leading Clara into a false sense of security. But that was not the case. They were more prepared than she would think possible.

Her dragon descended into the village, and she dismounted instantly. She stood there looking around, trying to understand what was going on. First she studied the fire, discarded cups, bowls and food. She then turned her attention to the empty, silent huts but, apart from a few cleverly placed items strewn around, there was nothing for her to find. Terry remembered how he had laughed when he hung a small sheet on a tree on the opposite side of the clearing, giving a false impression of their escape route.

He watched as she turned to the creatures stood behind her.

'They won't have gone far. Just look at this place,' she bent down and inspected the food spilt on the floor. It was still warm. 'This is fresh. The fire is still lit, and they've even dropped bedding, clothing and food as they left, giving us an obvious sign of where they've gone.' Clara said, pointing to the trail leading into the jungle.

'You,' she said pointing to the Kaxons, Tebilisks, and Graklors. 'Hunt them down and find him. He's the only one I need. Sinka, you go too. Follow the trail. They must have gone through there,' she said gesturing towards the sheet hanging on the bush.

The Chimera roared and led the way. Once half of the creatures had disappeared along the decoy route into the jungle, something glowing to the left caught Terry's eye. He looked over and took a deep breath as he noticed the purple fletchings start to glow and pulse.

Here we go, he thought, just as Sue released the arrow.

Chapter 53
The Ambush Begins

Austin watched it all unfold in front of him, just as Janji had planned it. The carefully placed trail showing a path out of the village had given the creatures a false idea of their route. The bowls, filled with the last of the warm food that had been bubbling away on the fire, lay on the floor. Janji had even placed fresh logs on the fire as everyone took up their hiding positions. Everything worked a treat. Clara had sent half of her army away into the jungle, making things a little easier. Mr Robertson gave Austin a nudge and nodded to the opposite side of the village. Through the trees, he saw the faint glow of purple.

'Come on Sue, you got this,' he muttered. He picked up one of the balls lying in a pile next to his elbow and loaded it into his catapult. As Austin pulled it back and took aim, a blue glow surrounded the ball and the twine on the catapult began to pulse gold. Just like Sue, he was ready.

The purple glow from the arrow became brighter as Sue released it, sending the arrow towards the army of creatures standing around the fire. There were still so many of them, but that was about to change. Austin gasped at the magic as it unfolded.

******

Sue released the arrow, and it shot through the trees. As it did, she could not believe what she was seeing. Sparks flew from the arrow and there was a flash of purple as it multiplied. Soon four arrows headed unerringly towards the mass of creatures gathered in the middle of the village. None of them had time to react. All four arrows hit a target and the creatures fell instantly. Dead. Four down. They were already winning. The other creatures stood there, stunned. What was that? Clara spun to see who had fired the arrows, but there was no one there. Billy had grabbed Sue as soon as it connected with the creatures and dragged her to their secondary position.

Austin released his ball, as did Mr Robertson. Both projectiles flew through the air and exploded amongst the creatures, filling the area with a thick blue smoke that rendered them temporarily blind. The smoke did not dissipate, it was clinging to the creatures. They started growling and turning to try and escape the blue smog. Another arrow appeared, from the top of the clearing this time. One of the fastachees had copied Sue and was just as accurate as she had been. The arrow multiplied once again. Another four hits, another four enemies lying dead. Clara ran. The ambush had taken her by surprise and she had no choice but to flee. Sue looked over. She could not see Clara, but she had a perfect sight of the dragon. In one movement, she removed an arrow from her quiver, loaded her bow and sent it on its way. Four arrows approached the beast, but it was already airborne. The arrows all missed.

'Damn,' Sue cried, before being dragged away again by Billy. They couldn't stand still. They had to move, shoot, move, shoot and move again. That was the plan. The thick blue smoke lifted, and the creatures had full sight of the clearing once again. They looked for their leader, but she had fled, leaving them to deal with their attackers on their own. The creatures did not give up, they split up, and began searching the village, while others headed into the jungle. Austin and Mr Robertson loaded their catapults. Austin shot his to the left, Mr Robertson sent one flying to the right. Smoke billowed around the clearing. Billy picked up a coconut lying next to him. He had spotted several creatures scurrying past the fire and launched it. The coconut landed in the middle of a gaggle of beasts. Sue looked at him, frowning.

'Your aim is rubbish,' she said. Seconds later,

the coconut started glowing bright red and then, Boom, it exploded, sending red dye everywhere, covering the creatures. A pocket of red smoke circled their heads, before wrapping around them like a helmet. The creatures started turning around and shaking their heads, but the helmets didn't move.

'Is it?' Billy asked, smiling. 'Now, finish them.'

Sue loaded another arrow and sent it straight at the group, swiftly followed by another. They multiplied and hit their targets, another eight casualties. She turned and smiled at Billy, but he wasn't looking at her, he was already heading towards another position. The creatures were getting annihilated, their numbers dwindling faster and faster. The huge number of creatures that entered the village had been massively reduced due to the well-planned ambush. Several of them lay lifeless around the village. Austin caught himself smiling, they were going to win. But then there came a roar from inside the jungle. Moments later, the creatures that had left the village earlier returned, led by Sinka. They did not stand around stunned like the others, but attacked the villagers straight away. A fastachee flew through the air and smacked against a tree; dead before he hit the ground. They launched another onto the fire and set him alight, another casualty within seconds. The army of creatures were fighting back. They would not take this lying down. One-by-one the fastachees fell. Austin and Mr Robertson were firing off as many balls as they could, but the smoke was making no difference. In fact, it was now starting to make the battle harder. The creatures were using it as camouflage, hiding deep inside as they crept unseen towards the villagers, before lunging and taking their prey.

Terry was watching it all unfold. There was nothing he could do. He was under strict instructions to stay out of the way. The village was now a battle zone for both parties, so he would find it hard to single out the creatures as they moved quickly from target-to-target.

Mr Robertson grabbed hold of Austin and started dragging him away. They had to escape. The villagers numbers were reducing at a rapid rate. Billy was now ahead of Sue, throwing the fruit bombs, but he was too far away from any targets to make an impact. The fruit was exploding and dissipating in the air. Janji was running around and trying to provide support where it was most needed. He knew they were fighting a losing battle, but he continued to fight hard. Sinka then took three villagers out in one foul swoop, the lion's mouth swallowed one whole, the serpent lurched forwards and crushed another's head as the goat skewered a third with his black horns. There were over 100 villagers when the battle began and now barely 40 remained. The creatures had the survivors surrounded. Janji was at the front, leading by example, protecting his tribe who had put up a tremendous fight, but it was almost over. Mr Robertson and Austin could not get back to their ammunition. Sue had no arrows remaining and was too far away from the secondary position to make a run for it.

Sinka stood at the front of the creatures and started edging towards Janji, who was standing firm. The serpent hissed and the lion growled as it slowly crept forwards. It was about to strike, when there came a roar from overhead.

Clara had returned. She had not fled the scene after all. It was she who had brought the other monsters and Sinka back. Everyone watched as the dragon lowered itself back into the decimated village. Sue, Billy, Austin and Mr Robertson all stood at the back, looking dejected. It was over.

'We gotta protect Terry, no matter what,' Austin whispered.

'Too right,' Billy replied.

'Let's be realistic. We all know he can't survive this, no matter how hard we try,' Mr Robertson said.

Clara dismounted, walked over and stood by Sinka, placing her hand on the top of the lion's head.

'So, where is he?' She asked, looking around

the group as she continued stroking his head like he was a cat. No one answered.

'The goblin is the only one I want. He has the stone. The rest of you can go on your way once I have him.'

'You ain't having him, we ain't giving him up. We will fight till the end,' Austin screamed. She looked at him with utter amazement and started laughing.

'My dear boy, do you think you have a chance?' She tapped Sinka on the head, giving him the signal. The serpent lashed out and grabbed Austin by the throat, holding him a few inches from Clara's face.

'Now, you can either give the little creep up and save yourself, or you can continue to defy me and Sinka here will crush you. Nice and slow, right in front of your friends. And once you're lying dead on the floor, I'll grab another of you and do the same. How does that sound?'

Austin's eyes were full of fear, but he did not say a word. Clara let out a sigh.

'Well? I'm waiting.'

'Stop! Leave him alone,' screamed Billy, distracting Clara for a split second.

'Oh, don't worry. If he doesn't provide me with the information. I'll make sure you're next,' she said, before turning back to Austin.

'Okay, I'm going to count. If I get to three, then

you will never hear another sound. Fair enough?'

The serpent increased the pressure, causing Austin to gasp.

'Yes, I think so too,' Clara added. 'Okay, one... two...thr—'

'Stooooop.'

Clara looked across as Terry came out from behind a hut at the back of the village with the stone gripped in his left hand. Sinka dropped Austin immediately. He started gasping as his hands reached for his throat and he started coughing.

'Terry, what are you doing?' screamed Billy. 'You can't do this, we agreed.'

Terry looked at him.

'I can't let you boys come to any harm. This is all my fault. Enough is enough. It's over,' he said, before turning back to Clara.

'Okay. If you want this 'ere stone, it's yours. On two conditions,' he went on.

Clara stared at him for a moment, thinking.

'And why should I agree to any conditions? I can just take it if I want it,' she replied.

'Because my ansum, I can make this 'ere stone disappear if I want, will be no good to me or you then. If you is goin' kill us I will make it disappear, forever. So two conditions, or no one gets the treasure. Tis your choice.'

Clara continued to stare. He might bluffing, but

she was not prepared to take a chance now she had come this far.

'Okay. What conditions?'

Terry breathed a sigh of relief. His bluff had worked.

'Ansum. First, promise that no harm comes to these 'ere villagers, or my friends. I don't care if you 'ave to take me, but you have to make sure they is left alone and you get 'em all back 'ome.'

'Are you saying you want me to leave these cretins alone, but I still get to kill you?' She frowned, as if she couldn't understand the reasoning behind his crazy demand.

'Yep, you got it my ansum. Maybe you ain't so stupid after all,' he said, smiling.

'No. She has to leave you alone too, Terry,' said Mr Robertson. 'We're not leaving without you.'

Terry looked at him and gave a warm smile.

'I'll be fine,' he replied as he winked.

'And the second condition?' Asked Clara.

'Release 'er, now,' he said, pointing to the rear of the dragon.

'Who?' Clara asked.

'You know very well who. She's on the back of that over-sized chicken,' he said nodding at the dragon.

Clara stood, hands on hips, frowning.

'And that's all you want?' She confirmed.

'If you want this 'ere stone,' he said holding it

out to her, 'that's all you have to do and tis yours,' Terry added.

Clara shouted over her shoulder.

'Bring her out.'

There was some movement around the back of the dragon and seconds later, Jeremy appeared from the rear of the beast, holding a long pole. The other end of it was fastened around the neck of the prisoner. Clara untied her feet and hands and released her. Janji ran for her with his arms raised and swept her up in his arms. She flung her arms around him and lay there loosely. As Janji walked back past Terry, he stood there for a few seconds and nodded up and down.

'You're welcome, my ansum,' Terry said, smiling.

Janji turned and disappeared into his hut with his daughter held tightly and safely in his arms.

'Okay. Hand it over. I'm bored with this whole charade now,' Clara said.

Terry looked at the stone and then into the eyes of those gathered around him. He had loved having the stone; the fun, the games, the memories, but there was nothing he could do now. It would soon be hers. As soon as he placed it in her hands, she would have the power.

Clara walked towards him and held her hand out.

'I'm sorry my ansums, I didn't mean for any of

this to 'appen,' he said, sullenly looking around the group. They all looked downbeat. This was the end. There was nothing more any of them could do.

'Give,' she demanded.

Terry reached out and placed the stone in her hand. She smiled and started rubbing it between her fingers. She finally had it. She had won and would now complete Professor Thomas's mission. He would be so proud.

Everyone watched as she closed her eyes, took a deep breath, and threw the stone into the air. It landed with a dull thud in the earth. They all waited for the spinning to start, but nothing happened. Her smile faded as she looked at the motionless, colourless stone lying on the ground.

'What's the matter with it? Why is it not spinning. It's meant to spin, why is it not spinning?' She glared in Terry's direction.

'ave you not 'ad your magical Weetabix this mornin' my ansum?' He said as he chuckled.

The others looked at it. What was going on? Clara walked over, picked it up and tried again. Still nothing. She screamed, walked over, picked it up and frowned at it.

'Might 'ave it the wrong way round. Turn it over, might work a bit better,' Terry said.

Everyone watched as she turned the stone over, the anger in her face exploded and she went bright red. If this was a cartoon, there would be steam coming out of her ears right now.

'What is this? Where is the stone?'

'Well, the stone is in your hands, can't you see it? You asked me for the stone, so I gave it to you. Is that not what you wanted? First you want the stone, then you don't want it, make your blinkin' mind up,' he struggled to not burst out laughing.

Everyone gathered did not understand what was going on. The creatures all growled and edged forwards, ready to pounce if needed. Clara raised her head skywards and screamed.

'Aaaaarrrrgggghhhh. That's it, you had your chance. Your friends will pay,' she said, looking at Billy and Austin. Then she stopped and started looking around.

'Wait, where's the girl?' Clara said, looking around the village.

'What girl?' Terry asked, sounding like he had no idea what she was going on about.

'The girl. Where's the girl?'

Terry started frowning and scratching his head.

'No idea what you is on about. You is the only girl 'ere. Huh, unless you are on about Austin. He acts like a girl sometimes. Honestly, you sh—'

'Shut-up!' Clara screamed at Terry.

'The girl. She has the stone. Quick, find the girl. Find the girl!' She screamed at the clueless creatures stood behind her.

They turned to move, but they did not know which way she had gone. Clara threw the stone on the floor and ran to her dragon. The stone landed right in front of Austin and Mr Robertson, who both read the single word scratched into it, *'Gotcha'*. Billy wasn't looking at the stone, his eyes were darting around, and he began panicking as he realised who Clara had been talking about.

Sue was gone.

Chapter 54
Sue's Mission

Sue took off as soon as she felt the stone land in her pocket. That was the sign Terry told her to wait for, the sign to run and escape. He came up with the idea while they were creating the bows.

'I don't know, Terry. I'm not sure I'm brave enough,' Sue had said.

'Yes you are, my ansum. I trust you more than anyone else. You 'ave to do it. If we end up in trouble and get cornered, wait for the signal and go. Don't wait, just go. You must run as soon as you feel it. Sneak behind the huts, and when you're clear, run. Don't let anyone see you, don't tell anyone about this, and don't freeze. I have total faith. I'll buy you as much time as I can, but you must keep runnin' and head for the cave. Don't stop until you get there,' Terry said.

'But how will I know which way to go? It'll be dark,' she was panicking at the task she was being entrusted with, but also pleased that he had such faith in her.

Terry shook his head and started tutting.

'Ave you not learnt anyfin' today?' He said.

Sue stood there, deep in thought and as it came to her, she smiled. Terry nodded and smiled back.

'Precisely.'

So, when the battle ended, Sue made sure to position herself away from everyone, including Billy. She had to be on her own for it to work. Once the serpent grabbed Austin, Billy's attention switched to his best friend, giving Sue the perfect opportunity to make a break for it, unnoticed. As she felt it land in her pocket, Sue dropped to the floor and commando-crawled behind the huts. She heard Billy screaming and pleading for the Chimera to let Austin go. Next, Terry was there, giving himself up and bargaining for the stone to buy her time. That was the last thing she heard. She snuck past the village, jumped to her feet and ran, faster than she ever had before. This was all on her now. Sue needed to be braver than ever. The adrenaline was coursing through her veins, giving her a massive rush.

She kept running into the darkness. The only light was coming from the full moon hanging high above her in the clear evening sky. Her heart raced and her eyes were wide open as she kept moving through the jungle at pace. One false slip and it could be over. She had to be careful. Her eyes were darting from side-to-side, looking for a sign that she was going the right way. Her heart was pounding as the panic increased. There was nothing there. Where was it? Had she gone the wrong way? Please god, no, she thought. And then, she saw it, up ahead, reaching high above the treetops. Her pace increased, and she smiled at the sight of the red beam. A location marker appeared beside it and started counting down. She had 80m to go.

Sue headed towards the marker as fast as her legs would take her.

******

The creatures were on the hunt. They did not know which way Sue had gone, but they had to find her. She was the one they needed now. Their focus had switched from the goblin. She had the stone. The darkness made the search even more difficult for the gaggle of creatures trampling through the dense jungle and thick bushes.They searched everywhere, listening for any sounds that might lead them to her. Seconds later, there was rustling and movement behind them as Sinka burst through the trees and took charge.

'The cave. She's heading for the cave. Follow me,'

The Chimera headed straight towards the cave entrance up ahead. He bounded over logs as if they were nothing and led the creatures through the jungle with renewed energy. The army of monsters had one goal – to find the schoolgirl who was running to the treasure with the magical stone clasped tightly in her hand.

******

Sue was now fast approaching the target, she only had 30m left. Suddenly there were scurrying noises behind and to the right. She gasped and took a quick look but saw nothing. She re-focused on the red beam. Could she get there in time? Growling sounds soon joined the scurrying noises. The creatures were close, but so was the red beam, just 25m, almost within touching distance. The threatening, animalistic roar of the monsters on her tail were getting closer, but Sue kept moving. She was trying to make as little noise as possible while also covering the ground in front of her with purpose. Suddenly, she tripped and fell over, trapping her foot under a log. She started panicking, but turned her foot sideways, pulled it free, and re-checked the marker. She kept moving, 20m, 18m, almost there, 15m. Come on, come on. The flapping of wings could be heard overhead, followed by a loud shriek. Sue glanced up. The dragon was back and had joined the creatures on the ground that were looking for her. Just 12m to the beam and beyond that, the entrance to the cave, marked by the second target. A glowing white curtain. Terry had told her the plan from start to finish. This was another reason he chose her over the boys. She actually listened and would remember every single detail. Only 8m left now. She was tantalisingly close, but so were the creatures. Their breath! Sue was sure she could feel their hot, smelly breath right behind her! Was she imagining it? A shudder travelled down her spine as she realised it was not her imagination, something was literally breathing down her neck. Just 4m to go!

And then, as the dragon expelled a ball of fire in her direction, something grabbed her from behind and immediately covered her mouth. Sue couldn't look around or escape. The scream that wanted to explode from her mouth remained stuck in her throat. Whatever was behind her had caught her and there was nothing she could do. She had failed, just like she told Terry she would. Why had he trusted her? The creature hauled Sue to the ground, and was soon on top of her, pushing her into the cold, damp earth. This was how she would die, smothered to death and eaten, by whatever had her in its clutches.

And then, the grip around Sue's mouth loosened, allowing her to turn her head to the side and see her assailant. Her eyes widened, as the cover inside the beam was pulled over their heads, hiding them from the creatures, and the dragon who were all baying for her blood.

Chapter 55
Someone Else Is Missing

'What have you done?' Austin asked, clearly unimpressed. 'You've put Sue in danger! Anything could happen to her. I can't believe how stupid you are.'

Terry did not say a word. He waited for Austin to finish ranting. It would be useless trying to reason with him whilst he was in this emotional state.

Austin finally stopped and stood there panting away.

'Finished?' Asked Terry. 'She is goin' be fine, I trust 'er more than I trust you lot. She's strong, determined and will get it done. I saw it in her eyes when I challenged her wiv the arrows earlier. I 'ave put fings in place to make sure we protect her, so don't go worryin' you 'lil girl,' he chuckled.

'This is not a time for laughing, Terry, This is not funny,' Austin seethed.

'No, I agree, this situation is not funny, but the

way you is actin' is,' Terry raised his hands and danced around as he mimicked Austin in a silly voice. '*Oh no, a 'lil girl is braver than me, oh dear what is I goin' do. Maybe when I get 'ome mummy will give me a big cuddle,*' he shook his head, at Austin, insinuating he was over-reacting to the situation.

'Look, she is goin' be fine, 'tis all goin' work out. Trust me,' he added.

Before Austin could reply, Mr Robertson stepped in.

'So, what's the plan?'

'I got an idea,' said Terry. He looked over at the thirty or so creatures that remained in the village. Some were growling in their direction with saliva running from their mouths. They wanted to kill them, but they were not to attack anyone. Clara had given them clear instructions to only watch Terry and his allies - for now. She could not risk Terry being injured, or worse, being killed, before she had the treasure. He looked over at them and smiled.

'All right my lovers. Fancy a cup o' tea do 'e? No? Fair enough you moody buggers,' he then chuckled as he turned back to Austin and Mr Robertson. However, there was something wrong, something that worried him, but he couldn't put his finger on it. As he told them all about what he had done, and the next part of the plan, he realised what the problem was. Terry stopped talking and froze. His face dropped as he looked around the village. Someone else was missing.

'Oh, bugger,' he muttered.

******

Sue lay under the cover of the freshly dug ditch and the camouflage sheeting, as the creatures continued to hunt for her. Once they were a safe distance away, she turned her head to the side.

'What on earth are you doing here?' `She asked.

'I couldn't let you come here on your own. It's too dangerous. As soon as I knew what had happened I took-off, aimlessly at first, but then the red beam was there and the marker showed you were 40-meters away, so I ran faster. As long as the beam was in the air, I knew I had a chance. Then I spotted you just before you fell and realised I could catch up with you,' Billy explained.

Sue smiled. Knowing that he had risked himself to save her made her like him even more. Billy smiled back and poked his head out of their cover. The coast was clear, so he threw it back and they both breathed a sigh of relief as they looked around and gulped in the fresh air.

'So, why are you doing this?' He asked.

'It was Terry's idea. He said he had a plan in case things went wrong and that I was the one who could execute it,' she said.

371

'So Terry put you in this position?' Billy said, sounding annoyed.

'No, it was my choice. He told me the plan but if I didn't want to do it, I didn't have to. The plan sounded dangerous and scary, but he promised me everything would be okay and things had been put in place in case I got into trouble.'

'What things? Asked Billy, sounding dubious.

'I don't know. He just told me that all I had to do was concentrate on getting away from the village and then run. He said the stone would look after me until I returned,' Sue said, sounding unsure.

'I can't believe he put you in this position. I'll kill him!' Billy said through gritted teeth.

'No, you don't understand. I wanted to do it, I wanted to help. This was my choice, not Terry's,' she said. 'Mine.'

'But, why? I don't understand.'

'Because I do nothing fun, or dangerous, or scary, or important. Look at you and Austin, and what you did in the woods when you first met Terry. You both made tough choices, didn't you? Because you thought it was for the best? Well, that's all I done. I felt this was for the best, so I had to do it. You know what I mean?'

Billy stared at the ground. He was angry, but he understood. The only reason he was so mad was because he felt that Terry had put Sue in grave danger, but she was right. It was her decision.

As they sat there, they both looked up into the sky. The dragon was heading away from them as the howling from the creatures faded into the distance. They both breathed a huge sigh of relief and relaxed.

Then it came. A thunderous, ground shaking roar, rose out of the gloomy cave and headed straight towards them like a warning cry. After a few seconds, and even before the first roar had disappeared, another followed, even louder this time. Billy grabbed Sue by the arm, pulled her down, and brought the sheeting over both of them, again.

'Don't move,' Billy whispered.

Sue lay there, motionless, holding her breath.

The ground shook again, and the sound of heavy, monstrous feet came echoing over their heads. Whatever it was, was on its way out. Billy felt Sue shaking and pulled her towards him. As they lay there, watching, a pair of huge nostrils emerged from the cave entrance twenty meters away. Sue grabbed onto Billy's arm so tightly, it felt like she was cutting off his blood supply. Billy pulled her closer and tried not to move as he quietly told Sue to 'shush.' Air flowed in and out of the beast's flaring nostrils, enjoying the smell of fresh air, just as Billy and Sue had moments before. His long thick nose emerged from the cave and then the children saw his big round dinosaur-like yellow eyes for the first time. It took a deep breath and roared again. A powerful blast of air exploded through the jungle causing the trees to shake, as saliva splattered all around Billy and Sue, giving the feeling that it had started raining. The mouth contained hundreds of long, razor-sharp teeth. They looked like those of a Tyrannosaurus Rex. Billy felt himself shudder as he imagined being grabbed by them, before feeling the full force of their pressure as it snapped you in two.

The ground shook again as the enormous beast advanced out of the cave. The vicious gnarling mouth was attached to a long thick neck that reminded Sue of the giraffes she liked to pet on safari in South Africa, but she was not too keen about petting this beast.

The children waited for it to exit the cave, but what they saw next almost made both of them scream.

What was this thing?

******

There she was, down below, running through the jungle as if her life depended on it. She kept glancing behind to check for the creatures that were hot on her trail. Clara was about to descend and strike, when she saw someone chasing the girl down - a boy. This was perfect, she would use him as bait to get the stone. Suddenly, the girl slipped and fell to the ground. For a moment it looked like she was trapped, but then she climbed back to her feet and continued moving forwards. Clara switched her gaze to the creatures. They were covering the ground so quickly and would be on them in the next few seconds. Sinka was at the front, jumping logs and creating a path through the jungle for the others to follow as they swallowed up the ground in front of them. They almost had them. The stone would be in her possession within minutes. In her excitement Clara yanked the chain wrapped around the dragon's neck. It responded by roaring and expelling a ball of fire. She smiled as she turned back to watch the girl and her boyfriend, but she couldn't see them. She frantically looked around, but they were gone. They had both disappeared, like some sort of magic trick. She screamed with anger before flying over the top of the cave and landing her dragon while she waited for Sinka and the rest of the creatures to appear.

******

'Yes master,' Sinka confirmed.

Clara sent her dragon off, high into the sky, and instructed a few of the creatures to head further away from the cave and start growling, howling, and shrieking. She wanted them to create as much chaos and noise as possible to make the children think they were still searching for them. The creatures were frightened. They knew the monster would eat them once it exited the cave and spotted them, but they could not disobey her command. Perhaps they could find some cover out there?

Suddenly, a cry exploded from the cave. Clara froze. She knew it was coming, but it still made her feel uneasy.

'Quick. Over there. A sniff of us and he will come,' she said, pointing to a large overgrown area down a gully. They reached it and tucked in as tight as they could, covering themselves with any undergrowth they could find. Another cry came, louder this time, followed by the sound of thunderous footsteps. The monster was leaving the cave. Clara, who was normally so cold and calculated, became nervous. Not because of the monster, but because this was it. She knew that once it had taken flight, the children would emerge from wherever they were hiding and run inside to recover the ring, and when they came back out, she would pounce.

As Clara lay there, hiding, and thinking over her plan, a ferocious-looking head appeared from around the corner of the cave and as it did, she felt the biggest smile creep across her face.

Chapter 56
The Hydra

Billy and Sue could not believe what they were looking at. As the long neck emerged from the cave, they heard another roar, but this one was not from the mouth of the monster, it came from behind it. It seemed there was another monster in the cave. Seconds later, an identical head appeared from behind the first one. Just like the first head, its nostrils were flaring as it took in the fresh air. The monsters looked at each other, exhaled, turned and bellowed into the jungle, causing the treetops to shake even more violently than before. Once again, saliva flew towards Billy and Sue, soaking through their cover and dripping onto them. Sue almost squealed, but Billy sensed this just in time and put his hand over her mouth.

As the gigantic body slid out from the cave, Billy realised they were wrong. There were not two monsters in the cave, but one monster with two heads. Its thick necks joined together at the top of the body. Billy took a sharp breath as he watched it edge towards them. This enormous beast stood half-in, half-out of the cave. It turned and roared, causing Sue to grab Billy's arm even tighter.

The monster stomped out and stood at the mouth of the cave containing the treasure. To Billy and Sue's astonishment, another two heads began unfurling themselves from either side of the body. Four identical stone-grey heads were now sweeping the area in front of them. Billy could swear one set of beady eyes were staring right at him. Sue had buried her head deep into Billy's chest, so she did not have to look into its piercing yellow eyes. The monster snorted, expelling a slimy-snotty substance, which drenched the surrounding area. The eight tree-sized legs then marched forwards, revealing the last part of the monster - a huge 20-foot-long tail which swayed from side-to-side. The monster came to a stop in front of the jungle and gave one final almighty scream. Sue quickly reached for her ears as the ground shook violently. Billy reached up and grabbed their cover to stop it blowing away. The colossal beast stood there for a few seconds, as if allowing them to take it all in.

Four dragon-like heads, complete with long razor-sharp teeth, atop long thick necks were all attached to its enormous dinosaur-shaped body.

Large spiky fins ran down each of its necks and met at the top of its back before joining at the centre and tracking down to the tip of its tail. It walked towards the edge of the jungle stretched out in front of it, roared again and unfurled a pair of gigantic, purple wings. The wings began flapping and within seconds it was airborne, off in search of its nightly feed. Billy and Sue were transfixed. It almost seemed magical. The Hydra glided through the air with the full moon glistening on the crystal clear water in the distance. Another ear-splitting shriek shook both of them.

'Right, let's go,' said Billy, as he threw the cover back, stood and helped Sue to her feet.

'The clock is ticking,' he said.

'Then we better get going,' Sue said, as she pulled the stone out of her pocket and headed towards the entrance of the cave.

******

Clara, Sinka, and the remaining creatures watched the monster emerge from the safety of their hiding spot. Like every other creature on the island, Clara had always remained hidden at night. Legend told that if the monster saw you, he would hunt you down and strike. There was no chance of escape. However, she had no choice now. She had to take the risk and hope she could remain hidden until the monster was far enough away for her to come out. She would follow the children, track them down, and take what was hers.

The sight of its four heads and enormous body stunned Clara. She watched as it screamed before unfolding its huge wings and taking to the skies.

'Let's go,' she demanded as she set off to get her hands on the stone and the ring at long last.

******

He watched it all unfold from inside the jungle. Billy and Sue reached the cave entrance first. He watched their reaction change from fear to relief as soon as they saw the surprise awaiting them and ran into the cave. Moments later, he saw Clara and her small army emerge from around the corner and stop at the cave entrance. His eyes narrowed as he watched her. Was she going to enter? Was she as brave as two school children? He wasn't sure so he stayed there, hiding and waiting to see how this would pan out. When the time was right, he would attack. A smile crept across his face as he edged back into the darkness, hiding from sight once again. Then he settled down on a log and watched. His time would come, and he couldn't wait.

Chapter 57
Austin's Plan

Austin moved across to Terry and bent down to do his shoelace up.

'Here, Terry?' He whispered.

'Yes, my ansum?'

'Where's the secondary stash of ammunition?' Austin whispered, keeping his eyes on the creatures.

'Same place we put it earlier, not that we can get to it though, not wiv this lot watching us like hawks.'

'We still got the sacks from earlier?' Austin asked.

'Yeah, behind the huts. Why?'

'Did you take the spells off of them,' Austin was still watching the creatures and pretending to do his shoelace up. He changed feet to avoid suspicion.

'Oh bugger. No I didn't,' Terry said, putting his head in his hands. Austin smiled.

'At last, you've done something right,' he said, looking around the clearing.

'Why, what the blinkin' 'eck are you thinkin'?' Terry asked, sounding dubious.

'I need a distraction. I have a plan,' Austin said. 'Do whatever you have to do to get their attention. Create a scene, cause a fight, dance, anything. As long as you all stay in this area for a few minutes, it will be fine. Then I need you all situated over there,' Austin said, throwing his eyes towards the cold camp-fires. Terry looked concerned but said nothing.

'This is your chance to redeem yourself for bringing us here and putting us in danger,' Austin said, smiling.

Terry was unsure, but they had to do something.

'You sure you know what you 'is doin'?' Asked a worried-looking Terry.

'Positive. Distract them and it'll be fine. I'll be back before you know it,' Austin didn't wait for an answer.

Before Terry knew it, Austin was rolling around on the floor, screaming in pain and clutching his belly. Mr Robertson looked across and came running over, oblivious to what was going on.

'Austin, what is it? What's wrong?' He said as he knelt down beside him. All the creatures looked over at the boy wriggling around on the floor.

'Aaahhhhhhh, my belly, aaahhhhhh. It hurts so

much,' he continued screaming. 'I'm going to be sick.'

Terry twigged immediately.

Austin tried standing up, but fell to the floor again as he continued screaming in pain.

'Quick, take him in there put 'im on the bed and grab him some water, see if that 'elps,' Terry said, pointing to the hut near the sacks.

Mr Robertson picked Austin up and started walking towards the hut. The creatures all started growling and edging forwards.

'And what on earth are you lot going to do, eh? The boy is sick. I'm going to lie him down, and make sure he's okay. You wanna eat us then be my guest, but I don't think your master will be too pleased, do you?'

Without waiting, he disappeared through the curtain entrance to the hut. The creatures all stayed where they were, watching as the curtain settled again, hiding the teacher and his pupil inside.

******

'Okay, what are you doing?' Asked Mr Robertson as he put Austin down on the bed. 'I know there's nothing wrong. I've seen this too many times from you,' he said, before walking towards the entrance and peeking out. The creatures were still watching, but thankfully they weren't coming over to investigate.

'Sir, you need to trust me. I have a plan but need a diversion. You and Terry need to do whatever you can to cause a scene. Once you have done that you need to move everyone over to where we made the weapons earlier,' Austin explained. 'But you need to do it now. We don't have time to waste.'

Mr Robertson stood there, listening, before nodding up and down. He didn't even question Austin.

'Okay, well, feast your eyes on this. I'll await my Oscar,' he then winked and turned to exit.

'Sir?' said Austin.

The teacher turned to him.

'You know, you're alright to be honest.'

'Yeah, I suppose you're okay too... for the class clown. Be careful,' Mr Robertson then created the scene that would allow Austin to escape and do whatever he had planned.

Chapter 58
Austin Escapes

Billy and Sue raced to the cave's entrance. The white glow covering it, which had disappeared momentarily when the monster emerged, was now back. They stood there, not sure if they wanted to go inside or not, but knowing there was no other choice if they wanted to get home. It looked so gloomy and scary, how were they going to work their way through it? As they looked nervously at each other, the white curtain peeled away from the entrance and fell to the ground, covering the cave floor in a bright glow. Suddenly, big white arrows appeared along the wall, identifying their route.

'Clever little Knocker,' Billy muttered, before they both entered the now bright cave and followed the path that would take them to the long-lost treasure of Kaninjanga.

******

As the Hydra flew into the distance, Clara made her way towards the cave entrance, with Sinka following behind. She crept forwards, carefully measuring each footstep to ensure she made as little noise as possible. After a few minutes she reached the trees separating the cave from the jungle and then edged around them. Sinka was given the signal to stay back, as Clara eased forwards and positioned herself behind the final tree. With her hands holding onto the bark, she inched her way around it. She looked across to her right and noticed a green sheet that had been abandoned, half-in, half-out of a freshly dug ditch that was just big enough for two young schoolchildren. The sight of it made Clara smile. So that's how they hid! They must be in the cave. All she had to do was be patient for a little while longer and it would be hers. She motioned for Sinka to get the others ready. He nodded and headed back, as she waited for the treasure to come to her.

******

As Mr Robertson exited the hut, Austin rose from the bed. Seconds later he heard commotion and shouting outside. He allowed himself a smile at what he heard, and then got back to the task at hand. He loosened part of the cloth sheeting at the back of the hut, just enough to allow him to slide underneath. Once outside he looked both ways to ensure the coast was clear. The noise from the other side of the hut was increasing. Raised voices and shouting confirmed that the diversion was well underway, exactly as Austin had asked. He crawled to the edge of the hut and saw the sacks lying there. He reached out a hand, grabbed them and pulled them towards him. Just then he heard growling from the other side of the hut. He hoped that the ruse had not been uncovered. Before heading off, he took a peek at the chaos unfolding in the village. The sight he saw made him realise the diversion was going well. Mr Robertson was kneeling on the floor with Terry's left arm wrapped around his neck in a headlock. The Knocker was then using his right hand to drag his knuckles across the top of the teacher's head. Austin almost burst out laughing. A look at the creatures confirmed they didn't have a clue what was going on. Their eyes were trained on the would-be fighters. They were turning from side-to-side, growling at the teacher and the Knocker as they continued to brawl.

'Get off me you stupid little goblin,' Mr Robertson screamed as he tried to prize Terry's arm from around his neck.

'Cummon my ansum, you want a piece of me, let's go for it,' Terry said, playing his part, too. The sacks rustling under Austin reminded him he needed to hurry. He crawled behind the huts and headed towards the path on his left. Once he was clear from the village, he got to his feet and ran as fast as he could along the path. After a few minutes he burst through two trees on his right, and there they were, munching away. The hibknibs. Austin placed the sacks on one of their backs, jumped on, and seconds later he was flying through the Jungle at high speed. The creature headed straight towards the stash of emergency weapons that the villagers had made earlier, while Terry was running around trying to give Mr Robertson a wedgie.

Chapter 59
Into The Cave

'This way. Keep following the arrows,' said Sue.

Billy was a few steps back, keeping an eye out for anybody approaching from behind. The cave was so cramped. It was a surprise the monster could even fit down there. What struck Billy was the sheer complexity of the network of tunnels. They seemed to intertwine and crossover each other. They would never have found the treasure without a little help. Billy was sure they were going around in circles, as it felt like they were continually passing the same intersections. However, they followed the glowing and pulsing arrows hanging on the walls, confident they knew the way.

Ahead of him, Sue was on a mission. She had taken charge and seemed determined to find the treasure and get out of the cave as quick as possible. Soon a potent smell of fish filled his nostrils. In front of him, Sue brought her hand up to her nose. She obviously smelt it too, although her pace never wavered.

'This stench is getting ridiculous. We need to get out of here, quick,' said Sue.

Billy didn't respond. He was too busy holding his breath as best he could. The lights guided them around a bend to the left, but then they came to a dead-end.

'Oh brilliant! Where on earth do we go now?' He asked.

Sue let out a sigh and put her head in her hands.

Just then, an arrow slid down and pointed at the bottom of the adjoining wall. The light from the arrow uncovered a gap underneath the rock in front of them. It was only just big enough to crawl through, but there was nowhere else to go. The eagerness Sue had displayed until this point had vanished. She wasn't sure about this. Billy stepped in front and looked at her.

'I'll go first and let you know what's on the other side, okay?'

Before she could reply, he had lowered onto his belly and crawled into the gap. It was hard going but he managed to squeeze through. As he pulled himself along, a faint orange light appeared, as if welcoming him into the space. Another helping hand from Terry?

'Can you see anything?' Asked a very nervous Sue.

'Almost there,' Billy answered, as he shuffled

along. Moments later, he reached the entrance. One more pull forwards and he was through.

'You gotta see this,' he shouted back to her.

'What is it? What's in there?'

'Just get in here, but be careful when you crawl through.'

Sue copied Billy in lowering onto her belly and crawling through the gap. The floor was cold and wet. However, she was not paying attention. The orange light was welcoming her, as if pulling her towards it. Once she reached the end of the tunnel, a hand appeared in front of her face, and she looked up into Billy's eyes. As she grabbed his hand, he helped her to her feet. She looked up and let out a gasp.

'Not what we were expecting, eh?' Asked Billy, but Sue didn't say a word as her eyes danced around the space they had crawled into.

******

After Mr Robertson left the hut, he made a bee-line straight for Terry. He needed to start the distraction that would allow Austin to complete whatever task he had planned.

'Oi, what have you been saying about me, you over-sized frog,' he shouted at Terry. 'Austin just said you've been shouting your mouth off about me. So what drivel have you been spouting from that stupid goblin mouth of yours?' Mr Robertson said as he started rolling his sleeves up.

Terry looked shocked, he didn't know what was going on, but then he saw the wink and knew this was the distraction Austin needed. *Best make this look real*, he thought.

'What you fink I 'ave been sayin', said you woz nuffin but a big bully. Way you talk to them children is disgustin' ya gaet 'oaf. You 'umans is all stupid, but I gotta admit, for a teacher, you is the stupidest one I 'ave ever met. If you wanna make somfin' of it, then come 'ere my ansum,' Terry raised his hands and started bouncing up and down like a boxer.

The creatures stood looking from one to the other, confused about what was going on, and not sure what to do as the teacher and the Knocker started attacking each other.

As Mr Robertson reached him, Terry dropped to the floor, grabbed hold of Mr Robertson's right leg and started biting it. The teacher screamed, not a play-acting type scream, but a proper, full-on, get off me scream, as he felt Terry's teeth sink into his skin. He bent down to pull Terry off, however as quick as a flash, Terry let go of his ankle, stood up and grabbed the teacher around the neck and started knuckle dragging the top of his head. Mr Robertson reached for Terry's hands to prise them off as he started gasping for breath, but Terry hung on tight.

'Yeah, 'ow do you like them apples my ansum,' he said.

The teacher was not beaten yet. He reached around and grabbed for the top of Terry's trousers. Once he had a good handful, he pulled them up as hard as he could. Everyone heard the material rip as they were yanked up his butt-crack.

'Ooohh,' screamed Terry and his eyes widened. He released the teacher from his choke hold so he could prevent his trousers from disappearing up his bum like some awful magic trick. Mr Robertson's hands instantly went to his throat as he began gasping for breath. Once he had recovered, (and Terry had re-arranged himself) he started towards the Knocker again. The diversion they were creating had now turned into a backstreet brawl. The face-off continued, while they walked around, looking for the best time to attack. The villagers and the creatures all stood there, watching in disbelief at what was happening. Nobody had a clue what this was really about, but they would soon find out.

They continued to move around, as if weighing up the best time to launch a new attack, when Mr Robertson gave a slight nod to Terry, and they both stopped moving. They were positioned exactly where Austin had asked them to be. All the pair of them had to do now was wait, and maybe, fight a little bit more.

Chapter 60
The Fight

As they stood inside the cave, Sue and Billy could not believe what they were looking at. On the right-hand side, piled 10-feet high, lay a pile of old bones.

'Must be from its victims,' Billy said as he pointed towards them. Sue nodded up and down as her eyes continued wandering around the cave, looking from wall-to-wall. She noticed there was no other entrance, not that she could see. So how did the monster get in here? And if it was living somewhere else, where did those skeletons come from? As Billy headed towards the bone collection, Sue made her way down the left-hand side. The far end was pitch black and although she had no idea why, she was suddenly drawn to it. Maybe there was another way in down there? As she approached, the foul smell of rotten fish filled her nostrils once again, and then she stepped in something squishy. The stench seemed to rise up and punch her square on the nose. She looked down and could just make out the carcass of a dead animal. When her eyes focused and she saw what it was, it almost made her throw up. It was the half-eaten head of a killer whale and its one remaining eye was looking straight at her. Sue panicked, turned, and slipped in the putrid guts she was standing in. She almost fell but managed to get some purchase on the ground and ran straight to Billy, flinging her arms around him.

'Oh my god, this is definitely his cave. Either that or there is something else down here,' she mumbled into his chest.

Billy gave her a quick comforting hug and then pulled her away from him.

'Look. He's not back yet, but we need to hurry up and get out of here. Okay? The treasure has to be on the other side of these bones.'

Sue calmed herself down. Billy was right. After taking a few deep breaths, she got a grip of herself and re-focused. Suddenly, her thoughts were distracted by the sound of running water.

'Listen!' She said, extending her finger upward.

'What?'

'You hear that?' Sue asked, her eyes darting around. 'Water. You know what that means?'

'What?'

'Well, where's the only source of water you've seen on this island?' Billy thought for a moment.

'The sea?' It sounded more like a question than an answer when he said it.

'Correct. And if there is water above us, that means?'

He thought for a moment and then his eyes became almost as wide as the cave itself.

'This cave reaches under the sea.'

'Either that or very close to it,' Sue said.

'We better hurry then.'

'Don't panic. I'm sure we'll be okay. This island has been here for hundreds of years,' she said.

Billy's attention was drawn back to the bones. In life they would have given the body shape, and allowed it to move. Now they lay lifeless, on the floor of the dark, cold cave. The faint orange glow projected onto them was coming from whatever was on the other side.

'That has to be coming from the treasure,' he said.

'Well, let's go get it then,' Sue replied.

Billy made his way over. The smell of rotting fish was still there, but it seemed to be easing, either that or they were getting used to it. All they had to deal with now were a pile of old bones. He reached the front of them and took a deep breath. There was nothing to worry about, as long as he could keep moving forward and not think about where they were. He lifted his right foot and placed it on top of the bones. They instantly started shifting and moving, and he had to move his feet quickly to ensure he didn't land on top of them. It reminded Billy of trips to his local beach, where he had to walk over stones to get to the sea. They would shift and move around as he stood on them. On occasions, he had been so eager to get across them to splash in the waves he had ended up falling over, much to the amusement of his father.

After sorting his feet out, Billy started moving forwards again. Sue was right behind him. Although neither of them said a word, they were concentrating on the task in hand. They could not see how far back the bones stretched, but they were progressing over the treacherous surface quicker then Sue thought possible. Many of the bones slipped and fell to the bottom of the pile, but they both kept moving. The orange glow seemed to increase as they edged themselves closer. The sound of running water was still there, although Billy thought it had stopped for the moment as all he could hear was the crunch of broken bones under their feet.

Billy looked behind to check on Sue.

'You okay?' He asked.

Sue looked at him and smiled.

'Fine, you hanging in there princess?' She joked. Now fully recovered from standing in the dead wales guts.

'Oh, you're so funny,' he said, smiling at her. He turned back around and noticed that the glow was increasing, which gave him more impetus.

Billy was almost at the top of the pile of bones and looked up. He noticed the cave curved around to the left, about three metres in front of him. A quick glance to his right confirmed the water was still trickling down the wall and disappearing under the mass of bones, but he couldn't worry about that now. He kept moving, as did Sue, but then he stopped. Something landed on his shoulder, and as he glanced sideways, he saw what it was, a skeletal hand – the remains of a human hand to be precise. A shiver ran down his spine. He froze as the hand moved down the length of his shoulder and started to roll down his arm just as the sound of a growling voice filled his ears.

******

Austin saw the weapon stash up ahead. He only hoped that the others had done what he had asked. This was their only chance to help Billy and Sue, and if it didn't work, they were in deep trouble. But with so many creatures prowling around, and far fewer villagers left, he had to try something to reduce the numbers.

The hibknib arrived at the covered ammunition and came to an abrupt halt. Austin was out of the saddle and kneeling down with all four sacks open as soon as he had stopped. He pulled the sheet back that was covering the weapons. This was their secondary attack position, but they hadn't had the chance to draw the enemy here as it turned out. Luckily, the ammunition was still here and intact. Austin gave a sigh of relief, took a deep breath, and got to work.

He wasted no time at all in grabbing the first lot of weapons. Austin had to be quick, but he also needed to put them in the right sacks, or they would disappear forever. First up was the purple sack, he knelt down beside the arrows and shoved a handful in the bag. He closed his eyes as he placed them inside, hoping this would work. After a few seconds, he opened his eyes. The sack was empty, apart from the purple smoke billowing from it. Austin allowed himself a brief smile, and then moved as fast as he could with the others. He picked up another handful of arrows and shoved them into the sack. They disappeared with a pop as they were transported back to the village. He grabbed another handful and repeated the process, more popping as they vanished.

Once Austin had sent the last of the arrows, he flung the purple sack to one side, and in the same movement, grabbed the red sack and packed the fruit as fast as he could. Austin wiped the sweat from his brow as he continued to replenish the village with essential ammunition. All the fruit and arrows had gone, but he had not finished his task yet. He was feeling tired, and needed water. His mouth was so dry, but he couldn't worry about that now. The last two sacks were the easiest. Austin grabbed the balls of powder and shovelled them into the blue sack with ease, handful after handful went in. Soon only the catapults remained.

Austin loaded them two at a time and sent them back, ready for the second battle of the day. He looked around to make sure he had collected everything. This was too important and he didn't want to leave anything behind. Once he confirmed nothing was left, he jumped on his hibknib, raised the rope, and gave the 'go' command. They took off at high-speed and headed through the jungle to catch up with the weapons that were flying back to the village in the battle for Kaninjanga.

Austin was travelling so fast that he didn't even hear the Hydra as it exited the cave and set out on its nightly feed.

******

Terry started growling as Mr Robertson goaded him.

'I thought you Knockers were talented fighters, but you're all talk. My three-year-old niece is tougher than you.'

Terry began growling at him.

'I mean who brings two 14-year-old boys to complete their work? Oh, not forgetting a 14-year-old girl too,' Mr Robertson added with a smile.

Terry was getting wound up now. Mr Robertson was fighting dirty. Well, two could play that game. Terry smiled as he prepared to land his own punches.

'Well, ain't you the clever clogs. I wouldn't say too much if I were you though, we all knows your 'lil secret,' said Terry.

'What do you mean?' Asked Mr Robertson.

'I mean, didn't want that drink earlier diddee and we all know why, don't we?'

The pair of them stood, motionless, but ready to attack when the time was right.

'What do you mean?' Asked Mr Robertson. Still unsure what Terry was chirping on about.

'Well, put it this way my ansum. You didn't want to show your wildest dreams, not in front of Billy, anyway! Tell me, 'ow long as you liked 'is mum?'

Mr Robertson stopped rocking and stood straight. All eyes were fixed on the bickering couple.

'What did you say?' He growled at the Knocker.

'I know you went to school wiv Billy's parents and you and his mum dated for a bit before Frank Gibson came along and took her off your hands. I mean, she needed a proper man, so you 'ad no chance diddee' my cocker?' Terry stood there laughing.

Mr Robertson didn't wait for another word to tumble out of his mouth, he balled his hands into fists, screamed and charged at him.

Ding-Ding! Round two.

The teacher hit Terry and they started rolling around on the floor again. Everyone watching was so confused about what was going on, as the pair of them continued to brawl. They rolled around on the floor like they were trying to kill each other, and then it happened. Terry tapped Mr Robertson on the shoulder.

'Look.'

But Mr Robertson was not paying attention, he was kneeling over the Knocker and trying to wrap his hands around his throat. Leaving Terry with no choice. He brought his foot up and caught Mr Robertson in a very delicate area. As the teacher rolled off him, moaning, Terry scrambled forwards, grabbed a glowing ball in front of him and threw it toward the creatures, followed by another one. They both exploded on impact and covered the creatures in blue powder, causing them to growl, but they could see nothing. They were turning one way and then the other. Mr Robertson regained his focus and grabbed a coconut sat in front of him. He launched it into the same area that Terry had sent the balls. Popping sounds filled the air as ammunition appeared as if by magic. The villagers saw what was happening and ran over to join them. The coconut Mr Robertson launched seconds earlier landed amongst the disorientated group and as it ruptured, its contents wrapped around the heads of the creatures, rendering them blind. The monsters had been taken by surprise, but those that remained soon got their bearings and started fighting back. However, they were up against it because the villagers had a new lease of life thanks to the weapons that had appeared, popping and fizzing, before their very eyes. They grabbed the catapults and loaded them with fruit and blue balls of powder. Several of them picked up arrows that were lying on the floor, but with no bows, they could not fire them. However, this did not prove a problem. The fastachees pulled them back and threw them as hard as they could like javelins. The arrows flew through the air and as before, they multiplied, into pairs this time, and searched out their targets, striking them with unerring accuracy and killing them immediately. These creatures had come into their village and taken it as their own, but it was not theirs. The fastachees fought as if their lives depended on it. Janji led from the front, picking up arrow after arrow, each one sent on its way, multiplying and piercing straight through the hearts of these vile beings. Coconuts, dates, kiwis, avocados and more were picked up and launched at the intruders. No sooner had a projectile been launched then another would follow soon after. The creatures continued to battle back, one had snuck up behind them and took a fastachee in its mouth. He was dead before he hit the tree the creature had flung him against. Janji turned and sent three arrows in its direction, and seconds later the creature joined its victim lying lifeless on the floor. The evil beasts had lost control of the situation. They were beaten and withdrew from the village, growling and showing their teeth, but they knew they had lost. More ammunition was thrown and fired as the villagers continued to attack the retreating enemy. The war was not over, but they had won this battle, and they would be ready if they ever came back.

As the villagers started celebrating and hugging each other, Mr Robertson and Terry stood in the middle of the clearing staring at each other.

'Oops' said Terry and started laughing. Mr Robertson didn't look too pleased with the Knocker, not now that he knew his deepest secret.

Chapter 61
The Treasure

Once Billy's heart finally stopped trying to jump out of his chest, he turned around.

'You idiot,' he said to Sue, who was in hysterics behind him.

'My God. Your reaction was so funny,' she said, and waved the skeleton arm at Billy.

'Hello, my name is Captain Boney, how do-you-do, do you need the toilet, or have you just been?' She said in a silly voice.

'You need help,' he said, as he shook his head.

He turned back around and continued forwards. Sue threw the lifeless arm down and followed him.

They continued climbing the mountain of bones and as they reached the top, the orange glow intensified. Billy placed his hand on the cold, damp wall and edged himself around the corner, closely followed by Sue. The cause of the orange glow immediately became clear. Sue let out a gasp and moved with more purpose. She caught up with Billy and they both stood, staring into the small alcove of the cave. Billy turned towards Sue and they smiled in unison. They made their way down the other side and headed towards the treasure that had been hidden for more than 300 years.

******

The Hydra finished feasting on its seven whales and began the return journey back to the cave. As it soared high above the jungle, it noticed movement down below. There were two creatures running through the jungle, so the monster let out an ear-piercing scream.

The Hydra watched as they started darting around looking for somewhere safe to hide, but it was too late, they were already dead. It swooped down and realised there were not two creatures, but a group that were running together, frantically looking for a way out. Some tried to camouflage themselves in the bushes, while others attempted to flee, but they would get nowhere. The monster landed with a thud and went straight to work. Within seconds all four heads were busy crushing bodies and ripping them to pieces. Some put up a good fight, while others died instantly. Screams and shrieks filled the jungle as they were all slaughtered. Seconds later the monster took to the skies again, leaving a pile of warm dead creatures lying in the middle of the jungle. They had not been killed for food, but for fun. Blood dripped from all four mouths as the Hydra let out another cry and headed home.

******

Austin was working his way through the jungle at a pace. Up ahead he saw a plume of blue smoke, followed by shouting and screaming. Faint growls came drifting through the jungle to meet him, followed by the unmistakable sound of more explosions. He pulled the ropes around the hibknibs neck and brought them down as hard as he could, dropped his head low, and dug his heels in as the animal increased its speed. Austin moved through the terrain as fast as the creature would take him. The battle had begun and he needed to get back and help the village. Little did he know, they would not need him. He had already done his bit in the battle for Kaninjanga.

******

Clara sat waiting. Where were they? What were they doing? They should have found it by now. It had been 25 minutes already. She looked over at Sinka who was waiting for the signal to advance, with his serpent head swaying expectantly above him. She heard what sounded like faint screaming coming from the village. An icy shiver ran down her spine. Had the creatures got bored and attacked them? They were under strict instructions not to attack. She needed the goblin alive until she had the ring and the stone. Only then could they kill him, not before. While she was wondering what was going on in the village, more screaming came from the other side of the jungle, near the water. She flicked her head to the left. Oh no, this was not good. Clara ran, pointing at Sinka to move. They made it back to the other creatures and hid, just as the flapping of wings could be heard approaching.

******

Billy and Sue stood with their mouths open as their orange faces looked down on the mass of items in front of them. They'd found it. The treasure, which had been hidden for over 300 years, was shining away. The golden glow of it made them both feel warm and cosy in the cold, wet cave. Billy looked at Sue.

'What?' She said.

'How are we meant to find the ring? We can't take all of this and the ring is the only item we need,' he said.

Sue looked around. Billy was right. The treasure consisted of golden swords, shields, cups, goblets, coins, helmets, ornaments, and countless rings. To the left of the pile lay three enormous broken chests. The discarded lids lay to one side.

'How do you think they were broken?' Sue

asked.

Billy turned around and pointed towards the skeleton bones behind them.

'Explorers who didn't quite make it out I expect,' he suggested.

The children stood there trying to think how to tackle the monstrous task in front of them, when Sue felt her pocket become very warm. She put her hand in and pulled out the stone, which started glowing and floated up into the air. The children watched as it made its way over to the treasure and hovered just above it. Sue gasped as the stone started spinning and the glowing increased. Within seconds the treasure started shifting and moving around, filling the cave with clattering noises as a hole was formed in the middle. Billy glanced at Sue who had a big smile on her face as she watched it all unfold. He turned his attention back to the treasure just as something started to emerge. An item in the shape of a horseshoe rose from the hole. It sat six inches above everything else and began spinning and glowing. The stone made its way back over to Sue, followed by the spinning horseshoe. Sue held her hands out as the stone approached and it landed in her palms. The horseshoe made its way over to Billy, who also had his hands held out, and caught it. The ring looked like it was made of wood, but it had the weight of something far more substantial.

Sue returned the now cold stone to her pocket and they both looked at the item in Billy's hands.

'This can't be the ring, surely?' He said, but as he turned it around he saw something that made them both realise this was the sacred ring. Inscribed on the back were words they both immediately recognized, *Quod Occultatum Regno*.

Billy looked at Sue and smiled.

'The Hidden Kingdom. This is it,' he said.

Sue smiled and nodded in agreement. They'd found it.

'Right, let's get out of here,' Sue said and made a move towards the exit. As they stepped back onto the bones, they heard a noise which terrified them. From around the corner came ominous growling and the sound of thunderous feet that made the ground shake. They dropped to the floor and hid as best they could amongst the bones. Seconds later, the cave filled with a deafening scream and the strongest smell of fish engulfed the children.

The Hydra was home.

Chapter 62
Unexpected Help

Austin reached the edge of the village and saw them all jumping around and hugging each other. He smiled as he noticed there were no creatures anywhere, except those lying dead on the floor. It had worked. He entered the village, climbed off the hibknib, and headed for Terry and Mr Robertson. They stopped talking when Austin arrived, beaming from ear-to-ear. Terry looked up at him.

'You is some clever, my ansum, not to mention brave. Where's that 'lil scaredy-cat I first met in the woods?' He said and winked. Austin smiled.

'Thanks, Terry,' he said before turning his attention to Mr Robertson who seemed tense.

'You okay, sir?' Austin asked.

'Umm, yes, I'm fine. Well done young man. I'm very proud of you,' he said.

Austin smiled once again. He could get used to this.

'Anyway, what's the plan?' He asked.

Terry sat them down and explained everything, including how he had told Sue about his back-up plan if they lost the battle, and that he needed her to carry it out. She had taken some convincing, but he had managed it. Then he had used the stone to prepare the cave so that the task was as easy as possible for Sue. Invisible direction arrows had been positioned along the wall which would appear and glow to show her the route to the treasure when the time was right. Terry explained all about the ditch and the red beam that would appear and guide her, the same beam they used earlier. She would not be in any danger if she moved quickly. After he finished telling them everything he waited.

'We need to go. Clara will be after them, so we need to get moving.'

A scream from the distance interrupted the conversation. The villagers all started panicking and ran for their huts as quick as they could. The others followed them, and as another scream echoed through the jungle they hid from sight. Austin got down on his belly and crawled over to the doorway to take a sneak at what it was. The fastachees were motioning for him to hide, but he took no notice. In the distance, flying through the sky, he saw a massive monster. There was something strange about it and as he focused harder, he realised what it was - it had four heads, which were all looking in different directions. At that moment, another scream echoed and the monster descended into the jungle. Austin turned to the others.

'We ain't goin' anywhere yet my ansum, they is goin' 'ave to deal with this by themselves,' said Terry.

Austin stood up and looked at the Knocker.

'But we have to help them. We can't abandon them. They're my friends!' Austin screamed. 'They're my only friends!' The cracking in his voice showed he was close to tears.

'Austin, we will help them, but not yet. If we're spotted, we're dead, do you understand that?' Mr Robertson said, trying to bring a sense of realism to the conversation. Austin looked at him and nodded, before dropping his gaze to the floor.

'Yes, sir,' he said.

'We will go, but not yet.'

Austin brought his gaze up, and the steely look in his eyes let them know this conversation was not over.

'As long as I'm careful, he won't spot me,' said Austin. Mr Robertson frowned at him.

'What do you mean?' He asked.

'You lot stay here. I'm going to help my friends,' Austin added.

Before anyone could do anything to stop him, Austin had turned and exited the hut. Mr

Robertson reached for him, but it was no use. Austin had gone.

******

Billy and Sue held their breath as they crouched behind the pile of old bones. The Hydra was growling and snorting as it ambled around on the other side of the cave. They could hear its ferocious heads sweeping from side-to-side.

'How on earth did he get in here?' Asked Sue, the quiver in her voice showing how scared she was.

'There must be another entrance. The tunnels down here lead everywhere, so who knows where it came from,' whispered Billy. 'The problem now is, how on earth are we going to get out of here?'

Grunting noises started coming from the Hydra as it settled down, hopefully to have a sleep after feeding. Billy slowly stood and started to move forwards.

'What are you doing?' Sue whispered anxiously.

'I'm just going to check something.'

As he took one pace forward, the sound of sniffing crept towards him. He quickly dropped back down as a huge head appeared from around the corner. A set of flaring nostrils sniffed the old dead bones Billy and Sue were trying to hide behind. The monstrous beast had picked up something that did not smell right and one of its four heads had decided to have a look. As they lay

414

there trying to figure out an escape route, Sue felt her pocket become warm again. She reached in and removed the stone, it jumped from her hand and dived into the bones.

'No!' Sue almost screamed and tried to grab it, but it was too late, it was gone. Another head emerged from around the corner, the nostrils were once again flaring in and out, snorting as it picked up the same scent. The heads moved even closer and continued sniffing. It would see them in seconds. They couldn't move any further forwards without disturbing the bones, which would have confirmed the monster's suspicions. Billy grabbed hold of Sue. This was the end. He could do nothing to save them so he pulled her in tight and let her bury her head into his chest. His beating heart brought her some comfort in their final moments. They both closed their eyes as Billy pulled Sue in tighter. Then, just as the creatures heads crept closer, Billy felt something fly over his head. It passed so close that it caused his hair to ruffle. It was quickly followed by another and then another. What was happening? Seconds later, the sound of clattering could be heard as the bones in front of them started shifting and moving around. Another sound, this time from the Hydra. The two heads nearest the children growled and screamed. As the huge monster expelled the air from its lungs, the stench of fish surrounding them made

Sue feel nauseous. Billy let go of her and they both slowly peered over the top of the bones. What had happened? The huge mountain of bones had vastly reduced. More swooshing was coming from behind now. Helmets, swords, shields were all floating up from the treasure and flying over their heads. Another flew so close to Sue that it made her hair swirl around her face. She brushed it back and looked at Billy. His shocked look matched hers. There was another scream as the bones continued to shift and move in the air. The pile in front of them was now almost non-existent. They had all been put to good use. The Hydra filled its lungs again and roared once more. Billy and Sue did not have long, but they might just have enough time to escape. Stood between them and the Hydra was an army of skeletons, all prepared to fight with the swords and shields that had floated over the children's heads from the treasure. One skeleton turned to face the children as he pointed his sword at the gap which they had used to enter the cave earlier.

'Go! Save the ring!' He growled.

Then he turned back to face the monster, and raised his sword, ready to battle and help them escape.

Billy did not check on Sue. He rose, grabbed her hand, and ran for the exit, as the stone jumped up and landed back in her pocket.

Chapter 63
The Escape

Austin was panting hard. He kept looking straight ahead, but occasionally glanced around to ensure he was not being chased. The noise up ahead had stopped. The battle must be over, which meant only one thing. The monster was heading back home. Soon he would have to hide, but he had to get as close to the cave as possible before then. Austin was getting tired. His breathing was heavy, his speed was decreasing, and there was sweat on his brow. He started thinking that maybe he should have grabbed a hibknib, but it was too late for that now. Then he saw something up ahead that gave him fresh impetus. He put his head down and pushed on. The tiredness he felt was forgotten as he sprinted towards the red beam rising high into the black sky above. According to the floating marker next to it, he was only 60 metres away. *Come on Austin, you can do this*, he thought as he moved his tired, aching legs as fast as they would take him.

Sue reached the opening first and wasted no time in dropping to her belly. The ground was uncomfortable, but she didn't care about her knees scraping on it or her head banging against the rock above her. She had to get out fast so that Billy could follow. She was panting and could feel the ground slicing her skin, especially at the speed she was moving. But that didn't matter, she gritted her teeth and pushed on as quick as she could.

As Billy waited for Sue to crawl through the gap, he crouched low and watched the battle. The skeletons were putting up a good fight, several were piercing the Hydra's belly with their swords, others were trying to sever the tail, and groups of three were attacking each head. The Hydra let out a scream as one sword went right through one of its neck and came out the other side. It swept a head in the skeleton's direction. It connected and sent the bones flying towards the wall. They smashed against the hard surface and once again became a pile of old lifeless bones. Another head swept across the cave, creating another pile of bones. Sue screamed, startling Billy into action. He dropped to his knees and started to enter the gap. A sudden roar from behind made him look back. One head had spotted him and the menacing look on its face confirmed it was not pleased. It growled and attacked. Billy quickly slid into the gap, pulling his legs in just as the monster smashed against the rock above him. He felt the snort from the monster's nostrils blow up his trouser leg. The rock wobbled and Billy thought he was about to be crushed, but he wasn't. The skeletons behind were keeping the monster at bay, allowing Billy to pull himself forwards. He could hear the crack in the rock above his head as it worked its way towards him. The narrow gap would soon collapse. Just then, there was another smash against the rock above his head and he felt it shift even more than the first time. He definitely didn't have long. As he pulled himself the last of the way he felt the skin covering his kneecap tear on a sharp rock. He winced but continued moving. He tried pulling his legs out, but his trousers got caught. At that moment, there was another crash as the rock above his head was hit again by the furious Hydra trying to break through. The splitting sound filled his ears as he frantically tried to free his trapped leg. The rocks around them began to crumble. Billy yanked his leg as hard as he could, tearing his trousers and screaming in pain as he sliced his shin. Sue had a handful of his clothes and was pulling him before he was crushed. He dragged his legs free just as the rock finally split in two and came crashing down. Billy had made it, but only just.

'Go!' Billy screamed, getting to his feet. Sue did not need asking twice, she was off at high-speed, following the glowing arrows on the walls. Their direction had magically changed and they were now highlighting their escape route. Sue looked back. Billy was right behind her and catching up. She put her head down and ran. Another scream filled the cave, but the Hydra would not catch them... not yet anyway.

As Billy came shoulder to shoulder with Sue, they rounded a corner together and there it was - the entrance and their chance to escape. As they ran for it, they smiled, but the smiles soon faded and they came to an abrupt stop. It was not over yet. A gaggle of creatures stood there with Sinka positioned at the front, his serpent head raised high, hissing and swaying from side-to-side, as the lion was being stroked like it was a pet cat.

Clara was waiting for them.

******

He continued to watch, hidden under the cover of the jungle. There was no danger of the monster spotting him, or Clara, or even the children. The screaming and the growling of the Hydra had disappeared. There was nothing but the gentle wind blowing through the trees of the jungle. Then there came screaming from deep inside the cave, an angry roar that once again made the ground shake. Were they going to make it out, or had they been attacked and killed? The jungle was in total darkness, all except for the light offered by the full moon high above.

There was nobody else around until a few minutes ago when Austin arrived. Clara had only just darted back around the corner to hide when he appeared and dived into the ditch and pulled the sheeting over his head. Seconds later, the Hydra had landed and headed into the cave. Then Clara reappeared with her small army. Their numbers had dwindled to almost nothing, but she was so close to what she wanted now that it didn't matter. The serpent raised its ugly head and started swaying as she patted the lion head. A few minutes later Billy and Sue were on their way out. Billy was holding something in his hand - the ring!

Until this moment, the trees and bushes had offered him camouflage, keeping him hidden from everyone. He had waited patiently and now here they all were. He had done as asked and waited until this moment. The instructions had been easy to follow. 'Hide and watch. When the time is right, you must strike. Protect the ring.' He had been eager to get involved and now he emerged from the shadows, ready to attack.

It was time to battle for the sacred ring.

Chapter 64
The Final Battle

Austin waited. He had reached the ditch located inside the red beam and pulled the cover over him seconds before the monster landed and entered the cave. As he lay there catching his breath, he heard rustling and movement to the left. He peered out and there was Clara, with Sinka and the other creatures following close behind. Austin couldn't help but smile as he saw how pathetic her army looked now. They had come to the village in huge numbers, but only a handful remained. He watched as they all lined up in front of the entrance. Billy and Sue must be inside searching for the ring.

The musky smell of the earth was now starting to make Austin feel sick and he needed to get out. He eased the sheet back and suddenly froze. His eyes widened, his mouth went dry, and he couldn't speak. A pair of eyes were staring right at him. It was as if they had pinned him against the cold, wet ground.

******

As they walked out of the cave, Clara held her hand out to them.

'Give!' She demanded.

'Give what?' Billy asked.

'Well, how about you give me that,' she said pointing to the ring in Billy's hand. 'And you...' she said as she switched her attention to Sue.

'...can hand over the stone,' Clara added.

She held her right hand out in front of Billy and her left hand out in front of Sue with a triumphant look on her face.

'Now give! Both of you!' She demanded.

They looked at each other. They hadn't been through all of this to just hand the ring and the stone over now. Billy tried to sneak a peek around, looking for reinforcements, but Clara noticed and laughed.

'Oh, the others are all gone. You're the only ones left. So hand them over and I may let you live here on this pathetic, stinking island,' she said, stepping closer. 'I said give!'

Billy and Sue both lowered their heads. It was over. They really had lost. Sue put her hand in her pocket and removed the stone. They both extended their hands to relinquish the items when they heard a screaming voice coming from the darkness of the jungle.

'Canonballlllll!'

Clara turned around in time to see the blurred image of what looked like a bowling ball fly into the gaggle of creatures behind her. The group were sent flying and barged into her, almost knocking her over. Billy grabbed Sue by the hand and dragged her into the jungle. Clara turned back around to face them and was hit around the waist. Someone had rugby tackled her and this time she went crashing to the ground. Sinka started growling as Austin scrambled back to his feet. The serpent raised up and hissed at him. Austin was in trouble, but then his partner in crime returned.

'Geronimooooooooo,' he screamed as he hit them.

Sinka tumbled, causing the serpent to recoil and allow Austin to run for it. But he wasn't going anywhere. The creatures were all lying prone on the floor, desperately trying to get up. Clara turned and whistled. Within seconds, her dragon descended and she jumped on-board. Austin tried to clamber on, but he was too slow. The beast was quickly airborne again. They had to stop her, but how? Billy and Sue were on the run too. They had to protect the stone and the ring, but Clara was right on their tail. The dragon was frantically flapping its wings as it chased after them. Clara didn't care about her army. There were only two things she cared about and she was chasing them down.

Sinka was back up and started towards Austin. The creatures were behind the Chimera too, backing him up. Austin started retreating, glancing around to see if he had anywhere to go, but he didn't. He had no protection, no help. He continued searched but could not see his partner-in-crime. He was alone. Just as he thought his time was up, a glowing purple light flew right past his head. The arrow multiplied and struck four creatures. They died instantly. Another arrow followed and took another four.

'Austin, run!' screamed a voice from behind.

He turned and did as he was told. A ball zipped past his ear and exploded, sending blue smoke into the air and obscuring the Chimera's vision. Then something flew over his head. It landed amongst the creatures and seconds later exploded, releasing red mist which started wrapping itself around the heads of the remaining creatures. Austin stopped and turned as another arrow emerged. It was unerringly accurate, hitting four of the blind army. Only a handful remained.

'Brace for impact!' His partner was back. It swiped through all of them. They lay there, bruised and battered, but their torture was about to end. Two arrows followed in quick succession and the army were wiped out. All of them except for Sinka. As the Chimera lay there, he knew they had won. The forlorn figure gingerly got to his feet and stared at them, before growling and retreating to the darkness of the jungle. They let him go. He would no longer be any danger now that it was over. Austin turned and walked away, smiling. As he made his way over to meet the others, he heard another scream.

'Austin, look out!'

Austin turned and stumbled backwards, eyes wide and panicking as the Chimera leapt towards him. The fangs of the serpent, the ferocious mouth of the lion, and the horns of the goat were all headed right for him. Austin tried to react, but he tripped on one of the dead creatures. Sinka was about to strike when there was another whoosh and Austin felt the fletchings brush against his cheek. The arrow multiplied into four and hit their targets. One punctured Sinka's belly, another entered the serpent's open mouth and shot out the back of its head, and the third one pierced the side of the goat's head where it remained lodged like a skewer. The final arrow penetrated the lion's head, right between the eyes and the Chimera dropped to the floor. Sinka was dead. Austin continued looking into the empty eyes of the beast for awhile before he allowed himself a huge sigh of relief. It was over for real this time. They were all gone. The bowling ball rolled up and smiled at him.

'Enjoy that my cocker?' He asked.

'Thanks for your help, Denzel,' Austin said.

'That's alright. I've been here waiting all night. Terry gave me an important job to do and I fink I did okay, don't you?'

Austin nodded.

'You were awesome,' he said.

'I know,' Denzel said as they smiled at each other. There was movement behind them and then the remaining fastachees emerged from the trees, all holding catapults. They were followed by Terry who walked out with a finger stuck up his nose, before removing it and waving at Austin. And then, from the darkness of the jungle, the last member of the team, Mr Robertson, gripping something loosely in his right hand - Sue's bow.

'You, sir?' Austin said, sounding surprised.

'I may seem like a boring school teacher who's not any good on a paddle-board, but I love my archery. So, yeah, me,' he said and smiled. Austin smiled back, but then he realised it wasn't over yet.

'Sue and Billy,' he screamed, they were still on the run and Clara was chasing them. Without saying a word, Austin grabbed, something from a fastachee's hand and ran back towards the jungle. The others all stood there as he disappeared from view once again.

Chapter 65
The Chase

Billy was panting and his heart continued to race as he tried his hardest to pull Sue along with him. He didn't know where they were going, but they needed to escape somehow. The ring was stuffed down the back of his trousers, digging into his skin, but at least it reminded him it was still there. The black shadow of the dragon hung high above them, tracking their movement, but it could not attack as long as they stayed close to the wall. There was another scream from above, followed by the explosion of a ball of fire, which gave enough light to allow Billy to see ahead. He almost froze. They were approaching the sea and there was nowhere to go. Their path to freedom would soon end. He looked to the right, but there was nothing there except the dense jungle. They were nearing the end of the cave wall. Their escape was about to end and there were no options left.

******

Sue was keeping up, panting as Billy pulled her along. She was struggling, but the alternative was much worse. The dragon screamed again, letting them know it was not going anywhere. Then Sue heard another sound. It was Clara, laughing hysterically as she stayed on their trail. A ball of fire exploded from the dragon, lighting their path. Sue could see they were fast approaching the sea and were running out of time. They kept going, kept moving. They were not beaten yet, but time was running out. What were they going to do?

******

Clara had sight of them down below. There was nowhere for them to go. The path led to the sea and beyond that, there was nothing. The jungle was too overgrown to contemplate turning right and wading through. The end was near and she would soon have them. After all her work, all the waiting, all the battles, all the planning, they would soon be in her grasp, and she could flee this pathetic island and move on. Her army was dead, probably Sinka too, not that she cared. The children were only 20 meters away from the end of the wall. They had nowhere to go, their time was up.

After eight years it was almost over. Clara let out another hysterical scream and continued to watch Billy and Sue as they ran to oblivion.

******

Austin was working his way through the jungle. The dragon was flying in a straight line in the distance, letting him know he was heading the right way. He was unsure how this would end, but he had to try whatever he could to help. Billy and Sue would do the same for him and that's what gave him the push he needed. The three of them had been inseparable since the second day of the school year. They were like the three musketeers.

'*All for one and one for all,*' Austin muttered and picked up his pace once more. His best friends needed him and he had no intention of letting them down.

Chapter 66
The Three Musketeers

Billy and Sue backed up against the wall as the dragon hung overhead. They had reached the water's edge and there was nowhere for them to go. Clara started laughing as Billy and Sue looked from side-to-side, searching for an escape route, but realising there wasn't one.

'Well, well, well, here we are again, nowhere left for you two imbeciles to go now,' she said, sounding triumphant.

The dragon lowered itself and hovered above their heads. It was breathing through its nostrils, causing snot to spray out over them. Sue turned her head to the side to avoid being covered in dragon gunk. As she did, she looked down and that's when she saw it, a slight crack in the wall. Water lapped against the rock and ran along a small channel before seeping into the crack and entering the cave. Sue gasped, she knew exactly what was below them and it gave her an idea. It may be their only option, and it was risky, but it was worth a shot. As the dragon landed, Clara stepped off and gave a sigh.

'Right, hand them over. I'm tired of this now. You have no back-up, no weapons, and no friends to save you, so give them to me.'

'I think you'll find they do have a friend, you old battleaxe.'

Clara, Billy and Sue all turned to see Austin walking along the wall, heading right for them. Billy and Sue smiled at the sight of him while Clara rubbed her head as he approached.

'And what are you going to do about it?' She looked at him, arms outstretched with a '*please explain*' expression on her face.

'I've come to save my friends and finish this,' he said.

Clara stared at him and started laughing.

'Hahahaha, and how are you proposing you do that? Three children against us,' she turned and pointed to the dragon who snorted in agreement.

'What you seem to be forgetting is, you have nobody else, you have no help, and you have no clue what you are dealing with. It's over, the sooner you realise that the better,' she said. 'There's nothing you can do to save yourselves now.' She began to laugh even harder.

Austin said nothing. He simply gripped the item he had grabbed earlier and stared at her. Sue put her hand in her pocket and slowly removed the stone. Austin noticed and twisted his arm to secretly show Sue the ball that was sat in his hand. Sue nodded at him and nudged Billy.

'Now!' Sue screamed.

Clara was taken by surprise as Austin launched the item in his hand at her. It started glowing as it connected with her chest and exploded on impact, covering her and the dragon in blue smoke. Sue threw the stone at the wall, and then Billy grabbed her by the arm and dragged her into the water. Austin dived into the nearest bush and a massive explosion was followed by the sound of a wall crumbling. Clara was trying to waft away the blue smoke that was circling around her head, as the dragon continued to cry and tried to take off.

Suddenly, debris was sent skywards as two heads burst up through the collapsed wall. One grabbed the head of the dragon and the other wrapped its teeth around Clara. They started screaming as a third head appeared and wrapped its mouth around the body of the dragon. The children sat transfixed as the Hydra returned to the cave, dragging Clara, and the creature she had raised since it was a baby, away to their grisly and well-deserved deaths.

Billy jumped out of the water and helped Sue out. Austin set-off back along the path, closely followed by the others. As they ran past the collapsed wall, Sue felt the stone land in her pocket once again. The screams of the dragon and Clara continued for a few seconds and then finally, there was silence.

The three musketeers ran, no talking, no stopping, no turning around, they just put their heads down and ran, as the screams of the monstrous Hydra burst up through the collapsed wall and filled the jungle once more.

Chapter 67
Back In The Village

Two hours later, they were all sat around the campfire; eating, laughing and joking. The children suggested putting on a talent show, which mainly involved Mr Robertson doing poor impressions, much to the amusement of everyone.

Sue walked over and sat next to Terry.

'You okay, my ansum?' He asked.

Sue smiled and looked at him.

'I believe this is yours?' She said, handing him the stone.

'You know, you did blinkin' amazin' today,' Terry said.

'Thanks, it was some adventure,' she said, before glancing across at Billy.

'He's a gooden that one. Make sure you keep 'old of 'im. He likes you,' Terry said, pointing at Billy.

'I like him too. Thank you, Terry,'

'For what?'

'For trusting me. My dad controls every aspect of my life these days. It's nice to do something where I don't have to explain myself and I have a bit of freedom,' she said.

'You know, things will be different when you get home,' Terry said, as he gave her a reassuring smile.

'What do you mean? About my dad letting me go on the school trip?' Are you sure he won't remember saying no?' She asked, sounding anxious.

'You'll see. Things are gonna change when you get 'ome,' Terry took a step closer and stared into her deep brown eyes as he took her hand.

'Thank you, Sue, we couldn't have done this wivout you.'

They smiled at each other for a few seconds, and then he let go of her hand and pointed at Billy.

'Now, go over to boy wonder. I'm sure he's missin' you by now.'

Sue nodded, stood and headed over, sitting down beside Billy in time to see Mr Robertson's awful Mrs Doubtfire impression. Once everyone finished laughing at him, he was asked to stop.

'Fair enough, you don't know talent when you see it,' he said, as he walked over to Terry and offered him his hand.

'Friends?' He said.

Terry stood, smiled, and shook it.

'Friends,' he agreed.

'Terry, about what you said earlier, you know, about Billy's mum...,' he whispered, awkwardly rubbing the back of his head as he glanced over at Billy.

'Relax my ansum, my lips are sealed, just wanted to get you all fired up, that's all. Blinkin' worked, too, I thought you woz goin' kill me. Now, promise me one thing?' Terry asked.

'What's that?' Asked Mr Robertson.

'Never call me an over-sized frog again. I is more like Yoda, don't you fink?' He chuckled.

'I promise. Although I'm not sure about the Yoda comparison.'

Terry mockingly gasped at the teacher.

'Lies tell you do,' he said, mimicking the Star Wars character.

They both laughed as Mr Robertson walked over to treat the children to his Mr Bean impersonation.

Terry sat back down and watched the boys and Sue talking, laughing, and joking by the fire. Mr Robertson was performing again - making silly noises and walking around like he'd had an accident in his trousers. Terry was pleased Sue had come. The boys were fond of her and she had proven to be a useful member of the team, as had Mr Robertson. The children had shown they would do anything to help each other, even if it meant putting themselves in danger. Mr Robertson had proven not all teachers were boring old farts who didn't have any better skills than shouting for children to keep quiet and giving detentions for forgetting homework.

As Terry sat there watching them, Denzel floated over and stopped in front of his fellow Cornishman.

'Some day that wan't it, my cocker?' He asked.

Terry looked up and smiled.

'It was, and now I need to sleep. We 'ave got a long journey back in the mornin',' he said.

'Must be fun travellin' 'round like that though?' Said Denzel.

Terry frowned at him and smiled.

'What are you smilin' about?' Asked Denzel, suspiciously eyeing the Knocker.

'Oh nuffin, just finkin'.'

Everyone carried on drinking and chatting for another hour before heading off to bed. They were all exhausted after everything they had been through and were ready for some well-needed rest before setting off for home the following day.

******

As the embers on the fire died down, Terry wandered off to his bed for the night. The hut was quiet, all except for Denzel who was floating in mid-air, snoring away and shouting something out about pasties in his sleep. Terry smiled, closed his eyes and was soon dreaming about pasties too.

******

Sue, Billy, and Austin were all chatting in the hut next to Terry.

'I'm too excited to sleep,' said Austin, contradicting what he just said by yawning. 'What a day.'

'Yeah was a bit crazy. Fun though, don't you think?' Said Billy, rubbing his eyes.

'It was different! I'll give you that,' Sue added.

Mr Robertson was asleep in the corner, no shouting about pasties from him. The children lay down, and seconds later the boys were sound asleep.

Sue was still awake. She lay there, staring at the ceiling and thinking about the day. The meal onboard HMS Victory had seemed so long ago. She had been so disappointed when the chaos onboard had meant they'd had to leave the ship, but little did she know how her day would pan out. She closed her eyes and seconds later joined the boys in drifting off to a well-earned sleep.

Epilogue

The following morning Billy, Austin, and Sue left the hut and walked out into bright sunshine. Terry was sitting on the logs eating a bowl of food, whilst Janji was over by the fire-pit cooking breakfast with his daughter. Mr Robertson was walking around and helping the fastachees tidy up, whilst the hibknibs were doing their part in eating any food scraps they could find.

Billy stretched, yawned and walked over to Terry, closely followed by Austin and Sue.

'Yours I believe?' Billy said as he handed him the ring.

'Oh yeah, forgot all about that,' Terry said, causing Austin and Billy to frown at him.

'Forgot about it?' Said Billy.

Terry stared up at him, unsure why there was surprise in his voice.

'Yeah, wots problem?' He asked.

'That is the whole reason we came here, Terry,' Austin said, pointing at the ring. 'How could you forget about it?'

'Oh yeah, I suppose so. I don't fink it does anyfin' anyway,' he said very matter-of-factly. 'Prob'ly just a nice souvenir.'

'What?' Said Billy. 'You better be joking?'

Terry stared at him and shoved another spoonful of food in his mouth, before screwing his face up at the funny taste.

'Are you being serious?' Asked Austin.

Sue stood there, watching, unsure if this was a wind-up or if Terry really was stupid.

'Wots matter? We 'ad fun, didn't we? Better than bloomin' campin' wiv stupid school kids, don't you fink?' He said as he continued to munch away, still persevering with the strange tasting delight in his mouth.

As they continued to wonder if Terry was joking, Mr Robertson walked over and joined in the conversation.

'What's up?'

'This clown said he doesn't think the ring is any good,' Austin explained as he pointed at Terry.

'Oh well, never mind, these things happen,' Mr Robertson said, as he sat down next to Terry, picked out a piece of fruit from his bowl and popped it into his mouth.

'Hmm, tasty,' he said, much to the surprise of Terry.

The children could not believe their ears.

There was an awkward silence as they looked at each other, but then it started. Terry burst out laughing and seconds later Mr Robertson joined him. They were like two naughty school children playing a prank. The others couldn't help it. They started laughing and shaking their heads too.

'I suppose we better see what this is all about once everyone is 'ere,' Terry said as he held the ring up and looked around.

'We are all here,' Billy said.

'Not quite,' said Terry and pointed behind them. 'Ere 'e is.'

The children turned around and saw someone walking over. His hair was blue on one side and red on the other, he had green bushy eyebrows and different coloured eyes, one gold, one silver. But, what made him look extra weird was that he was dressed in the same outfit as Terry. He looked most odd, but waved and smiled as he reached them.

'Alright, my cockers,' said Denzel.

'Are you coming back with us?' Asked Austin, excitedly looking from Terry to Denzel.

'I certainly am, if that's okay with you?' Austin nodded up and down.

'Of course it is. Nice legs by the way,' said Sue, causing everyone to laugh.

'Fanks, grew 'em myself,' Denzel chuckled.

'Right, let's see what this is all about,' said an

excited Terry, as he knelt down and put the ring on the ground. He reached into his sack, removed the map, unfolded it and lay it down beside the ring. Then his hand returned to the sack, removed the stone and slotted it into the centre of the horseshoe-shaped-ring. Everyone watched as a blue coloured dot appeared at the top of the ring and instantly traced down either side. As it made its way around, the ends of the horseshoe moved towards each other, fusing together as they touched to form a circle around the stone, as if protecting it. With the circle complete, and the band of colour glowing brightly around the outside, it started turning one way as the stone spun in the opposite direction.

'Look!' Sue screamed as the map lifted off the ground, flipped over and lowered back down again. The stone, which had now filled with black ink, moved to the top of the map and dropped one tiny dot onto it. Then it moved down and produced another dot, right underneath the first one, followed by another and then another. It continued to move down the page, producing dot after dot, until it reached the bottom, leaving the map marked with twenty dots running down the left hand side. As everyone watched, the tiny dots wobbled and stretched across the full width of the map. Once they reached the opposite end, they stopped moving and the previously blank map was now marked with twenty identical lines. There was no further movement, no wobbling, no turning, twisting, or any other magical effects.

The group remained silent. Nobody knew what to say, until Austin piped up.

'Well, that was worth the last couple of days, Terry. You could have bought a notebook if you needed lined paper mate,' he joked.

'What the blinkin' 'eck is this?' Terry moaned, as he threw his hands out to the side and frowned in frustration.

Suddenly, there was a *popping* sound, and a gap appeared in the top line as part of the ink vanished. Seconds later, there was another pop and a gap appeared in the second line, followed by another in the third. Before long, there was pop after pop piercing the air all around, like balloons bursting at a party. Once the popping had ceased, several gaps had penetrated each line. Billy and Austin looked at each other and smiled. It reminded them of the scroll they had found in the woods before they met Terry.

Every line on the page now comprised of four or five much smaller lines. And then a *bang* and flash of light exploded from the middle of the map, making everyone jump as they shielded their eyes against the brightness in front of them. They lowered their hands as the light began to fade. What they saw made them all gasp. Each individual line had transformed into a single word. Ten lines comprised of four words, while the other ten consisted of five.

What they were looking at was something the boys had seen many times before.

'Go on Terry,' said Billy. 'This is your adventure.'

Terry looked around at everyone and then back to the map. He cleared his throat and rubbed his hands before reading the poem aloud.

> *'This task is complete,*
> *The ring has been found,*
> *You defeated the beast,*
> *And are now homeward bound,*
> *You have won the battle,*
> *But not the war,*
> *You must go again,*
> *As there's still one more,*
> *Just pick up the stone,*
> *And hold it up high,*
> *Peer through the centre,*
> *And look into the sky,*
> *Away to the past,*
> *Is where you must head,*
> *The image you see,*
> *May fill you with dread,*
> *But the future depends,*
> *On the action you take,*
> *So think hard about,*
> *The decision you make.'*

Sue broke the silence that was surrounding the group.

'What does it mean, there's still one more?'

'Only one way to find out,' said Austin. 'Go on Terry, do as it says.'

Terry didn't need asking twice. He picked up the ring with the stone sat in the middle and lifted it high. They watched him as he searched the skyline for a hidden message. He moved his arm all around and as it passed over the top of the mountains, Sue noticed something strange. The words inside the ring, *Quod Occultatum Regno*, flickered for a few seconds. But as soon as Terry's arm moved away from the mountains, it disappeared. He lowered the stone and looked disappointed.

'That's blinkin' weird,' said Terry. 'Nuffin to see. Nuffin at all,' he stood there scratching his head.

'Do it again,' said Sue.

'What? Why? It's a waste of time. There's nuffin there,' he moaned.

'Point it over the mountains and hold it there, don't move it too fast and concentrate,' she said, sounding impatient.

The boys and Mr Robertson looked at each other and shrugged. They didn't have a clue what she was going on about.

Terry frowned but did as he was told. He held it up and slowly moved it towards the mountains. As the ring reached the peak, the words filled with colour once more. This time they did not flicker, they did not disappear, they stayed there, shining bright. Austin nudged Billy and Mr Robertson as he pointed at it. Their eyes became wide as they held their breath. Terry also noticed and started smiling. He had found it.

'Alright. Now what?' He asked.

'Bring the stone towards your eye and look through it,' she told him.

'I blinkin' 'ate technology,' he complained, causing Billy and Austin to snigger.

Terry slowly brought the stone towards his right eye and looked through it as he closed his left to enhance the image.

'Well?' Asked an impatient Mr Robertson.

Terry lowered the ring and the biggest grin covered his furry little face.

'Fancy goin' on an adventure?'

They all looked at each other, smiled, and nodded. Billy then asked the question Terry was dying to hear.

'Where did you have in mind?'

Terry winked at him and returned the ring to the centre of the map.

'That, my ansum, is the right question,' he

said, as the ring and the stone started spinning in opposite directions. Then, as they both began to glow, the words on the page started to transform into the most beautiful map...

THE END